PLACE

Beverley Farmer was born in Melbourne in 1941 and studied Arts at the University of Melbourne. She was married to a Greek immigrant for thirteen years, three of which she spent in his village. Now she lives on the coast south of Melbourne. She has a son aged eighteen. She has been writer-in-residence at the University of Tasmania, the Geelong College and Deakin University. The stories in this collection are selected from two short story volumes – *Milk* and *Home Time*.

Place of Birth

BEVERLEY FARMER

faber and faber
LONDON · BOSTON

This collection first published in 1990
by Faber and Faber Limited
3 Queen Square WC1N 3AU

Phototypeset by Input Typesetting Ltd London
Printed in Great Britain by
Cox and Wyman Ltd, Reading, Berkshire

All rights reserved

© Beverley Farmer, 1983, 1985, 1990
Beverley Farmer is hereby identified as author of
this work in accordance with Section 77 of the
Copyright, Designs and Patents Act 1988.

'Milk', 'Melpo', 'At the Airport', 'Darling Odile', 'Snake',
'Inheritance', 'Maria's Girl' in *Milk*,
first published in 1983 by McPhee Gribble Publishers, Victoria, Australia, in association with Penguin Books Australia
and simultaneously by Penguin Books Ltd, London and
Penguin, New Zealand
'Place of Birth', 'Caffe Veneto', 'The Harem', 'Home Time',
'A Man in the Laundrette', 'A Girl on the Sand',
'Pomegranates', 'Our Lady of the Beehives' in *Home Time*,
first published in 1985 by McPhee Gribble Publishers, Victoria, Australia in association with Penguin Books Australia
and
simultaneously by Penguin Books Ltd, London and
Penguin, New Zealand

A CIP record of this book is
available from the British Library

ISBN 0-571-14148-X

For Domna and Stratos Talihmanidis

CONTENTS

ACKNOWLEDGEMENTS viii

PLACE OF BIRTH 1

A GIRL ON THE SAND 24

THE HAREM 42

MARKET DAY 54

CAFFE VENETO 62

MILK 76

MELPO 90

DARLING ODILE 103

AT THE AIRPORT 116

INHERITANCE 127

MARIA'S GIRL 137

HOME TIME 146

SNAKE 156

POMEGRANATES 169

A MAN IN THE LAUNDRETTE 177

OUR LADY OF THE BEEHIVES 188

ACKNOWLEDGEMENTS

Acknowledgement is made to the publications in which these stories first appeared: 'Milk' in *Island*, 1983; 'Melpo' in the *Bulletin*, 1982; 'Darling Odile' in *Cleo*, 1982; 'Snake' in *Meanjin*, 1982; 'Inheritance' in *Westerly*, 1982; 'Maria's Girl' in *Tabloid Story* (*National Times*), 1982; 'Caffe Veneto' in *Follow Me*; 'The Harem' in *Australian Short Stories*; 'A Man in the Laundrette' in the *Australian Literary Supplement*; 'Pomegranates' in *The Canberra Times*; 'Our Lady of the Beehives' in *Meanjin*.

Ὅλοι γιά προσώρας εἴμαστε ὅπου καί να πᾶμε . . .

All of us are passing through no matter where we go . . .
                    Stratis Myrivilis, *The Mermaid Madonna*

φτενὸ οτὰ πόδια σου τὸ χῶμα
   γιὰ νὰ μὴν ἔχεις ποῦ ν' ἁπλώσεις ρίζα
   καὶ νὰ τραβᾶς τοῦ βάθους ὁλοένα

let the soil at your feet be thin
   so that you will have nowhere to spread roots
   and have to delve in the depths continually
                    Odysseus Elytis, *To Axion Esti*, from *Genesis*

PLACE OF BIRTH

On the last day Bell will remember before the snow, on a blue-grey morning of high cloud, the old woman brings out a *tapsi* rolling with walnuts that she has cracked for the Christmas *baklava*. 'We'll be shut in soon enough,' she sighs, perching on a plaited stool under the grapevine with the *tapsi* on her lap. Bell, her son Grigori's wife, pulls up stools for herself and Chloe, the other daughter-in-law, the Greek one who has come to the village for Christmas; her husband's ship is at sea. The women huddle over the *tapsi* picking out and dropping curled walnuts here, shells there. Chloe's little girl, Sophoula, leans on her mother.

'Me too?' she murmurs.

'Go ahead.'

Sophoula, biting her lips, scowls over her slow fingers. With a trill of laughter Chloe pops a walnut into the child's mouth. 'My darling! Eat,' she says.

'Don't tell me she has nuts at her age?' the old woman says. 'You'll choke the child.'

'Mama, she's three.' Chloe's face and neck turn red.

'Just the same – '

'Oh, I don't like it!' Sophoula spits and dribbles specks of walnut. The shelling goes on; under their bent heads Chloe and the old woman put on a fierce burst of speed. Suddenly all of them flare bright with sunlight and are printed over with black branches and coils of the grapevine as a gap opens in the cloud. Bell leaps to her feet and lumbers inside.

'What's wrong with you?' Chloe frowns.

'Nothing. I'm getting my camera.'

'*Aman*. Always photographs,' her mother-in-law sighs.

'It's too cold to sit out here,' Chloe says.

'Oh, please,' Bell wails from the window. 'All stay where you are!'

PLACE OF BIRTH

But the gap in the cloud has closed over by the time she gets back, so that what she will always have is a photograph all cold blues, whites, greys and browns: brittle twigs and branches against walls and clouds, the washing hung along the wire, a white hen pricking holes in mud that mirrors her, and the three heads, black, brown and bone-white, suspended over the *tapsi* of walnuts.

Because she takes all the photographs, she won't find herself in any of them.

Six weeks ago, as soon as she knew for certain, Bell wrote to her parents that they would be grandparents some time in May. 'You're the first to know,' she added, though by the time the letter got to Australia the whole village probably knew. There's no hope now of an answer until after Christmas. But at noon the postman's motor-cycle roars past, a fountain of mud in his wake, and stops at the village office, so she wanders down just in case and is handed an Australian aerogram. It has taken a month to get here and is one she will mark with a cross and keep as long as she lives.

Grandma and Grand Pop, eh, scrawls her father. *And about time too. Tell Greg to take that grin off his face.*

'Are they pleased, Bella?' The old woman is kneading the pastry for the *baklava*. Her arms are floured to the shoulders.

'Of course. Dad says, "And about time too." '

'No wonder! Considering that you're thirty-one – '

'Thirty – '

'– or will be when it's born.'

'Hasten slowly.' Bell reads her mother's exclamatory, incoherent half-page, laboriously copied, then goes back to her father's.

It's been three years. You could leave it too late, you know, Bell. With a bub and all that you could find yourselves tied down before you know it. It's hard to think we mightn't live to see our only grandchild. Mum's been having dizzy turns again lately. She's had one stroke, as you know.

PLACE OF BIRTH

If money's the problem, I can help you there. Also book you into the Queen Vic or wherever you like.

'What else, Bella?'
'Oh, questions. Money, hospitals. All that.'
'Surely you're booked into the Kliniki?' Chloe stares.
'No, not yet.'
'Well, you'd better do it soon! You don't want to have it in the Public Hospital! *They* have women in labour two to a bed in the corridors, it's so crowded.'

'I think I want to have it at home,' Bell hears herself say.

'At home!' Kyria Sophia is delighted. 'Why not? I had all mine here. Grigori was born in the room you sleep in!'

'It wouldn't be safe.' Chloe raised her eyebrows. 'Not with a first child. Anything can go wrong.'

'Thank you, Chloe.'

'It's the truth. Look what happened to the *papas*'s daughter!'

'The *papas*'s daughter? You know why that happened? She got a craving for fried bananas in the middle of the night and her husband wouldn't go and try to find her any. And sure enough –'

'Mama, the cord got round her baby's neck and strangled it.'

'Mama, not because of the bananas!'

'You're both fools! Of course it was because of the bananas!' The old woman rams a grey branch into the firebox of the *somba*. '*Aman!* How come I'm the only one who ever stokes the fire?' She brushes a wisp of hair out of her eyes and flours her face. White like her hair and arms, it sags into its net of wrinkles.

Lunch, Bell's chore today, isn't ready when the old man comes in from the *kafeneion* and finds her alone in the kitchen. Kyria Sophia has taken Sophoula with her to the bakery to leave the *baklava*, Chloe is at a neighbour's place with the baby. He sits by the *somba*, small and grey and muddy, rolling and smoking one fat cigarette after another. The *makaronia* have to be boiled to a mush, Bell knows, before she can toss them in oil and butter and crumble *feta* cheese over them. Kyria Sophia comes back exhausted hand-in-hand with Sophoula and as if the day's work wasn't enough, now she has her to spoonfeed.

They eat the *makaronia* in silence. At every mouthful a twinge, a jab of pain drills through Bell's jaw. Not a toothache, please, she prays. Not now, not here.

Sophoula pushes the spoon and her grandmother's hand away. 'Yiayia! You have to tell a story!'

'What story?' sighs the old woman.

'A story about princesses.'

'Eat up and then I will.'

'Now!' Sophoula bats the spoon on to the floor. The old woman gets another one and shovels cold lumps into the child's mouth, chanting a story by heart. Whenever she falters, the child clamps her mouth shut. Bell, stacking the dishes, isn't really listening, but when the bowl is almost empty she exclaims aloud in English, 'Snow White! No, Snow White and Rose Red!'

The old woman giggles. 'Zno Quaeet,' she mocks. 'No Zno Quaeet End – '

'Yiayia, *pes*!'

'*Aman*, Sophoula!'

'*Pes*.' She spits into the bowl.

After lunch these days Bell sleeps until it's dark. Now that she is into her fifth month she is sleepy most of the time. From under the white *flokati* she can hear Grigori's voice (so he is back from Thessaloniki with the shopping) and then Kyria Sophia's shrill one. When she wakes properly, ready for another long yellow evening by the *somba*, he is still there in the kitchen finishing a coffee. So is Chloe, red from her sleep, with the baby at her breast. 'Hullo,' Bell says, kissing Grigori's woolly crown. She fumbles with the *briki*.

'Coffee again?' Chloe mutters.

'Just one to wake me up.'

'It's so bad for the baby.'

'One won't hurt.'

'Oh well, you'd know.'

PLACE OF BIRTH

Bell turns her back to light the gas. 'Where are the old people?' She touches Grigori's shoulder.

'Milking.' His father's grey head grins in at the window; he leaves the milk saucepans on the sill. 'You got a letter, Mama said. Are Mum and Dad all right?'

'Yes, they send their love and congratulations.' Bell rubs her jaw. There's a hollow ache in her back teeth. She empties the sizzling *briki* into a little cup and takes a furry sip of her hot coffee. The *baklava* is on the table, baked and brought home already, its pastry glossy with the syrup it's soaking in. Grigori's shopping is all around it: oranges in net bags, chestnuts, a blue can of olive oil, lemons and mandarines and – she can hardly believe it – six yellow-green crescent bananas blue-stamped *Chiquita*. 'Oh, bananas! Oh, darling, thank you!' she cries out. 'We were just talking about bananas!'

'I'm so extravagant,' Chloe simpers, 'but Sophoula simply loves them. So I gave Grigori the money to buy her some.' Her eyes dare Bell to ask for one. A pregnant woman can ask even strangers in the street for food. Bell grins at Chloe, remembering her frying mussels one day in Thessaloniki when a pregnant neighbour squealed from a balcony, 'Ach, Kyria Chloe! Mussels! I can smell them!' and Chloe had to let her have a couple. 'She never smells anything cheap,' Chloe grumbled to Bell.

'Is that so, Kyria Chloe?' Bell contents herself with saying. 'Ah, so much lovely food. We'll never eat it.'

'*You* won't.' The old woman comes in and lifts the milk saucepans inside. '*Aman*, the cold!' She slams the window. '*You* won't eat. You're fading, look at you. White as snow.'

'I *will*. That was when I had morning sickness.'

'We don't want a kitten, you know, we want a big strong baby.'

'Believe you me,' Chloe mutters, 'the bigger it is, the harder it comes out.'

'Ah, *bravo*, Chloe, *bravo*!' The old woman clatters the saucepans, straining the warm milk. 'Don't you crave anything, Bella? You must crave something.'

'Why must she?'

'Well, to tell the truth, I'd love a banana,' says Bell. 'It seems like years! Can I buy one from you, Chloe?'

'I'm sorry. There aren't enough.'

'We share in this house, Chloe! If you want a banana, Bella, you have one! Don't even ask!'

'No, no, it's all right.'

Grigori stands up. 'See you later,' he says. He grabs a mandarine and saunters outside.

'Not to the *kafeneion* already?' his mother pleads. 'You just got here.' She stares bleakly after him. 'And what would you expect?' She rounds on her daughters-in-law. 'Doesn't a man have a right to peace and quiet?'

'Auntie?' Chloe has taught Sophoula this English word. 'Auntie Bella? Do they have Christmas where you come from?'

'Yes, of course.'

'Did you go to church?'

'No.'

'You stayed home at Christmas!'

'We went to the beach,' Bell says.

'At Christmas! You're funny, Auntie!'

'Funny, am I?' Bell crosses her eyes. With a giggle, Sophoula sits in her lap.

'Where's your baby?'

'You're sitting on it. Oh, poor baby.'

'What's its name going to be?'

'I don't know. What's your baby's name going to be?'

'We won't know till he's been christened.'

'Oh, no, I forgot.'

'If it's a girl, they'll call it after Yiayia,' Chloe interposes. 'The same as we did with you.'

'Good idea. I'll call my baby Yiayia.'

'Auntie, you can't!'

'Why can't I? Not if it's a boy, you mean?' Bell winks. 'Then

I'll call it Pappou,' and she is rewarded with a peal of laughter so loud that it wakes the old woman.

'Let's eat, Mama,' Chloe says.

'Is it late?' She blinks, squinting in the light. 'The men'll be home any minute.'

'No, they won't.' Bell lifts Sophoula down. 'Can we cut the *baklava* now? I crave *baklava*.'

'Oh. All right.' Smiling in spite of herself, Kyria Sophia cuts her a dripping slice. As Bell bites into it, the ache that has been lying in wait all day drills through her tooth and she shrieks aloud, letting syrup and specks of walnut dribble down her chin. She swills water round her mouth. The women cluck and fluster. Sophoula clings to her mother in tears of fright. The old woman mixes Bell an aspirin and she gulps it. She is helped to bed, where she curls up moaning in the darkness under the *flokati*. The light flashes on once, twice. She lies still until the door quietly closes.

Grigori is undressing with the light on. Bell rubs her watery eyes. The ache is duller now.

'Were you asleep? How's the tooth?'

'Bad.' She probes with her tongue.

He turns off the light and lies on his back with one cold arm against her. 'What's all this about having the baby here at home?'

'No! I'd be terrified.'

'Mama said you said you wanted to.'

'No. She misunderstood. I meant – I just feel – I want to go home and have it.' She holds her breath. 'Home to Australia.'

'How come?'

'Oh. Mum and Dad. You know. Mostly, I suppose. Yes.'

'We can't afford the fares.'

'One way, we can. Dad said they'd help.'

'Ah. One way? I see.'

The moon must have risen. In the hollow glow through the shutters the *flokati* looks like a fall of snow on rough ground. 'I wonder if it'll snow for Christmas?' she says. 'It didn't the other times.'

He snorts. 'You spring a thing like this on me. What I might feel – you couldn't care less, could you! I wanted to stay in Australia three years ago, but no, you uprooted us, you – felt – you had to go and live in Greece. And now what? Come along, doggy, I want to go home. To Australia!'

She takes a shaky breath. 'I feel guilty, I suppose. They're old, they're not well. "You could leave it too late," Dad said.'

'You know what a pessimist he is. You used to joke about it.'

'Can we bank on it, though?' She ploughs on. 'It's not as if it would be for ever.'

'It might.'

'We can always come back.'

'Always, can we? Backwards and forwards.' He turns his back to her. 'I'll need time to think it over. I'm tired.'

'There's not much time. We've got till the end of February. That's when my smallpox vaccination expires. I can't have another one while I'm pregnant and I can't enter Australia without it.'

Lying along his back, she feels him tightening against her. The nape of his neck is damp and has his hot smell. Once he pelted past her down a sand dune and was out of sight in the white waves when the hot smell from him buffeted her face. That was at Christmas.

We went to the beach at Christmas when I was little, she remembers. On Phillip Island we had dinner at the guesthouse and then Dad and I followed a track called Lovers' Walk – there was a board nailed up, Lovers' Walk – to look for koalas as they awoke in the trees. First we walked down the wooden pier where men and their sons were fishing. Red water winding and hollowing. Crickets fell silent when I walked in the tea-tree. After sunset the waves were grey and clear rolling and unrolling shadows on the sand. The trees, black now, still had their hot smell.

Some time in the early hours the toothache jerks her out of sleep. Grigori breathes on deeply. Tossing, feverish, close to tears, she stumbles to the kitchen for an aspirin and Chloe, passing through to the lavatory annexe, sees and scolds her. 'You shouldn't take any medicines now,' she says.

'One little aspirin!' Bell's smile is a snarl.

'Any medicine at all.'

'I have toothache!'

'Still, for the baby's sake.'

Bell turns and gulps it down. Back in bed the pain is relentless, it drills into her brain. After an hour, two, of whimpering in her sweat she creeps back to the kitchen and in a flash of bilious light swallows down three more aspirins. No one catches her. In the passage she trips over Sophoula's potty, which they leave outside their door until morning. Splashing away over cold urine, she lets it lie where it fell. Grigori is snoring. 'Turn over,' she hisses in Greek, and he turns.

A rooster calls, the same one as every morning, then hens, then a crow, so loud it must be in the yard. How long since she last heard a gull? It must be only a couple of weeks. When was the last time she was in Thessaloniki? Gulls are as common as pigeons in the city. It seems like years.

What does tea-tree smell like in summer?

Their bedroom is white and takes up one corner of the house and of the street, 21st of April Street these days, in honour of the Colonels' coup. The two-roomed school that Grigori went to is opposite. They are on one of the busiest crossroads in the village. All through Christmas Day, Boxing Day and the next day Bell sleeps and wakes to the uproar of tractors, donkeys, carol-singers, carts, trucks with loud-speakers bellowing in her windows. Snow falls. She sits sipping milk at the family table in her pyjamas, staggers to the lavatory annexe and back to her cooling hollow under the *flokati*. She coughs. Her head pulsates. She loses count of how many aspirins. The toothache goes through her in waves. Sweat soaks her pyjamas and sheets and Kyria Sophia dries them again by the *somba*. Grigori takes refuge for two nights at his cousin Angelo's place behind the bakery. Children throwing snowballs yell and swear. The baby wails.

PLACE OF BIRTH

From time to time Sophoula opens Bell's door, but slams it in panic when Bell stirs to see who it is. Chloe keeps away in case she and the children catch something. Kyria Sophia comes and sits at the end of the bed crocheting with a pan of hot coals at her feet.

Penicillin, somebody suggests, a shot of penicillin, there's a woman down the street who's qualified. Bell says yes, oh yes, please. Chloe is appalled. But no one ever comes to give the injection. Time has broken down. Sand slides shifting under the scorched soles of her feet. The scream of a gull makes her slip and clutch at the stringy trunk of a tea-tree, but it must be the grapevine. No, she is flat on her back, she is clutching the *flokati* when her eyes open. It looks like snow on rough ground. That scream comes again and it's the baby screaming, Chloe's baby though, not her own, that she can hear, then all the sounds of hushing and commotion as he sobs, then whimpering and quiet.

One morning she wakes and is well, clear-headed, free of toothache and of fever. She opens the windows but the shutters won't move. She is weak, look, trembling. But it's not that: snow is heaped on the sill. She patters to the door and stares down the white street. The sun is rising behind white roofs and trees, turning the snow sand-yellow, shading in the printed feet of birds and a stray dog. The stringy grapevine has grown spindles of ice.

Stooped panting over buckets and *tapsia* of water, she spends the day washing her stiff, sour clothes and her hair, stuck in yellow strings to her head by now; and sitting with hair and clothes spread out to dry by the *somba*. She would love a bath, but not in the dank ice-chamber that the lavatory annexe has become. For one thing, other people are always wanting to get in. And in any case, it's not as if they'll notice whether she does or not, not even Grigori: for fear of a miscarriage, now that she has finally conceived they don't make love. She's well again, she won't risk catching cold. She wraps a scarf over her mouth

PLACE OF BIRTH

whenever she goes outside. Now and then a twinge through her tooth alarms her, but the rivetting ache is gone.

Every day there is washing and cooking of which she does her share. When the sun is out she walks around the village photographing crystals and shadows, tufty snow and smooth. The narrowed river is crinkled, slow, with white domes on its rocks. Ovens in the deserted yards have a cap of snow over two sooty airvents and stare back at the camera like ancient helmets. White hens are invisible except for their jerking legs and combs. The storks' nest is piled high; it could be a linen basket up on top of the church tower. In the schoolyard a snowman has appeared – no, a snow woman two metres tall in a widow's scarf and a cloak of sacking under which her great round breasts and belly glisten naked.

She takes photographs of the snow woman and of children hiding to throw snowballs and of the *papas* as he flaps by, his hair and beard like a stuffing of straw that has burst out of his black robes. The family and the neighbours line up for portraits under the grey grapevine. The old man leads the cows out of the barn and poses for her standing between them on the soiled snow while they shift and blink in the light, mother and daughter.

'You can show them to your parents,' he says. So all the family knows that she is going home. No one talks about it.

She takes time exposures in the blue of evening as the windows in the houses light up and throw their long shapes on the snow outside. As often as not, Kyria Sophia, Chloe, Grigori, even the old man, can be found in one or other of the rooms, the little golden theatres, that Bell used to love being in. Now she knows the sets, the characters, the parts too well. She would rather stay home alone; she is quite happy babysitting. Having read her own few books too often, she reads Sophoula's story books about princesses. If Souphoula wakes, Bell reads aloud with the warm child in her lap. When the old man comes in they roast chestnuts on top of the *somba* until the others come. They listen in to the clandestine broadcasts on Deutsche Welle, which he calls Dolce

Vita: these are banned by the Junta and the penalty for listening could be imprisonment, could be torture. He has enemies who would report him if they knew. 'The walls have ears,' he growls, the radio pressed to his grey head; he is hard of hearing himself. His wrinkles are so deep that they pull his hooded eyes into a slant and his lips into a perpetual smile around his cigarette.

On New Year's Eve Kyria Sophia announces that she is too tired even to dream of making the family *vassilopita*. 'Thank goodness my nephew's the baker,' she says. 'Angelo says he'll bring us one.'

Chloe fluffs up her hair. 'My mother always makes ours.'

'It's a lot of bother for nothing, if you ask me!' snaps the old woman. 'Who appreciates it? Look at all my *baklava* that none of you will eat!'

'Mama, it's a wonderful *baklava*!' Bell hugs her.

'You say that. Eat some then.'

'And what about my tooth?'

'*Aman*, that woman!' Bell hears her whisper to Grigori. 'I could wring her neck,' meaning Chloe, or so Bell hopes.

Then to her further exasperation the old woman looks everywhere and can't find the *flouri*, the lucky coin that she hides in each year's *vassilopita*. Bell gives her the lucky sixpence that she brought from home, the one her mother used to put in the plum pudding.

After dinner, while Grigori and his father are still at the *kafeneion*, Angelo and his mother, Aunt Magdalini, arrive with the *vassilopita*. An elderly doll in long skirts, she falls asleep by the *somba*, steam rising from her woollen socks. Bell wakes her to eat a floury *kourabie*, and again to drink coffee. Angelo has ouzo. It blurs his sharp brown features, so like Grigori's, and makes him jocular.

'What can you see out there, Bella?' She turns from the window. 'Your man coming home?'

'The moon rising.'

'*Fengaraki mou lambro*,' recites Sophoula proudly.

PLACE OF BIRTH

'Good! What comes next?'

'*Fexe mou na perpato!*'

'I'll give you twenty drachmas,' Angelo drawls, 'if you can tell me what the moon's made of.'

'Rock?'

'You lost. It's a snowball, silly. It was thrown so high it can't ever come back to earth.'

Sophoula's jaw drops. 'Who threw it?'

'Guess.' He scratches the black wool on his head.

'A giant?'

'*I* think a bear. There's one up the mountain. There were tracks up there the other day. The hunters are out after her.'

'The poor bear!'

He peers out the window. 'That's not her in the school yard, is it? A huge white bear?'

'Silly.' She giggles. 'That's only the snow woman.'

'The snow woman, is it?' hisses Angelo. 'So that's who threw the moon up there!' and Sophoula screams in terror.

Kyria Sophia glares up over her glasses. 'God put the moon there.'

'Supposing she comes alive at night time? Supposing she comes and stares in all the windows while we're asleep?'

'No, no!' Sophoula clamps herself to Bell. 'Auntie, make him stop it!'

'Angelo, please?'

'Of course she doesn't!' cries Kyria Sophia. 'Aren't you ashamed to put an idea like that in the child's head?'

The door bursts open on Chloe red-faced and turbulent. 'You'll wake the baby! Can't I leave you alone here for one minute?' She drags the child by the arm into their room. There they both stay until Angelo and Aunt Magdalini have gone and Grigori and his father are home for the midnight ceremony of cutting the *vassilopita*. Then Chloe sidles sullenly in with her black hair stuck to cheeks still red with sleep or crying. 'Sophoula will have to miss it. She's asleep,' she mutters.

The old man, as head of the household, carefully divides the

PLACE OF BIRTH

loaf. He sets aside a piece for the church and then for every member of the family, present and absent. The lucky sixpence turns up in Chloe's baby's piece, as it was bound to, and they all pretend surprise. Bell stuffs the sweet bread into the safe side of her mouth. Next New Year, she knows, wherever they all are by then, the *flouri* or the sixpence will turn up in her child's piece.

The New Year card games at the *kafeneion* will go on all night. Grigori walking back is a shadow among other shadows that the moon makes in the snow.

On New Year's Day no bus comes to the village. The road in has been declared dangerous because the two narrow wooden bridges that it crosses are thick with frozen snow. No buses until further notice, bellows the village loudspeaker. People grumble. This happens every winter and every winter the government promises a new road. The mountain villages are worse off, of course; they'll be snowed in for weeks, not just a few days. Still, since no one has a car, everyone is trapped here while it lasts, except Angelo with his bread van.

Angelo goes on delivering his bread around the villages using chains, risking unmade tracks on hills and across fields to bypass the bridges. Grigori has been joining him lately for the sake of the ride and the company; now he goes on every trip in case Angelo strikes trouble and needs a hand. But Angelo won't take anyone else. 'It's not legal,' he tells everyone, 'and it's not safe.' He broke his rule twice last year, he says, and look what happened. The old man that he took to the district hospital in the back of the van survived; but the woman in labour? She lost her baby when the van hit a buried rock miles from anywhere and broke an axle. 'Never again, not for a million drachmas,' he says. 'Don't ask me.'

So that evening Bell and Chloe, sitting by the small *somba* in Chloe's room with the work done and the children asleep, are thunderstruck when Kyria Sophia – who has made herself scarce all day – puts her head round the door to announce that by the way she and Grigori are off first thing in the morning to Thessaloniki to see her other grandchildren. Angelo is giving them a lift.

'She can't do that!' Chloe cries out, and follows her into the kitchen. 'You can't do that!' Bell hears.

'What? What can't I do?'

'What about *me*?'

'What about you?'

'I brought the children all this way to visit you and it wasn't easy on the bus and now you take it into your head to go off to Thessaloniki just like that and – '

'Look, when I need you to tell *me* what – '

'– and leave us stranded here!'

'What would you do there, anyway?' Kyria Sophia shouts. 'Your husband's away at sea for two more weeks!'

'I happen to live there. *Your* husband's here, remember? How will he feel if you go? This is your house, it's not mine. I could have gone to my own village for Christmas and New Year when they begged me to. *My* mother – '

'You're a married woman. It's your duty to come to us.'

'Duty? Oh, duty? What about your duty, then? Aren't *you* a married woman?'

'You dare to talk to me like – '

'Mama, you have *no right* – '

'Get out of my kitchen, Chloe. You say one more word and I swear I'll hit you. I'll hit you!'

Chloe strides into the room where Bell and now Sophoula too are listening in horror; she slams the door behind her. Thuds and crashes of glass hit the wall between them.

'*Oriste mas! Oriste mas!*' come her shrieks. 'Now *she'll* tell *me* if I can go or not, will she? Twenty-five years old! *She'll* tell *me* what I can and can't do?'

'Mama, what's Yiayia saying?' Sophoula whimpers.

'Never you mind. She's wicked. She doesn't love you or any of us.' Chloe bites her lips. 'Let the old bitch howl,' she mutters.

'She would have slapped my face in there! She knows she's in the wrong.'

The outside door slams and they jump. Footsteps splash past the shuttered window. The three of them creep to their beds. Bell is still wide awake when at last Grigori comes in and starts undressing in the dark.

'Grigori?'

'You're awake, are you? What happened here? Mama's in a frenzy. She's beside herself.'

'She had a fight with Chloe.'

'And you?'

'Me? No! I stayed out of it.'

'You didn't try to stop her.'

'As soon try stopping a train! If Chloe wants a fight, I suppose that's her business, isn't it?'

'If she fights with her own mother it's her business. If she fights with mine it's my business and yours and all the family's.'

'So I should have stopped her.'

'You were there.' He has slid into bed without touching her. 'And your place in the family gives you the right.'

'Because I'm older than Chloe?'

'No. Because I'm the older brother and you're my wife.'

'Oh. I think Chloe was right to be upset. Is it fair of Mama to go off and leave us like this?'

'One more day of Chloe, she says, and she'll go mad.'

'Chloe's hard to take. It's the children. They tire her out, you see.'

'Mama does everything.'

'No, she doesn't. Chloe pulls her weight. I'm here all day and I know.'

'*You* know! You live in a world of your own! Chloe pulls her weight, does she? And what about you?'

'Tell me, what do the men do here while the women are pulling their weight? Play cards in the *kafeneion*? Stroll around Thessaloniki? If it comes to that, I'm the one who really needs to go. If I don't get to a dentist, I might lose this tooth.'

PLACE OF BIRTH

'Nice timing.'

'For every child a tooth, they say. It's to do with lack of calcium.'

She feels him shrug. 'Drink more milk.'

'I'm awash with milk already. Milk won't fill a rotten tooth, though, will it?'

'Well, bad luck,' he says wearily. 'It's stopped aching, hasn't it? There'll be a bus soon anyway, go on that. The fact is Angelo only has room for two and he needs me.'

'Well, let *me* come, then! Explain to Mama!'

'*You* explain to Mama.' He waits for her to think that over. 'Why all this fuss, I wonder?'

'You're going and leaving me here.'

'It's not as if it's for ever, is it?'

'Oh, that's it. I see. You want revenge.'

'You're happy to go off to Australia and leave me here.'

'Happy? I'm hoping you'll come.'

'It's more than hoping, I think. It's closer to force.'

They are lying rigidly side by side on their backs and neither moves. 'You'd be taking my child with you.'

She snorts. 'Not much choice at this stage!'

'No. There's not. So I want you to wait.'

'I can't, I told you. My smallpox vaccination.'

'I know that! I mean wait till after it's born.'

She opens her eyes wide in the darkness, so suddenly alarmed that she thinks he will hear the blood thumping through her. 'No. I'd be trapped here then,' she dares to say.

'Trapped!'

'Besides, the whole point is to be home with Mum and Dad before the birth. And then come back. If you want.'

'*Why*? Why does it matter *where* you are for the birth?'

'It just does,' she mutters. 'I'll feel safer there.'

'You're a stubborn, selfish, cold-blooded woman, Bell. You always have been and you always will be.'

'Always?'

'You want your own way in everything. Well, you're not getting it.'

Calming herself, she strokes the long arch of her belly, fingering the navel which has turned inside out and then the new feathery line of dark hair down to her groin. Once or twice a flutter inside her has made her think the baby has quickened, but it might have been only wind. Soon there'll be no mistaking it, her whole belly will hop, quake and ripple. She runs a finger along the lips that the head will burst through. 'What the fuck are you doing?' he mutters.

'Nothing.'

'You're breathing hard.'

'No, I'm not.' She forces herself to count as she breathes slowly in one two three, out one two three.

'I can hear you.'

'No.' She moves to the cold edge and listens motionless, breathing very slowly. He is silent. He has had his say.

She wakes at cockcrow when he gets dressed. She hears the van come, then go. She has stayed in bed through all the flurry of their departure, and so has Chloe. They open the kitchen door to find the *somba* burning with a bright flame, the milk boiled, the baby's napkins dried and folded, the day's eggs brought in from the barn and the table laid with bread and cheese and honey under a cloth.

'Oh, lovely!' cries Bell.

'You see?' Chloe snorts. 'She's sorry.'

'She must have been up all night!' Bell could hug the old woman.

'She was. I heard her.'

'She didn't have to do all this for us!'

Chloe stares and shrugs. 'Why shouldn't she?'

Chloe spends the morning washing and rinsing clothes, Bell taking Sophoula for a walk with the camera. The piles of soft snow were frozen overnight; so were the puddles and the clothes hung out on wires and bare brambles. There are no clouds this morning to block the sun or the faded half-moon, and everywhere they go water trickles and drips and glitters. As they come near the schoolyard Sophoula cringes, pulling at Bell.

'Carry me, Auntie Bella.'

'Why, for heaven's sake?'

'The snow woman's there.'

'It's only snow! It's only a big doll made of snow.'

'It's the wicked witch.' She huddles against Bell. 'She comes alive at night and stares in the window.'

'She does not! Look, she's melted. The poor old thing, she's vanished away.' A heap of pitted snow sits under the pines.

'The moon's melting too, Auntie Bella!'

Sophoula keeps Bell company while she boils the potatoes and fries eggs for the four of them for lunch; Chloe is with the baby in the bedroom. But the child is grizzly and cross now and says she isn't hungry: she doesn't want potato or egg or bread or anything. 'Have a bit of banana?' Bell pleads. One banana is left. Chloe has made them last, feeding them to Sophoula inch by inch and folding the black soft skin over the stump. But no, Sophoula won't. 'I know!' On impulse Bell peels the last banana, flours it and fries it in the pan with the eggs for Sophoula. 'My darling, eat,' she says. The old man trudges in. Lunch is late again. 'Try it? For Auntie? Have some milk with it?'

'Tell a story.'

'Once upon a time,' she slips a spoonful of banana in, 'in a little cottage in the woods – '

Sophoula gags and splutters. The old man stares. 'Eat,' he growls. 'It's good for you.'

'No! Auntie, I don't like it!'

'All right, you don't have to eat it.' Blushing with shame, Bell gobbles the banana herself before Chloe comes.

'There was a banana,' Chloe says when they are peeling fruit into their empty plates later, and Bell tries to explain. Sophoula announces smugly that Auntie ate it all up. So as not to let it go to waste, Bell says, red-faced. 'You know she has them raw,'

Chloe accuses. 'No more bananas!' Chloe kisses the child's hair. 'Wicked Auntie! Where will I get my darling some more?'

The old man, groping in his pockets, finds a bag of peanuts in their shells and presses it into Sophoula's hand.

'Is it *safe* to give her nuts?' Bell wonders aloud. 'They'll choke the child.'

In silence she rinses the dishes while Chloe shells peanuts by the *somba*. Abruptly Sophoula hoots and stiffens. Her back arches. Chloe bangs her, shakes her, shoves her head forward, and at last a great gush of sour curds and speckles pours out of her mouth all over her mother.

'Thank God!' Chloe hauls her jumper over her head. '*Aman*, my poor darling!' she moans, dabbing Sophoula's white face. 'They're bad, don't ever eat them! Wicked Pappou!' She pushes the whole bag into the firebox and slams the iron door. The old man plods to his room. 'There,' she says, 'let them burn. He won't tell Her,' she mutters at Bell, who has brought a glass of water. 'Thanks. Don't you tell either, or we'll never hear the end of it.'

It is dark these days before the old man wakes to do the afternoon milking. The torch he takes into the barn lights up the ridge of snow at the door. His approach to the house is a clank and slop of saucepans past the window and a red point and trail of smoke, his cigarette. This time he dumps the saucepans caked with dung and hay inside on the kitchen floor and covers them. 'Who'll strain the milk?' he says loudly to no one. 'Will you boil it or use if for cheese?'

Sullen with sleep in their doorways, the women exchange looks. He is waiting. Chloe tweaks a curl off her baby's damp cheek and kisses it.

'Two daughters-in-law!' barks the old man and they all jump. The baby whines.

'Sssh.' Chloe frowns.

'Two daughters-in-law and I do it, do I? I strain the milk! I make the cheese! It's not enough to look after the cows and milk them. I can do the lot!'

The kitchen door slams. Chloe pulls Bell into her room, where they stand listening behind the door as he unlatches the windows and clatters the saucepans. Then the front door clangs shut and his boots crunch away.

'He's thrown it out!' Bell mutters.
'Two daughters-in-law and I do it, do I?'
'Sssh. He'll hear!'
'Him, hear?'
'Sssh.'

They creep to the kitchen and turn the light on. In the square of yellow it throws outside, Bell can just make out the saucepans on end against the barn wall. The sun never comes there and the snow is still thick, with a pale puddle in it, a cat crouched at the edge, and all around a wide shawl of creamier snow. 'Oh! What a waste,' Bell sighs.

'Who cares?' Chloe looks in a jug. 'Look, there's all this left from this morning.'
'He's right, though.'
'It's Mama's job!'
'But since she's not here.'
'I have two small children I have to do everything for.'
'Yes, I should have done it.'
'You're pregnant!'
'Only five months.' She sits down. 'I need a coffee.'
'No, come on, let's get out of this place before we go mad! We'll take the children to Aunt Magdalini's. Come on.'

At Aunt Magdalini's, the village secretary's wife tells them that the bridges have been declared safe for the time being and that a bus to Thessaloniki will run in the morning. Rowdy in her elation and relief and scorn of Kyria Sophia, who might just as well have waited, Chloe hauls Bell and Aunt Magdalini's three daughters-in-law along the crusted, muddy street to celebrate her release at the *kafeneion*.

Inside its misted windows men are smoking at small tables,

watching the soccer on the grey television screen (the only one in the village) or looking on while Grigori's father plays the champion at *tavli*. The men all sit with their elbows on the chairback and their hands flat on their chest, glancing sidelong from time to time at the table of women drinking orangeade. When Grigori's father wins the game he sends the *kafedji* over with another round, and the women raise the bottles smiling in a salute to him.

Chloe tells joke after joke uproariously and the other three are soon helpless with laughter. 'What are the men staring at?' she asks, gazing round. 'Oh, Bella, it's you!' She swoops and whispers, 'Bella, look how you're sitting.' Startled, Bell looks. 'Bella, your hands!' She has them open over each breast exactly as the men's are, but women never sit like that. She moves them to the slopes of her belly and Chloe giggles and nudges but Bell is too torpid in the smoky heat to be bothered. When the others are ready to go they wake her. The sky is all white stars, frost crackles as they tread. They link arms with Bell in the middle to keep her from a fall. Scarves of mist trail behind them. They drop her at home on the way to Aunt Magdalini's.

Alone in the cold bed, Bell is awake for the first unmistakable tremor of the quickening.

Before daybreak Bell is up to strain the milk – twice carefully through the gauze – and boil it in time for breakfast. Chloe's noisy desperation surges all around her. At last the kisses crushing or missing cheeks and she is away with the children, the old man carrying their bags to the bus, and Bell has the house to herself.

She scrubs the saucepans and puts clean water on to boil. The table is littered with crusts, plates and cups under the yellow bulb that only now she remembers to switch off; she tidies up. She has the packing to do as well, letters and lists to write, but that had better wait until Grigori decides whether or not to go with her.

PLACE OF BIRTH

When her saucepans boil she carries them and another of cold water into the lavatory annexe that the old man spent all autumn building and is proud of. In case he tries to come in and wash, she pushes the heavy can of olive oil against the door. There is no light bulb in here yet, only an air vent and a candle stuck on a plate. She leans over to put a match to it and its flame lights her breasts: they are as she has never seen them, white and full, clasped with dark veins like tree roots. Shuddering in the cold, she stands in the *tapsi*, wets and soaps herself urgently, rinses the soap off. Flames go down her in runnels. She is rough all over with goosepimples except for her belly, domed in her hands, warm and smooth like some great egg.

All the water is swilling round her legs in the *tapsi* before she has got all the soap off but she rubs herself dry anyway, pulls on her clean clothes and with a grunt hoists up the *tapsi* and pours all the water into the lavatory bowl. It brims, then sinks gurgling down in froth and a gust of sweet cold rottenness from the sewer belches up in her face.

Still shuddering, she hugs herself close to the *somba*, propping the iron door open while she crams pine cones in. She sits with her clothes open. Perhaps the baby can see and hear the fire, she thinks: did he see my hands in there, by the light of the candle? They must have made shadows on his red wall.

Here we are in a cold white house with icicles under the eaves and winter has hardly begun, but inside its walls are warm to the touch, full of firelight.

She has a couple of hours before she needs to start cooking lunch, and one full roll of fast film left: she will use them to take her last photographs. Bare interiors of sun and shade and firelight, in which as always she appears absent.

A GIRL ON THE SAND

I think I could live in almost any country now so long as I was not beyond the range of seagulls and the smell of water, salt water, lifted in on the wind.

'We Greeks, we can make a life in any country, Dimitri,' I remember my mother insisting. We chose Australia because there was work, and we have made a life. We have more or less mastered the language. We are here to stay.

This part of the coast of Australia, facing Bass Strait and the Southern Ocean, is where I want to build a house when I can afford one. Not because it reminds me of Greece. Except in its wildness it hasn't the least resemblance to any part of Greece that I knew. Maybe the wildness is why. The village of my childhood was on the plains under a ledge of mountains. Thunderstorms along this coast have all the savagery of the ones I remember, when lightning bolts struck farmers down in the fields and fireballs burst in at windows and burned children in their beds.

We talk a lot at home about the storms, the floods and droughts and iron winters, what was done in the War and then the Civil War. We feel it proves what we are made of. I have heard Australians talk with the same pride in having endured. Our countries have barrenness in common: the centre of ours is jagged rock, the centre of Australia dry sand and rock, and we take pride in this even if we never set foot there. May your soil be barren, one of our great modern poets has written – I forget his exact words. May your soil be barren so you don't have room to spread roots and so you keep groping deep.

It must be every day of fifteen years since I came to Australia with my mother and my married sisters. After the first months at General Motors I've mostly worked in restaurants and hotel kitchens, studying part time in the last few years to get a science degree. All I need now is a Diploma of Education and my mother will have a teacher for a son. This will impel her to try even harder to find me a bride. I'm forty this year and one failed marriage is more than enough, I tell her. I left all thought of marriage behind in Greece.

I spend a lot of time in this town on the coast, in the water when I'm free during the day and fishing on the pier at night. A lot of us sit in a row on the planks with a crayfish boat on props towering over us on each side. (Two cranes on the pier lower the boats into the water and hoist them out again.) There are the lights of the town slithering over the water, and far across it the slow red flicker of the lighthouse. There is the creak and lap of water on wood, as if we were in a boat on calm water. It was like that, fishing from a *varka* with a lamp on the gulf at night, out of Thessaloniki. But the sea wasn't icy and wild like this sea, or not often.

If my family has found life full of harshness here, it hasn't been any more so than we were bred for.

This afternoon, the lunch rush over, the rest of the staff have gone across the road for a swim: I'm going as well as soon as I clean up. Too tired to hurry, I trudge round collecting the last cups with their saucers full of slops and sodden butts. The door handle jiggles. Someone is making wild signs against the blue glitter of the sea: Jake, a local, a friend I go fishing with, so I have to unlock the door.

'Jesus, Jim. *Jesus.*' He shakes his head. His face is yellow, his eyes wide.

'Cup of coffee?' I'm being offhand to make it clear that whatever has happened I'm not turning round to make him lunch at this time of the afternoon.

He nods. Sitting at a smeared table, he covers his face with tight hands while I make a strong short black for the both of us.

'Well?'

'I've been up at the police station.'

I wait. Jake's a journalist. He makes the most of the stories he has to tell.

'Well, I went round to Western River.' I know that; he asked me if I wanted to come. 'Went for a swim, fished off the rocks for a while, you know, times goes by.' He catches my look. 'Listen, you bastard. There'd been a quick shower, heavy for a moment but only enough to make pits in the sand and raise a hot smell. A rainbow was forming out at sea.' I know those rainbows stretched from cape to cape. 'I was looking at it and paddling back through the warm water along the edge of the river and so' – he takes a deep breath – 'I nearly trod on her before I saw she was there.'

'A woman?' A lot of Jake's stories involve a woman.

'She had her legs in the water, half in, half out. Wide apart. And not a stitch on. She was – white all over. Long black hair full of seaweed and things hopping, sandflies. Oh, Jesus.' He stirs his coffee and takes a gulp. 'She was white and sort of grainy like – I don't know – white sugar. Or sand, a sand sculpture, seaweed for hair. She had dark stains on her.'

'Was she dead?'

'Of course she bloody was.'

'There's a bit of a rip along there.'

'She was dead before she got into the water, it looks like. Or so the cops say.'

'Murdered.'

'That's what Bill reckons.' Bill, the local sergeant, is a friend of Jake's. 'Smothered or strangled. They'll have to have an autopsy. Can you manage another coffee, Jim?'

I take the cups to the machine. I know the spot he means, where the river curves past a cliff of jagged brown rocks as bright as snakeskins. The cliffs that face the ocean at Western Beach are black, damp from noon on, and their shadows darken the sea at their base. I was fishing there just the other day. The high yellow slopes of scrub and autumn grass were heat-shaken. An undertone of insects would suddenly lurch close, sun-jewelled, then away out of sound. In the dark under the ocean cliffs the beach was as cold as a cave.

'She wasn't on the ocean beach?' I put down the coffees.

'Thanks. No, up the river a bit. The tide was going out.'

'You could tell she was dead.'

'Oh, Jesus, yes, right away. There was this sweetish – funny, though, I couldn't leave her there while I went and reported it. I don't know why. I couldn't bring myself to touch her – try to drag her up on to the sand or whatever. What if I gave her arm a tug and it came off in my hand? That's been known to happen. Anyway, in the end I dropped my shirt over her and got up on to the road and stopped the first local that came past – the new bloke from the fruit shop, it was – and told him to send the police. Then I went back and waited with her. Jesus. The silence.'

'How old was she? Roughly, I mean.'

'Fucked if I know, mate. I couldn't – Jesus, how are you supposed to tell?' He knits his fingers together and stares at them. 'Bill reckons about sixteen and they're pretty sure she was pregnant. She was bloody huge. I just thought she was bloated.'

'Blotted?' A word new to me.

'Swollen up, blown up?' His hands shape a dome over his belly. 'Corpses do at a certain stage. I couldn't tell you how long it takes. Ever seen one?'

'Yes, often. In 1941 when the Germans occupied Greece. I was only a boy. I can't remember how long it took them to – blot.'

'Bloat.'

'People died in their sleep then, side by side on footpaths. When I woke up there would be a head bent back further along the row. A mouth open on broken teeth, eyes rolled back. Rats ate the noses off live babies.'

'Jesus. I never saw her face, come to think of it. Her hair was all over it. Can I have one more coffee and then I'll go?' But as I get up to make it he grabs my wrist. 'Wait on. I haven't told you the worst thing yet, have I? Jesus. The fucking worst thing.'

'Wait till I get the coffee.'

I make one cup. When I bring it he is leaning into the corner with his head flung back so that nothing of his face shows but his trowel of ginger beard.

'Coffee.'

'Yeah. Thanks, mate.' The beard waggles.

'This worst thing.'

He heaves himself round with a sigh to face me: 'She only had one hand.'

'One – '.

'Hand. Bitten off in the water. I thought. But then I got a better look after the cops arrived. Her arm ended smoothly at the wrist. It must have come off a long time ago. Maybe she was born like that.'

'Little buds of fingers on the end of her wrist,' I say.

'That's right.' He narrows his eyes. 'How did you know?'

I shrug. 'I've seen it before.' (Where have I?) 'Why is that the worst thing?'

'Fucked if I know. It just is.' He sips the coffee. 'Ah! Good one, Jim.' I've put whisky in it.

He has nothing more to say. Neither of us has. Once he has finished his coffee and driven off, I lock the door and walk down to the beach. No one knows yet that a girl has been found, nudged by yellow ripples of water and sand. Her legs were open in the shape of a gulf. *Kolpos* means gulf in Greek; it also means vagina, which shocks my Australian friends – a word like that all over the map. The sea froths over my feet and tugs and furrows the sand under them. I no longer feel like a swim. I walk round as far as the rocks on the point (something is rising like a bubble in water to the surface of my mind) and lie down on the sand.

Kitchens have been my life. Ploughed fields were meant to be, as they were for my father; but when he was away fighting in the War and the Civil War we had to move to the city for safety. We found two downstairs rooms in a tenement in the red-light district of Thessaloniki, not far from the railway station. We slept on the floor on *kilimia*, all five of us, I and my two sisters, our

A GIRL ON THE SAND

mother and our grandmother. What hope did the girls have of growing up chaste, I overheard our mother ask our grandmother one night: ours would be like all the other families where brothers dishonoured sisters and ended up pimping for them.

'What rubbish, Melpo,' my grandmother said. 'Dimitri's not like that. You know he has a sense of honour.'

A sense of honour: *philotimo*. Or rather, a pride in one's honour. Of all things to saddle me with. A very selective honour, since I stole, or we would have starved. Perhaps there's no honour free of paradox; no pride either.

In 1964 when I was twelve I started work as a kitchen and water boy in a *taverna* owned by a friend of my father's. All the *tavernes* had one or two boys who worked from the early morning until midnight with an hour off in the afternoon, their shaven heads cuffed for the smallest mistake. They could scrounge a living from tips and food scraps. My tips came from the girls in a couple of nearby hotels and in the brothel, when I took meals to their rooms. They were fond of me and tried to keep me talking. They passed the time making coffee and telling fortunes in the grounds, gossiping about pimps and raids and abortions, and who had fought over whose girlfriend in what hashish den, and who had syphilis or consumption.

My mother knew this was part of my job. She wept over me and made me swear not to dishonour the family.

I wonder why I'm remembering this, after all these years. Is it because a girl with only one hand has been thrown up on the beach? She had long black hair. Maybe she was Greek. This is the moment when the bubble rises to the surface and bursts. I remember who she was.

At about half past two one dusty yellow afternoon she sidled into the *taverna* and ordered a *pilafi* and a lemonade at the counter. Our customers were working men, on the railways mostly: women didn't eat there alone. I saw her glancing nervously around, though no one, after the first stare, was taking any notice. She was a stranger, a country girl judging by her clothes (my mother would have known exactly where from) and by her bundle too, her *bogos* of worn home-woven wool which she balanced on the chair beside her. She wore a white scarf over her hair, and white gloves, in all that heat. I brought her bread and a glass of water. When her meal was served she drank the lemonade in one gulp and with the fork in her gloved hand she scooped up all the yellow rice and then she scrubbed the oil off her plate with the bread. Then she called me to ask for more water.

After I'd brought it she called me again. '*Mikre,*' she said: little one. It was how everyone called us boys. I went over, wiping my hands on my apron and wondering what she wanted this time. She had paid the waiter already. The last customers were getting up to go. 'Tell me your name?' she said, and slipped a coin into my hand.

'Why?'

She smiled. 'It's awful, calling you "*mikre*".'

'His name's Dimitri,' grinned a waiter on his way past.

'Mine's Dimitroula,' she said to me. 'Strange, isn't it? The same name.'

I shrugged. What was she getting at?

'Have your worked here long?'

'Two years,' I muttered.

'Will you help me then?' I had to bend down to hear her. 'I don't know a soul in Thessaloniki. I only just got off the bus. Do you know if there's a very cheap hotel round here that's – you know – suitable for families?'

I knew one. She sat back in relief, her hands clasped, and I saw her face, broad and brown with heavy-lidded dark eyes and a full mouth with a mole at one corner: an *elia*, an olive, as it's called in Greek.

I explained that she would have to wait outside for me. We could all see her standing there in the sun, shading her eyes to glance in from time to time. My friends and enemies all thought it was a great joke. 'What does she see in you, Dimitri?' one said. 'Can't she wait till your voice has finished breaking?'

'Shut up,' I said. 'You've got it wrong. She's my cousin on my mother's side.' They gave a yell of joy. 'She is. It's years since we saw each other. She lives in – Katerini.'

'And what's her name, Dimitri?' The waiter opened his eyes wide.

'None of your business.' She had opened her eyes like that as she said her name: I didn't believe it was Dimitroula. I had said Dimitri and she had said the first name that came into her head.

'He can't remember!'

'He forgot to ask!'

'Dimitroula!' I squeaked, to a burst of applause.

'Get on with the job, come on,' the cook growled. But he crooned 'Dimitroula *mou*' under his foul breath the whole time I was scrubbing his pots and pans. 'You've got one hour,' he called as I rushed out, and raised another laugh.

Red-faced, I hoisted the girl's bundle over my shoulder and set off with her trotting beside me down the gravelled laneways to the Hotel Epiros.

'Epiros!' She made a face.

'Well, it's respectable. It's for families.'

'Yes, all right. It was just the name. My parents live there, in a village near Albania.'

I put down her bundle on the doorstep. 'I told them at work that you're from Katerini. I had to say something.'

'A lot further than that.'

'I *know*.' Did she think I didn't know Epiros was near Albania?

'No. Where I live is much further than Katerini. Skala – I live in Skala with my aunt. I haven't seen my parents since the Germans came.'

'Seven years!'

'That's right. I don't care. Neither do they. Now the *andartes* have taken over.'

'You'd have been conscripted! They're conscripting girls.' She shrugged. 'Skala where?' There are villages called Skala this or Skala that all over the coast of Greece. She bit her lip and looked down. 'All right, don't tell me then. Suit yourself.'

The manager came: he knew me. If she hadn't been with me she would never have got in, since she had no papers on her. He handed her key to me.

The passages of the Epiros were dingy and rank and had cockroaches. Piss glistened on the bathroom floor; on the enamel footplates and in the holes of the lavatories shit of various shades was clumped. A country girl would be used to worse, I knew. The air in her room was hot, striped with dusty yellow light. But the sheets on the bed were washed and starched and the blankets were old army ones, thin but solid. Families from the villages stayed there regularly: no one would molest her.

I dropped her bundle on the stiff blanket and she sank down beside it, her scarf slipping so that her hair fell along the pillow in a flow of black.

I opened the window and went to unfasten the shutters.

'No,' she said. 'Let's leave them shut.'

'I have to go,' I said.

'No, stay a minute. Don't go, Dimitri.'

I felt uncomfortable. She saw that I did, and sat up. 'I don't know a soul. What will I do?'

'I have to get back to work.'

'I have to find a doctor.'

'What's wrong with you?'

She gave a snort and her gloved hand shaped a dome over her belly.

'Ah,' I said as if I knew.

'Three months. I have to get rid of it.' *Na to petaxo* was what she said: to throw it away.

'Ah.' Now I knew. 'Can't you get married?'

Her nose reddened and her eyes spilled out tears which she wiped on her glove.

'I've got the money. My aunt gave me plenty. It has to be straight away. She said, "You come back in that condition and I'll stick a knife through it and you." '

I hid my shock. 'I think I can find out where there's a doctor.' The whores were certain to know a good one.

A GIRL ON THE SAND

'Oh, can you? Can you really? When?'

'Tonight. I'll come and tell you on my way home.'

'Will you? You promise?'

'Of course I will.'

'Dimitri, my life's in your hands.'

'I *know*. I said, I promise.'

I worked hard that night at the *taverna*, spurred on by jeers about how tired I looked. I knew who I could ask: Lina, the one I liked best, the one who made the most fuss of me. She had a lame leg, and that may have been another reason. When I went to pick up her dinner dishes – there'd been no time earlier – I asked if she'd do me a favour.

'Anything, anything, my darling,' she said.

So I stammered it out: where did she think my mother's cousin from Katerini could get a safe abortion? Lina lit a cigarette. 'You bad boy!' She goggled her black-rimmed eyes at me.

'Come on, Linaki. This is serious.'

'I'll say it is. You're telling me.' She passed me the cigarette for a quick puff. 'You could always marry the poor thing.'

I choked the smoke out. 'It isn't *mine*!'

'You all say that,' she sighed. 'Don't I know it?' She shrugged at herself in the wavy mirror, grabbing the cigarette and blowing a fan of smoke at her dark face staring back. She was enjoying herself. She went on like this for some time. Time was short, so was my temper, and the more thwarted and sullen I became, the more she teased. But she wrote a name and address at last. I grabbed her dishes and turned to go, but she took them back, put them on the dressing table and demanded a kiss. Angrily I jammed my mouth on her blotched lips.

'I won't tell,' she said. 'You be sure to take good care of your little cousin.' She stroked my cheek. 'She's in for a bad time. I should know.'

I kissed her again, and I meant it.

I ran to the hotel after work and told Dimitroula. She looked distraught and I felt bad about leaving her alone, but I was dropping with tiredness by then and my mother, as I explained, always waited up. Early next morning before work I took her to the address, a shuttered upstairs surgery. She was lucky, the nurse said: the doctor would do it that very morning. I knew I had no hope of getting off work early, so I told Dimitroula she would have to find her own way back to the hotel, but I would come straight after work and see if she needed anything.

It was well after three when I knocked on her door and called softly. 'Come in,' I heard. The door was unlocked, though she had the shutters and the window closed. In the thick heat I made out her face, a paleness as it moved on the pillow and made a ripple in her long strands of hair.

'Something to eat,' I muttered, having at great risk – a boy sacked for thieving wouldn't get another job – smuggled out a lump of stewed meat and potato wrapped in a teatowel. I presented it: the red sauce had soaked through. She gasped and turned abruptly away, flinging her brown arm up over her eyes and I saw that for the first time she wasn't wearing her gloves and – I peered closer in the dimness – *her hand had been cut off*.

I screamed.

'Take that thing away,' she groaned. 'Oh, it's all over blood. It looks like a – take it away, I'll be sick.'

I put the teatowel of food down on the floor outside her room and shut the door quietly. Her voice was thick, she had been crying. She was again, but she patted the blanket for me to sit down.

'Why did he cut your hand off?'

She sobbed, or laughed, and rubbed her wrist against my thigh. 'Don't be silly,' she said. 'Oh, why did you have to see it? I didn't want you to.'

'No, let me see.' I stared as she turned her arm, plump and brown on the top and white underneath like a loaf of bread. Her veined wrist ended in five small buds.

'How did it happen?'

'I was born with it like this. That's why my mother wouldn't have anything to do with me. My father's sister said she'd have me and they send her money every summer for my keep.'

'The same aunt? The one in – Skala?'

'Yes. She's fond of me in her way.' She caught my look. 'Well, she brought me up. A deformed child that no one wanted.'

'She made you come here by yourself and find a doctor.'

'She's letting me go back. Not everyone would.'

'Do you want to? After what she said about the knife?'

'Where else can I go? My own mother didn't want me to live.' Her eyes closed and tears ran into her ears and her loose hair. She whimpered something I didn't hear.

'Don't cry.'

'I'm worse than she is now. I've killed my baby.'

'They made you, though.'

'But I wanted to have it. You should have heard my aunt. "You're hard enough to marry off already," she said. I know that.' She held her arm up. 'Who wants a wife like this?'

'Can I feel it?'

She nodded. I touched the nodules with my long fingers: they felt like a baby's knuckles.

'It's not so terrible. It's only when you first – '.

'There's more to it than that. Don't you understand?' She leaned forward and whispered: 'Why am I like this? How would you like to be my husband and have to wait nine months to see if the child was the same as me?' She watched me understand. ' "No wonder he ran away," my aunt said. The father. She called me a whore.'

I'll bet! Just what my mother would say if it was one of my sisters. A silence fell. 'Did you love him?' I said at last.

'He didn't even know about the baby. And a lot of men are after me, you'll be surprised to know. Crippled or not.'

'You're not *crippled*.'

'He was different. He was a boy I've always known. We were at school together. He had big ideas about saving the world and feeding the poor and all that. He never said he was a Communist.

I wouldn't have cared anyway. He left home a few weeks ago. He's in Epiros with the *andartes* now. He never told me anything. That's what his best friend said.'

'You haven't heard from him?'

'No one has. He's dead or as good as dead. The *andartes* are going to get wiped out. Don't you read the newspapers?'

I didn't. 'He might come back when it's over,' I said.

'And be shot? His father's waiting. And his brothers.'

'But you still love him.'

'No.'

'Because he's an *andartis*?'

'No, because he left like that without a word. Because he didn't trust me.'

'Why did you love him?' I was, I realise now, jealous of the boy.

'Why! Why does anyone?'

'I don't know.'

'You will.' She smiled, but her face crumpled and she was whimpering again. I stroked her hair. My hands must have stunk of the meat stew but she stayed still, her eyes closed. 'I'm tired,' she said, 'and my belly hurts.' The hair close to her head was soaked with sweat, the ends dry and feathery. I smoothed it back off her forehead until her breathing went heavy. Then I crept out.

A squeal, the snake dash of a grey body, brought me up short. A rat was crouched in the corner. It had mauled the teatowel with the meat. Sick with loathing, I kicked the ragged mess down the passage a long way from her door.

On my rounds that night I took a dinner to the Epiros for her (Epiros, where her lover had gone): they could dock the money out of my pay, I didn't care. I chose *yemista*, one pepper and two tomatoes stuffed with rice, since she liked rice; and a serving of bread and a bunch of yellow grapes. I stumbled on the gravel in the dark, and trudged along the dank passages half-afraid of what I might find. But a light was on inside and she opened the door herself. The one dirty bulb in the ceiling made yellow waves on the walls, leaving the furniture in the darkness.

'Did you sleep?' I asked sternly as she laid herself down on the bed.

'Yes, I feel better.' When she smiled her face was sleek and brown again. 'Oh, look how much you've brought! You'll have to help me eat it.'

I ate some rice to please her. She was slow but she finished it all and sopped the bread in the red oil and made me have a bite before eating that too. She lay carefully back with a sigh.

'Was it good?' I was eager for praise.

'You saved my life.' That was something the whores often said, but not the way she said it.

'It's nothing.'

'Here.' She took more drachmas than the dinner cost out of her purse and pressed them into my hand.

'No, it's all right! I'll pay.'

'Don't be silly, take it. My aunt gave me enough for my expenses. You have a family to support, haven't you? Put it in your pocket, go on.' I put it in my pocket. 'Have you got a girlfriend, Dimitri?'

'No,' I muttered. 'I'm only fourteen.'

'Is that all? You look older. I'm sixteen.'

'What a shame. You're too old for me.'

'What a shame. And you're good-looking too.' Her tone, her teasing smile: it was just what I needed. On such familiar ground I could relax. 'Don't go thinking I can't do things,' she went on. 'I can. I have a sort of leather strap that I wear on my wrist. I can cook, sew, knit, mend nets. I can embroider and use the loom. Anything.'

'You mean you've got your *proika* ready?' Even in those hard times some girls had managed to make sheets and woven blankets and clothes for their *proika*. My sisters hadn't.

'Everything. Why not?'

'Well, I can't marry for a long time,' I assured her. 'I have two unmarried sisters.'

'Bad luck.'

Traditionally the brothers have to wait until their sisters marry. A few years later, as it happened, I did marry before them. It caused a lot of bitterness in my family and gossip outside it. After ten years of murderous turmoil – war, disease, hunger – the grip of tradition had loosened. Magda, the girl I was in so much of a hurry to have, was like Dimitroula to look at, broad-faced and full-lipped. She had no physical flaw. Not even a mole.

'Aren't you going to eat the grapes?' I had to go back to work. 'They're good. Very sweet.'

'I'm too full. I'll have them for breakfast.'

I put them on the dressing table. 'You're sure you'll be all right?'

'Yes. You have to be getting back.'

'I'd stay with you if I could.' I wanted to stay.

'I know. I'll be all right, don't worry. I'll be leaving in the morning.'

'Will you come past the *taverna* and say goodbye?'

'If you want.'

'Is it the Skala near Platamona?'

She smiled. 'No. It's another one. Bend down,' she said, 'and give me a kiss.' Balancing the dishes, I knelt and kissed the mole beside her mouth. She turned her head to kiss me on the mouth. 'Good night,' we both said. Her damp hair smelled of salt.

That night for all my tiredness I lay awake a long time listening to the four women who depended on me, two old and two young, breathing in the dark.

Next morning she looked in through the door of the *taverna* – I was keeping an eye out – and waited till I had a chance to come outside. She was scarved, gloved and her face was sombre. 'I should have died,' she said. 'I wish I had. Then I wouldn't have to go back.'

'You can always come and live here,' I said, sure even as I spoke that she would never want to come back here. 'I could find you a room.' I was about to lose her.

'How would I live? Or don't you know?' I did know. She kissed my cheek, smiled, and walked off with her bundle.

With the passing of time I suppose I fell in love with her, or with the thought of her. I relived every word, every look. If I saw a white scarf in the distance, it had to be hers (and it never was). In my daydreams she came to the *taverna*, only this time I stayed the two nights at the hotel to keep her company and on the second morning she told me she was never going back to Skala. I worried when I changed my job: where would she find me now? I made up scenes, chance meetings. I would be taking meals up to the whores one night, for example, and find her among them. Or she would pass me in the street one day with a man and a child, children, and know me, or not know me.

We were fated to meet again. I was certain of it.

In the village your family is your life, or it was in those days. I was too young then to understand how she felt. When my wife Magda was caught in the arms of a neighbour who was our mortal enemy, she ran away; and the dishonour to our family drove my mother to emigrate to Australia. Maybe Dimitroula escaped by coming here, if the authorities would let her in with only one hand. She might have run away to the city; she would be easy to trace, but her aunt would hardly bother. My feeling is that she stayed in Skala and endured the darting eyes of visitors and the chatter in the street that stopped as she came near and waited for her to move on. They all knew too much about her, but she was never one of them. They smiled and kept their distance. There's no Greek word for privacy, as it's understood in English – nor for intimacy, if it comes to that. There is for loneliness: *monaxia*.

To be Dimitroula and be confined to Skala, wherever it was! I can see her as the scarved woman posed to give depth to postcard photographs: walking by a white bell tower or against fishing boats mirrored in the shallows. I saw a lot of sea ports during my national service. She might have been any one of the women – if I ever happened on the right Skala – that I saw watering geraniums in kerosene tins, hanging up herbs to dry, mending a net in a doorway, seagulls at her feet. (Did she ever think of me?)

If I did see her again, neither of us knew it. Her story has long since lost any power to move me. It must be twenty-five years since it occurred to me to wonder if she was alive, if she was happy or not. Now our lives have crossed a second time – no, drawn close without touching, a second time. Lives with their roots not spread but sunk deep.

No tide of any ocean could have washed her round the world from Skala to Western River, I know that. Even if she was living on this coast, she's forty-two now, not sixteen, and the sergeant said the girl was sixteen. That's not the point. Whoever she turns out to have been, and whoever killed her and why, the girl that Jake found has nothing to do with me. The link is too fine and fragile.

Even if it is Dimitroula.

The police will call on the public to come forward with any information that might help them identify the body. Nothing I have to tell could do more than confuse them and raise false suspicions. (Even if it is Dimitroula.) For me to claim more part in her life than I have had would be to falsify it. My part has been to stand by once – now twice – and witness, and stay silent. Why this should be, who knows?

What do I know about her? She was a beautiful, lonely, passionate woman who took risks. They think she was also pregnant. She has died by violence and her death seems to be something I was meant to learn of. Maybe I was meant to find her body; I spend a lot of time round at Western River. She looked like white sugar, he said. Or sand. I spread hanks of hairy seaweed in a fan. With my palms I raise and smooth the shape of a breast out of the sand, a second breast and the high dome of a belly. I make her two arms and one hand. I spread her legs wide apart. Between them a gulf of sand was formed as the yellow river water sank away from her.

Surfers are riding past me in the green waves.

The rocks here on the point are blistered with sandy pools

where the water is blood-hot. There are limpets and blue-black mussels and grape weed. A beaded net in a pool below a rock is the reflection of the sun's glitter on lichen on the rock. I measure the slowness of bubbles as they rise. A small flathead sways and noses under shadows. Puckering the pool, an insect trails over the sand its own magnified shadow ringed with bubbles of light in the precise form of a tea-tree flower. A limpet lifts its lid as water nudges it: the tide is coming in.

What part, I wonder, does free will play? I talk of honour and endurance and love.

THE HAREM

When Bell was nine the SEC transferred her father from Melbourne to Wangalla for nine months. In no time he was sick and tired of living in a room at Doolan's pub. He sent Bell and her mother scrawled postcards full of loneliness. For the school holidays he found them a cheap house near the station, and they could have the run of it but for Mr Grey's own front room where he kept himself to himself. Bell sneaked in for a look. His double bed was a smelly bundle of grey sheets and blankets. Morning sunshine burned in fluff all over his oiled floor and the dusty mirror over his dressing table.

Mr Grey owned the house opposite too, where the Harem lived. He owned the woodyard next door, its stacks of red-furred wood guarded by a savage dog. It said so on the gate. He owned half of Grey Bros iceworks; sometimes they met him on hot afternoons, chipping out shimmering blocks and carrying them wrapped in sacking on his shoulder into the shaded houses, while his horse stamped. Mr Grey was a widower and childless, and ought to have been well off but for his drinking problem. Bell thought he was old, but her mother said no, but he'd let himself go. Mr Grey was affable in the evenings and surly before noon. His little wrinkled eyes had veins, and when he yawned he showed yellow pegs of teeth. He spent most afternoons in the pub and even ate there. He shambled in about seven, banging doors, and sometimes crashed and swore, and sometimes sang snatches of "Knees up, Mother Brown" or "Oh, you beautiful doll".

The yard at Mr Grey's was shaded by a red-leafed tree dripping with little red plums sweet and yellow inside and warm when the sun was in them. A tame bird lived behind the tree. A curlew, Mr Grey said. It squatted in the dust or minced around and cocked its gold eyes. Once Mr Grey caught Bell throwing plums at it to make it hop and bridle.

'Know what happens to kids ut do that, do yer?' he growled. 'Bird gets in at night. Pecks their eyes out and swallers um.'

All night in the dark it hovered. A weird cry, a scimitar beak. Her mother insisted on fresh air. Every night once her light was off Bell leapt up and latched her windows.

Down the lane from the house there was a long footbridge over the railway lines, and the Spirit of Progress surged under it gushing great clouds and hooting. The wheels pumped, grinding, glittering. The high blue engine whooped. Every morning Bell rushed to the bridge for the Spirit to wrap her in hot white billows.

Once as she tore out she saw that the woodshed gate was open, the red dog bounding up, barking, slavering. She propped, but he only wanted to prance and bow and lick her hands. The Spirit shrieked. Bell and the dog took off and reached the bridge in good time. When the train had slid away they sauntered back together.

'If yer gunna take Rover out,' Mr Grey warned, 'watch out yer bring um back. Worth a packet, that dorg is.'

After that whenever the dog saw Bell he bowed and whined, a slobbery wood-chip in his teeth for her to throw. At Spirit time he jumped at the gate with his tail whipping. She called him Red, not Rover. Red was covered in such tight curls he looked as if June had permed him with her lotions and pins.

June lived with Mr and Mrs Peterson and their daughter Kate in the Harem. Mr Malone the grocer called it that. Met the Harem yet? He winked at Bell's mother but she seemed not to notice.

'Mum, what's a harem?'

'Oh, a sort of Arab family.'

June was tall and heavy, with curly red hair – hennaed, Bell's mother said – as glossy as plum-skins. Advertisements in shop windows said that Miss June Smith did hairdressing in your own home by appointment. Bell's mother said June looked fast, and she was, pedalling along from head to head on a glittering bicycle with netted wheels. Women waited for her with their hair lank and wet in kitchens soaked in the waxen light of hot sun behind holland blinds. Often three or four women would wait in the kitchen of one of them, who laid on tea with buns, or scones, or fruitcake. The teapots wore their best knitted cosies. June's bicycle was parked on all the best Wangalla verandahs. Sometimes it was leaning on the hot brick wall of Doolan's for all the world to see.

When Bell's mother first had her hair done, she hadn't met the other SEC wives, so no one else was there until Mr Grey slouched in. June laughed and smoked and told long jokes, and ate more than her share of the buttered Boston bun at afternoon teatime. When she had gone, Mr Grey wiped crumbs off his whiskers, sighed, and muttered, 'Fine figure of a woman. They say she's got a temper, but. Stands to reason, eh? Hair like that.'

Bell's mother sniffed.

'I reckon it's a blasted waste,' Mr Grey droned on.

Bell and her mother met Mrs Peterson at the grocer's. She had a toothy grin and long hair coiled in a dun roll on the bone of her nape. She was so homesick for the Old Country. Here the neighbours were so standoffish, weren't they? Do call me Mary, she said. Bell's mother said to call her Judith. Well now, how would Judith's little girl like to come over and play with her Kate? Kate wasn't much older really, only eleven, and so awfully lonely, poor child.

Sullenly dressed up in frills and strap shoes Bell was sent over to play.

Kate was tall and slim with a white face and straight black hair. Bell was tubby and pink, her hair butter-coloured. Kate was allowed to be barefoot, and dressed all in black. She had bitten her scarlet nails. Her eyes when they met Bell's were long and scowling, unsmiling. With her light on in bright daylight she showed Bell her treasures, her jewels, her greasepaints. She was going to be an actress. She let Bell try on in the dressing table mirror her Arabian brass bangles – so they *were* Arabs – and the strings of green and gold glass beads she spent her time threading. She showed Bell fuzzy photos of her relatives back home, then they sat on her bed to read her Enid Blyton books, stealing glances at each other in the yellow glare of the lamp.

When Kate said 'grass' it rhymed with 'mass'. She said 'somethink' and 'anythink', and called lemonade 'pop'. Later Bell's mother was annoyed when she said things Kate's way: don't copy poor speech, Annabel, please.

Bell was asked to stay to dinner, and ran across to ask her mother, who said yes. With the door open, the Peterson's kitchen table only just fitted in between the stove and the ice chest. Mr Peterson squeezed in on one side between Mrs Peterson and June, and Bell and Kate sat opposite. The light bulb was on a cord and swilled shadows over them with every gust of the northerly. The table cloth of pages from the *Age* lifted, flapped. They had a sweetish red stew with lumps of meat and soft potatoes, and drank 'shandies' of beer and lemonade mixed. They all called the lemonade 'pop'. A rare treat for Bell, it was spoilt by the beer. The grown-ups had just beer. Their breaths smelled like the hot buffets of air when the bar doors opened at Doolan's. Bell's parents never touched liquor.

'Coom on, Mary. Drink oop, loov.' Mr Peterson cuddled Mrs Peterson, winking at Bell. But Mrs Peterson only shook her drooping head.

After the stew Bell thought she should say thank you for the lovely dinner and go home, but Mrs Peterson gave them all peaches and spotty apples from the ice chest. They peeled them on to their dinner plates. June, showing Bell how to cut her apple through its equator to make a star-apple, dropped it and splashed stew on Bell's dress. June peeled her own apple all in one piece and tossed the peel over her shoulder to see who she would marry. Mrs Peterson's bony nose turned red. You couldn't make out any letters in the coils of apple peel. June and Mr Peterson lit cigarettes and blew smoke.

'Cheer oop, Mary, for the loov of Mike,' Mr Peterson boomed.

THE HAREM

'Ah'll open another bottle. Put a bit of life into the blooming proceedings.'

'I'm making coffee, Bob,' was all Mrs Peterson said, putting the jug on. Their coffee wasn't boiled in a saucepan with grounds on top, but mixed with syrup from a long black bottle with a picture on the label of a turbanned Arab. At home Bell was only allowed a drop of tea or coffee in her milk. She and Kate filled their coffee with sugar. Not even Kate was taking any notice of Bell. They were all shiny with sweat.

After the coffee Mr Peterson and June left the table hand in hand and shut themselves in a bedroom. Mrs Peterson sighed and boiled the jug again for the dishes. Bell helped scrape plates. Footsteps shambling down the back path startled them all. 'The boogie man,' breathed Kate in Bell's ear. But with a cough Mr Grey's shabby head was thrust into the lamplight. He said no thanks to coffee. He'd just dropped in to pass the time of day. He'd better be orf home, thanks, Mary.

When Bell asked Kate in her room what her father and June were doing, Kate said that if she didn't know at her age, thut was too bud, wasn't it? She shrugged.

'Bob looves them both. Me moom and June.'

'Oh.'

'He likes me best. He said so.'

'Oh, really?' was all Bell's mother had to say to that when she heard.

That was another interesting thing: Kate's father would only answer to 'Bob', not 'Father' or 'Dud'. He wore a bristly brown moustache and once belted Kate with his razor strop, and worked as a foreman at the cannery.

'Mum, can we buy that Arab coffee?'

'No, we can't.'

'But it's lovely!'

'They had no business to give a child coffee. You've got sauce on your dress.'

'June did it. It's stew.'

'Don't answer back.'

'Mum, what's a four man?'

Her parents decided that if she was asked again she was to say thank you, but her tea would be ready at home, and then come straight home. Because we say so, they said when she asked why. But she could still go over and play. She kept quiet about the shandies.

Kate came over the next morning to see if Bell could go for a swim in the river with them. Mr Grey said he'd be in that : too right he would. 'Well, well, well. Here's K-K-K-Katy,' sang Bell's father jovially, and Kate said, 'My name's Kate.' Bell's mother said definitely not, what with snags and currents and tiger snakes in the river. Bell's mother and father were awful. Kate was, too. They all were.

That was the Sunday the roast leg of lamb got blown as it waited on the table for the vegetables to cook. Her mother said the flies had got to it, but Bell could only see little white threads in rows, like specks of fat. Her mother said she wasn't to tell a soul, did she hear, and ran over to the Harem to borrow some meat. Bell and Dad read the Sydney Sunday papers. The hot darkness by the firestove was full of the sweaty smell of the roast. A long time later her mother came back with a tin of Spam, and served it cold with the vegetables. Bell sulked and said it was a blasted waste, but had to eat Spam or starve, while in the woodyard Red tore and gulped the grey leg and lay dreaming afterwards with the bone in his paws. The treacly dripping had to be poured into a hole in the garden, not back into its hole in the speckled wax in the dripping-basin.

Bell's mother told Dad that she had found poor Mary alone and in such a state that she had had to stay and calm her down. They sent Bell out to play while she told him all about it.

'Oh. But there's nothing to *do*.'

'Go on, sticky-beak,' grinned Dad.

There were some very hot days that week. For hours Bell lay and read in nothing but bathing togs on the cool linoleum in the kitchen. She was allowed to spray herself with the hose in the yard, squinting through rainbows and sheets of wet light, water pounding her. Tawny butterflies shook their wings. She swung ropes of glittering water under the tree, where the dry lawn glowed all over with soft plums. Her mother spent one whole afternoon boiling and bottling jam, some for them and some for Mr Grey. At teatime she sighed, saying how in Melbourne they could have just hopped on a bus and been at the beach in no time. She and Dad quarrelled that night in their hot room beyond the wall. Things were scurrying on top of Bell's ceiling. Her mother was always hoping to high heaven it was nothing worse than possums.

At the window the curlew wailed.

Bell was sent over to the Harem with a jar of plum jam. In her yellow room Kate made her shut her eyes. 'Now open them,' Kate said. She had a solid glass egg. When Bell cupped it in her hands like a chicken it was cold and glowed, a heavy drop of stony water, magnifying her palms. Through it she could see all the bulging golden room. A rainbow light lay deep inside. The egg caught lamplight and sunlight and nursed them like seeds.

'It's crystal,' Kate whispered. 'Bob gave it me. It's valuable. I can tell fortunes in it. I can read minds.'

Bell peered again.

'No, it only works for me.'

'How does it work?'

'Never you mind.'

She swore Bell to secrecy. Even so, she hid the egg away and wouldn't say where, or even let Bell have another little look, however much she begged and wheedled.

For a week Bell clung to Kate's side. Every afternoon they walked Red along the river banks or behind the ice cart for chips of ice to suck. Kate showed Bell her school with its empty yard of asphalt and yellow tussocks. Bell showed Kate Mr Grey's curlew. Kate threw plums and one hit it. She wouldn't talk about the crystal egg.

At last, alone in Kate's room while Kate went to the WC, Bell gave in to temptation. Evening was falling from a hot sky the colour of apricots. In Kate's golden room Bell dared to kneel and go rummaging. But as she grasped it, hard and icy in a singlet in the bottom drawer of the dressing table, Kate's face appeared. It glared down at her in the lit mirror.

'Put it down, you thief!' Kate hissed.

Bell, sick with shock, turned to face Kate's white face. Had Kate read her mind? They were both shaking, both in pyjamas and slippers, as were the grown-ups, it was so hot, out in the kitchen playing a rowdy game of cards with Mr Grey.

'I only wanted a look!'

'Oh did you now? Well, joost for thut, you're never going to see it again. I've a good mind to tell Bob on you.'

'No, Kate, please!'

'He'll belt you till you bleed.'

'I wasn't going to take it! Why *can't* I have a look? Aren't I your friend?'

'No. You're not. Go home, Sneak.'

Bell stared and burned.

'Go on. Before I change me mind. Tell your moom you're a thief. Tell her I'm not her babysitter.'

Shaken with sobs, Bell ran home. No one saw. She latched her windows and got straight into bed to hide in her hot pillow. She pretended to be asleep when her mother looked in, opened a window and switched off the light. Bell latched it again. The slow night passed. Over breakfast the next day she told about the shandies and so was banned from the Harem forever. She brought up her breakfast though, and had to go back to bed. Her mother and father brought her cool drinks, and food that she couldn't face; they read to her, sponged her, took her temperature and worried all day whether to call the doctor. By teatime she felt a lot better. She had scrambled eggs and slept for fourteen hours.

Next morning Kate was out on the footpath with scrawny Cynthia Malone, the grocer's daughter, drawing with chalks, so Bell had to make herself go out for the Spirit, with Red for company, prancing. They whispered and giggled behind her back. Afterwards they were still there having snail races, prodding the frothed brown shells and barracking. Cynthia's baby brother that she was supposed to be minding picked one up and ate it.

The gas heater blew up that afternoon. No one could have a bath. Bell's mother cried. She said it was the last straw. Then she said that the last matinee of the panto at the Tivoli was next Saturday, so they could still see it if Bell wanted to, but only if they went home a week early. Bell was overjoyed. She wanted to go home very badly. Even though it would mean leaving Dad and Red. So that was all settled.

June came over after tea to give Bell's mother's hair a quick trim. She was in a hurry and took puffs of her cigarette as she snipped.

'No time for a coopa, thanks, dear,' she said. 'No rest for the wicked.'

'June?' Bell said. 'Can Kate really read minds with her crystal egg?'

'Not now, Bell, June's busy.'

'What's thut, Bell? Did Kate tell you she had a crystal egg?'

'She *showed* me. It's beautiful.'

'Well, well. And where does she keep it?'

'In her bottom drawer in a singlet. It's valuable.'

'I'm sure it is. I'd like to see it.'

'Oh, she won't show you. It's a secret.'

'Oh, I think she will.'

June's face was dark, her crimson lips thin and tight. Bell kept quiet, then.

Over the road that night the lights were still on late, all the lights, and there were shouts and doors slammed. Bell was up way past her bedtime helping her mother with the ironing that she'd put off till then in the cool of the night. Dad looked up from his crossword.

'Sounds like the Sheik's got a war on his hands. Might just pop over and help him out. Even up the odds, eh?'

'It's no laughing matter, Alan. It's a disgrace.'

'Who do you back to win? I'll have two bob on June.' He winked. 'Or one? One Bob on June.'

'Oh, Alan, really. That poor little girl, that's all I can say. What hope has she got?'

'Why's Kate a poor little girl?'

'Never you mind. Off you go now, lovey, it's high time you were in bed.'

'Oh, Mu-um.'

Bell lay awake for ages with her door half-open in the dark, listening to squeals and scamperings above; bird cries outside; silence from the Harem. Her parents' light and Mr Grey's were yellow stripes under their doors.

In the morning the Harem was still silent behind its blinds until, just before the Spirit was due, the front gate slammed. June was out there alone, holding a suitcase and wheeling her bicycle. Her eyes and hair were hidden by her black-veiled hat, but her plummy lips were tight, her head high for the benefit of starers in the gardens and front windows. As she faltered in the dazing sun, Mr Grey appeared in pyjamas in his doorway, padded to the front door, and opened it. Then June came striding over.

'Well, here I am, Tom Grey,' she said. 'If you still want me.'

'Too right I do,' he said, white under his whiskers. So in she came and snibbed the gate, propped up her bicycle, handed her suitcase to Mr Grey still sagging in the doorway in his fluffed pyjamas, and kissed him. Bell and her mother stood by openmouthed as Mr Grey and June, hand in hand, shut themselves in his bedroom.

Bell hung around as long as she could, until the Spirit hooted: there were only a few mornings left. That was the golden day they had sandwiches and cordial on a bank of the river where ruffled branches hung their shadows looping in brown water. Red capered then snoozed. Her mother let her take snaps with the Box Brownie, and asked if she was sorry to go and if she'd miss Kate. When Bell said she'd never really liked Kate, her mother nodded, and left it at that.

At teatime they went out for a fish-and-chip tea at the Bridge Cafe, for the first time ever, to give the lovebirds a go.

'How's that for calling a bloke's bluff, eh?' Dad couldn't get over it. 'Well, he's bitten off more than *he* can chew. What a woman!'

'Can I ask June for a ride on her bike?'

'No, you can't. Don't talk with your mouth full.'

'Must've really done her block to walk out,' Dad went on. 'What set her off, I wonder? That's redheads for you.'

'It's dyed.'

Dad went on about how the blokes at work would be all agog, especially the ones that drank at Doolan's and had seen it coming. Her mother's answers were in such long words, Bell lost the thread, watching how the white bubbles heaved in a milk shake when you blew down the straw. Her father paid the bill and slipped some pennies in Bell's pocket. They all strolled home arm in arm the long way as the sky turned green and stars showed.

The next few days were a flurry of washing and pegging out wrung sheets and shirts that flapped like yacht sails on the lines; packing suitcases; having goodbye cups of tea in waxy kitchens. Bell and her mother were booked on the Spirit, and Dad was moving back to Doolan's pub. The bicycle stayed proudly on the verandah, but June and Mr Grey never seemed to be in. No one saw Kate or her parents at all, but Mr Grey told Dad that Bob and Kate were moving to Sydney and Mrs Peterson was on her way back to the Old Country. He wrote down Bell's Melbourne address for the wedding invitation.

The day before they went Bell said goodbye to all the house and the yard, the glowing shaggy plum tree stripped of its plums, the ruffled curlew, and poor sad Red who sensed it and whined, thrusting his rough head into her hands. In the house she visited every corner, remembering moments. No one was home. Her heart thumping, she pushed open the door of Mr Grey's front

THE HAREM

room. His bed was flat now. Silver brushes and combs and bottles of green-gold scent stood on lace on his dressing table. The mirror, burning, reflected Bell's joy and amazement. There at last was the crystal egg. It was glowing with inner fire among the ornaments.

MARKET DAY

The market town stayed green even now, when the fields of ripe wheat and barley all around for mile after mile were scorched and the simmering air wavered in ripples over them. The stork, its long legs trailing back like a mosquito's, dipped over its frayed shadow, landing to prod the stubble. Over fields and cracked creek beds the crows flapped: ka ka ka ka-o.

But the market town stayed green. Everywhere leaves dripped over mossy stone and the carved wood of balconies, and the sound that underlay all other sounds there even in midsummer was the sound of water moving. Mikri Elpida had noticed that about the market town even as a child who could see. Now that she was blind, it was what she loved most. On every market day that the family went she insisted on going, jolting and stifled in the bus from the village. Even then there were all the sounds of water, even on market days, when the *pazari* drew in the buses roaring from every village, honking and farting; and tractors and motor *trikykla*, trucks and cars and horses-and-carts all crowded in; and felted donkeys minced along the damp streets between tiers of tomatoes, peppers, peaches packed in boxes. It was always the same. Then, as now, ragged women offered their crumbles of white butter folded in leaves. In the laneway, where whiffs of coffee and cumin and charring *souvlakia* caught at you as you passed, rows of plucked chickens hung their red necks out of windows. Soldiers and priests, gentlemen in suits, gypsies and grim little pigtailed widows pattered past, as they always had. Jostling strangers pounced, called your name and turned out to be relatives, all with some thrilling piece of news to tell.

When you were tired, you found a table outside one of the three *kafeneia* under the plane trees of the Square, as near to the spilling, rippling fountain as you could, and revived over a coffee, an ouzo with salty *mezedes* to eat, a cold *limonada*. It was

MARKET DAY

the same, year in year out, season by season. When it snowed you sat inside round the stove. The mountain thawed and all the street gutters swelled with ringing tunnels of glass, and soon the Square was overhung with wisteria in bunches. In midsummer all the great plane trees dropped darkness over the tables and the fountain, over your lifted face.

Mikri Elpida always took her knitting, for company, she said: and she was glad of it today. Her brother's daughter, Nitsa, sipping her *limonada* opposite was sunk in silence. Nitsa's silences were new these summer holidays, no one knew why. Her mother, Megali Elpida, had dumped her with Mikri Elpida and dragged the rest of the family off to carry shopping. Click click, chattered Mikri Elpida's needles. In the family, jokes – worn thin now – were still made sometimes about their names. Big Hope and Little Hope: just because Mikri Elpida's brother had happened to marry another, taller and slightly older, Elpida, and since they all lived in the one house . . . But Big Hope, Little Hope! People had to smile. Little hope indeed, for a blind girl with no dowry! Still, you never knew. Elpida smiled. Click click, click click. The wool tickled her cool hands.

'You're like a knitting machine,' Nitsa whined.

Elpida's hands clenched. 'I always knit. I'm sorry.'

'No – you're so good at it, that's what I mean.' Nitsa's voice warmed, by way of apology. Poor Aunt Elpida. But life was so cruel! Always alone, yet never alone for a moment! And must men keep staring like that? Those soldiers by the fountain . . . She had an impulse to tell Elpida her secret. What would Elpida know about love, though? She was like a quail in a cage. A dry little nun.

'You can knit just as well!' trilled Elpida. Hadn't she herself taught Nitsa? 'Don't you flatter me, now!' Nitsa, with a peevish shrug, decided: no. And now two of the soldiers were strolling over. Elpida went on laughing. Even her laugh was birdlike, in shrill staccato chirps. We must look like two schoolgirls, she was thinking, to anyone who doesn't know us. Maybe not *school*girls, no. Besides, wasn't Nitsa a full-bodied woman now? She had been for two summers: since she was – yes, fourteen . . .

Just then the two soldiers, as if they had every right, scraped back chairs at their table, and one said hotly, boldly, in Mikri Elpida's ear, 'You don't mind if we sit with you, do you, Yiayia?'

'Yiayia?' Did they take her for Nitsa's grandmother? 'Yiayia? Me? Imagine!' tinkled Elpida. Nobody heard. The soldiers and Nitsa were all suddenly talking at once: Nitsa was furious. The soldiers shambled off, Nitsa's shout of 'Who do you think you are?' lashing their backs.

'Imagine! He called me Yiayia,' Elpida persisted.

Nitsa snorted. 'They've got a nerve! Soldier boys! No, thank you!' She sucked on her straw. And burning behind her dark glasses, Elpida knitted.

A grandmother? Nitsa smiled. She looked nothing like one; just like a little brown aunt. She was thin, she was agile and sprightly. With her plaits and her always eagerly tilted face, she looked young: until you saw that the face had set as heavy as clay behind the black glasses, and the hair under the crown of plaits was grey. When she dried it in the sun, the bronze cape of it swept close to the ground. But down to her armpits it made a grey veil. 'Your plaits look as if you knitted them on,' Nitsa remarked.

'Really, do they?'

'Yes, a thick grey and brown knitted cap. If I bought the wool, what if you knitted me a pullover? Would you? Those exact colours, I think.'

Mikri Elpida was open-mouthed.

'Oh, not for me.' Nitsa hesitated. 'Listen – can you keep a secret?'

Grey! A thick grey and brown knitted cap! Worse, worse than being called Yiayia! Elpida's lips shook. Of course, there had to be some grey in it by now, but –

'*How* grey?' she burst out.

'. . . What? Oh, well, not at the ends, only on top. It's like the rings of a tree, isn't it? You can read your whole life in it. If I buy the wool, will you knit me a thick pullover? Will you? Say yes.'

'We'll see.' Elpida's lips were stiff now. No one had ever told her. She was a grey Yiayia, she who had hardly lived. She was a knitting machine.

Megali Elpida pounced on them then and bore them off to the hospital on the leafy hill, where an old aunt from another village had recently had a gangrenous leg amputated. The corridors and the wards breathed ether and phenol, sweat and hot linoleum. Eyes everywhere tracked them past. Megali and Mikri Elpida sat on Aunt Lena's bed, holding a papery hand each. Nitsa, discomforted, took the peaches they had brought over to the washbasin and rinsed them until their velvet skins darkened. The ward filled with the rosy smell of peaches. Now and then Aunt Lena muttered, clutching the hands to her cheeks, 'Ach, Elpida! Elpida!' That there was no hope all of them knew. Tears seeped down their faces.

Out in the sun, rowdy as children let out of school, they marched down arm-in-arm to sit by the fountain again and drink cold ouzo and savour the strong *mezedes* fiercely: the black bitterness of olives, sour peppered cheese with a green gloss of oil, hair-boned anchovies crusted with salt. Before they could finish, the family swooped and rushed them staggering off to catch the last bus. Bags of shopping punched their knees. Hoisted up by the elbows, stifling her gasps, Elpida stumbled along. *Bouzoukia* jangled. In the smoky oven of their bus – nobody would hear of opening a window – she fell asleep on Nitsa's shoulder, her stitches dropping, and woke only when the bus braked in its own dust at the village stop.

Oozing dusty sweat, Elpida said she was tired and went straight upstairs to lie down. In the kitchen, meatballs began to sputter in hot oil. The hens in the yard squabbled. Then the sun slid away and water was pounding into the bucket: the tired cow came clattering home. Elpida unplaited her hot hair. You can read your whole life in it! Your wasted life. I won't go to the *pazari* again, she decided. Never. Never. Coolness flowed in at the window. A cat wailed.

At nightfall the cats, sprawled moth-eaten furs all day, came alive and squatted outside to stab their green gaze at beetles and moths and mice. All the family sat in a circle in the yard, with only the kitchen light on, and the radio, though nobody listened. Neighbours and relatives strolling along the road were called over. Megali Elpida and Nitsa brought out plate after plate of meatballs, fried potatoes, bread. Our kitchen is a lantern in the dark, Nitsa thought, dropping crumbs for the cats: everyone gathers like moths outside it. Everyone, she saw, except Mikri Elpida – who more than anyone loved to sit outside in the dark.

'Where's my aunt?' she asked Megali Elpida.

'Lying down. Let her rest.'

Knocking, Nitsa swept in without waiting to be told. Mikri Elpida was huddled by the window, her loose hair pooling in her lap. 'Who? No!' Her voice quavered. 'Leave the light off!'

'Why are you up here by yourself?'

'I have a headache.'

'Oh, me too!' Nitsa flopped on the bed. 'It's the *pazari* The heat.' Against the light thrown up from the yard, Elpida was a draped bronze statuette. Nitsa told her so. The answer was like a sob. 'Don't *cry*!' she protested, going nearer. But you never knew when Elpida was crying, even when you could see her eyes. They always looked tightly squeezed; no white edge showed. 'You *are* crying, aren't you? What's wrong?'

'Nothing!'

'Then come down. Come on.'

'Later.'

'What's *wrong*?'

'*Aman*, Nitsa. Don't be such a baby.'

Nitsa dipped her hand under the hair to press it to her aunt's forehead. 'Is the pain there?'

'No, in my heart,' Elpida muttered unexpectedly; straight away her face burned Nitsa's palm.

'Ach, me too,' Nitsa crooned. 'Where's your brush?' She pulled

MARKET DAY

the brush through rustling handfuls of Elpida's split hair. 'Isn't it sad how cruel life is?'

'How would you know?'

'Everyone knows.'

Which might be so, for all Elpida knew.

'Is it Aunt Lena?'

'Oh, everything.'

'Because of your eyes too?' murmured Nitsa.

'It's my own business.'

'You can tell me, I won't tell.'

'Well, my eyes, I suppose. In a way. Yes.'

'Do you remember when you could see?'

'Of course. I'm not so old . . . I see dreams every night.'

'Tell me how it happened.'

'But I have.' Everyone knew the story.

'Again.'

'All right. We children had climbed that red hill above the road into town, where everyone's grapevines were. Some of those old vines are still bearing, they're hidden behind the fig trees.' Her hair crackled round her as Nitsa brushed. 'Our mothers had given us baskets to pick the figs and grapes. I remember figs that the birds had torn open, hanging down like thick purple flowers, the seeds spilling. Heavy rains had washed tree roots out and made gullies full of red mud. Saki found a smooth shape buried in one. It looked like glass. "Treasure!" he shouted. Yordani found a mattock and we all crowded round. Then the mud erupted, we were thrown down. That's all I remember. When I dream about it, that's how it ends: a blaze of noise and when I wake up – I can't see.'

Nitsa hugged her. 'It was a German shell,' she prompted.

'. . . A live German shell. There are still some left, people say. Six of us were injured. Saki and Yordani died, torn open like the ripe figs . . . I remember when I could see, but times change. So I can't be sure of knowing what anything looks like now, I suppose.' She swung her hair. 'Today, by the fountain – '

Nitsa stopped brushing. 'What do you think *I* look like?'

'Like a – silly, how would I know?'

'Am I pretty?'

'Well, are you?'

'I know someone who thinks so!'

'What's this?'

'You won't tell, if I tell you a secret?' she whispered. 'Well – I'm in love.'

'Don't *tell* me!' Elpida jumped up. 'And I *thought* maybe – by the fountain today – a thick pullover! *Oh yes*, I thought. *It's for a man*,' and instantly she was sure she had thought that by the fountain.

'So can we buy the wool at the next *pazari*?'

'Slow, slow. Who is he? Do we know him?'

'You won't tell?'

'Never.'

'Well, his name's Aleko. He lives in Thessaloniki and he's a student.'

'And is he in love with you?'

Nita giggled. '*Madly!*'

'So life's *cruel*, is it?' scoffed Elpida.

'But I can't see him, can I? Not for weeks! I'll be stuck here in a village all summer till school starts and he's in Thessaloniki!'

'You'll work something out. What if – could he come to our *pazari*, do you think?'

'*Yes!*' Nitsa hugged her. 'Will you help us?'

'How?'

'To be alone together for a while?'

'You be sensible! You hear?'

'I will, I will. Now come down and eat. Please?'

'My hair!' protested Elpida.

'*Nitsa*, are you upstairs? *Nitsa!*' shouted Megali Elpida from the yard.

'Now what?' Nitsa leaned out. 'Coming!' She sighed. ' "*Nitsa, Nitsa,*" ' Elpida's fingers were twitching in and out of her dim skeins of hair. 'Tomorrow,' Nitsa said, 'I want you to plait my hair like that.'

MARKET DAY

'You can do it. It's easy.'

'It isn't. I can't.'

'We'll make a thick black cap of it, will we?'

'Not as thick as yours.'

'Flattering me again! Go on down, I won't be long.'

'Let me get you something to eat. Meatballs? Salad? All right?'

Elpida bit back her usual proud rejection of help. 'All right,' she said.

'Remember – it's our secret!' Nitsa flung the door open, clattered downstairs. Elpida sighed. Market day certainly tired you out. But how exciting! What a thrilling piece of news! Tubby, wilful little Nitsa – a fine sweet woman she was turning out, and in what seemed no time at all! Yet wasn't it a little shocking? In love, already! Aleko. Was he handsome, young, brilliant? He must be. He loved Nitsa – *madly*. Remember, our secret. How mystified everyone would be when they saw her knitting, the same as always, a thick pullover – for no one knew who! For Aleko. She would sit in the dark of the plane trees, the water beside her bubbling, brimming over – she remembered how the water looked – with splashed shadows of leaves and clouds. People might even think *she* was the one . . . Mikri Elipida's laugh trilled out. Voices answered. Dancing with impatience in the doorway, she pinned up her bronze crown.

CAFFE VENETO

Her father is there already when Anne comes. She sees him first, smoking under a streetlamp outside the misted windows with their gilt scrawl: *Caffe Veneto*. The seedballs and fingered leaves of a plane tree are touching him with shadows.

'You found it, then,' she calls out. 'Sorry if I'm late. I was held up at rehearsal.' He is holding a bottle wrapped in brown paper. 'Is this a celebration?'

'A Cabernet Sauvignon. Good to see you!'

'Yes. It's been a while. Two months?'

'Or three. Since Easter.'

'That's right. Well. What a strange phone call!' This furtive smile of his is strange as well; and how much he has aged since then. In this light his skin seems to have faded and creased, settled more slackly in the hollows of bones. His eyes are smaller. Even his teeth seem smaller, patched and stained, exposed in his uneasy smiles. This austerity of age, in his of all faces, is at the same time intimidating and pitiable. She wonders if he has seen it himself in mirrors.

'Is this place fit for the Cabernet Sauvignon?' she says. 'We could look for somewhere fancier.'

'No, why? They've only changed the name. I have been here before, I remember now.'

'Student food.'

'I live on it. The spaghetti's good, come on.'

The glass door opens and a laughing group pushes out. The bead curtains rattle. Then two barefooted girls go inside; a warm gust, a smell of coffee and smoke, blow out as visibly as breath. He holds the beads aside for her, and the door open. Lamps hang inside, round and red like upturned glasses of wine. In the blurred light they shed, Anne leads him past crowded stools at the counter to the only table free, a long bench against a wall of theatre posters. Its top is carved like a school desk. Her father sits at her side tracing initials on it with his finger while their order is taken and the table set. Only when he pours the wine does he give her his usual undaunted, boyish smile.

'This whole table to ourselves? Well, cheers.'

'Cheers. A 1975! Napa Valley. Californian? Oh, it's nice.' The wine, plummy and dark, stings and makes her shudder. 'So we *are* celebrating?'

'No.'

'No?'

He shakes his head, lighting another cigarette.

'Is Mum all right?'

'Fine. She's minding the children for your Aunt Sheila. She said to give you her love and talk you into coming back for a coffee.'

'Oh. I only signed out for ten-thirty, though.'

He checks his watch. 'How's College?'

'Great.'

'What was that about a rehearsal?'

'Oh yes. The Drama Club's putting on *The Seagull*. Chekhov? You have to come.'

'Of course. Are you Nina?'

'No, only Masha. Poor dreary Masha in black.'

'Well, we must come.' His voice falters. 'When's it on?'

'In two weeks. I'll look after the tickets. Now tell me,' she smiles and holds up her wine glass, 'what we're *not* celebrating.'

'What if we eat first, talk later.'

'No, now. Come on.'

'Well – my study leave's come through.'

'Well, good! I thought you'd decided to withdraw your application.'

'I had. But I'd have missed out altogether. It was now or never.'

' "It's now or never. My love won't wait." So you'll be going to America after all?'

CAFFE VENETO

'That was the idea. Funny you should say that.' He gives a short laugh. 'I've fallen in love.'

'Oh Daddy, again?' Her smile is stiff from the wine. 'Not that I can talk. I have, too.'

'*Have* you? What's his name?'

'I don't know him very well.'

'Don't know his name.'

'Not telling. Not yet. He's – he's married. Separated.'

'That's what they all say, they say.'

'Is it now? Anyway, she's moved to Sydney and he's here.'

'Well. What can I say? So long as you're happy.'

'It has its moments. You?'

'Yes. And no.'

'Do I know this one?'

'No.' He hesitates. 'She's one of my post-grad students. She's doing her thesis on Sylvia Plath. Oh, she's mature age,' he adds quickly. 'She's thirty-nine.'

'Married?'

'Divorced with one daughter. As a matter of fact, she's a student here: Microbiology, I think. The daughter. Jenny.'

She nods. 'You've met the daughter. What's the mother's name?'

'Sandra.' He gulps more wine and wipes his lips with a finger.

'So this is not a celebration because now you wish you weren't going to America.'

'In a way.' He fixes earnest eyes on her. 'You haven't seen your mother all this time, Annie, have you?'

'There's never a moment free. There are extra tutorials when you live in at College. And this play. And the essays all – '

'I know.' He breathes out smoke. 'I just wondered. When you didn't come home at the end of the first term.'

'Did she complain, did she? But she knew I was going camping!'

'No. All I'm saying really, darling, is that now your mother's going to need all your love and support. Please.'

'She doesn't *know*, does she?'

64

'No. She doesn't.'

'Well. Good.'

'I may have to tell her.' He bows his head and she sees that his grizzled curls, redder under this lamp, are thinning at the crown. 'This time it's the real thing. I may have to leave your mother.'

'For this – for Sandra?'

'When you meet her, you'll understand.'

'Hang on. Hang on.' Bowls of spaghetti thud into place under their noses. She watches her own hand pick up a fork and coil red hanks round and round it, too disconcerted by his lack of composure to take in what he is saying. 'Why *me*?'

'We've always been close.' He tries to smile. 'Trial run?'

'Oh, so it's all *settled*?'

'Darling, nothing's *settled* yet.'

'It sounds settled to me.'

'Not so.'

He stubs out his cigarette and lights another. Anne bends over her spaghetti. She should eat, being unused to wine. She gulps one hot mouthful, feeling her whole head swill with tears; tears of shock.

'Annie.'

'It's the spaghetti. Hot.'

'Damn,' mutters her father. Two people are seating themselves opposite them at the table, backs to the wall, a boy in a football guernsey and a woman in black suede. As alike as the Mother and Child in an ikon – though he must be eight or nine, Anne thinks – they look at each other with pleased black eyes set widely under round brows in their amber faces. Anne moves the wine glasses to make room and the woman smiles.

'It's the only table left.' Anne shrugs, pushing her plate away. She wipes her nose. 'I won't meet Sandra. How could you suggest it? You should know better.'

'I admit I was hoping, well, at least that you'd be more – '

'Amenable?'

'Just understanding.'

CAFFE VENETO

'Oh yes. I under*stand*.'

'Not how I feel. Do you?'

'Why not? I've understood the other times. I've kept your secrets. Commiserated when it was over. Haven't I? What I *don't* understand is why this time my mother would deserve to be left.'

'Darling, you don't leave people because they *deserve* it. Or stay with them, either.'

'If that's true, then no one's ever secure.'

'That's how it is. There's no security.'

'If people were *faith*ful – '

'Yes, in an ideal world, people would all be faithful and all be secure. I agree. Or there'd be no love and so no insecurity.'

'They go together, do they?'

'I'd say so. Wouldn't you?'

'No!' At her tone the woman opposite glances up from her struggle to tuck the boy's napkin round his neck, while he digs into ravioli; full of mournful surprise, her eyes meet Anne's. She thinks we're lovers quarrelling, Anne thinks, and looks away, down at her hands. They have been tearing a hunk of bread into crumbs. She picks some up on a fingertip and eats them.

'When do you have until?' she whispers.

'Not long. America, you mean?'

'Yes. Mum must have been thrilled about that?'

'I haven't told her, Annie.'

'Why not?'

'I can't decide, don't you see?' His hand is crêpe-skinned and the bones show, bent round the red glass. He sees her looking and looks too, holding his thick fingers outspread.

'I just can't take it in. When will you tell her?'

He winces. 'Oh, we'll more than likely call the whole thing off.'

'Call America off? Because of Sandra?' He stares at her. 'She – Sandra – must have known all along you were married.'

'Of course. Of course. Sorry. I thought you meant when would I tell your mother about Sandra.'

CAFFE VENETO

Maybe I did, Anne thinks. She gulps down the tart red wine, feeling dazed. 'How long have you known her?'

'About six months.'

'Six *months*.'

'Sssh. We've been lovers for two. Three.'

'Since Easter. You can't be sure, then. It's too soon.'

'That's what she says.'

'Well?'

'Just that it isn't true. I do love her. I'm only not a hundred-per-cent sure if she's worth the price. If anyone is, I mean. No, I am sure.'

'You mean, worth what *you* will have to pay.'

'Yes.'

'That's – don't you see that's selfish?'

'In a sense it's selfish, I suppose.'

This is what love does, she thinks. Puts us at the mercy of the other's selfishness. And of our own.

'If you believe in love,' he says, 'you pay the price.'

'Except that Mum will be paying the most. And she's always been faithful to you, in spite of your other women.'

'Doesn't that in itself say something about our marriage?'

'Maybe just about marriage.'

'When you get married – '

'I won't.'

'Let's keep our voices down. What's he like?' He smiles. 'This fellow you're in love with? Not that History tutor, is it? What's his name again?'

'I'm never getting married. Never.'

He shrugs. 'Up to you.'

Already he doesn't care, then. 'You know,' she says, 'if you leave her now she'll feel that her life has been wasted.'

'Her love, perhaps. Not her life. Most love is wasted.'

'Her whole *life*.'

'Past life. OK. Which is it worse to waste, I wonder? The past or the future?'

'Mum, of course, would be concerned about *her* future.'

CAFFE VENETO

'She's still a very attractive woman, darling. She'll find someone else.'

'Will she, though? She hasn't had the practice you've had.' There is a grim silence. She stares at the peeling theatre posters: there is one for *The Seagull*. Her mouth is parched, her throat swollen and furred. 'Besides,' she whimpers, 'she loves *you*. Doesn't that count?'

'Annie,' he sighs, 'we have to be mature about this.'

'Are you being?'

'Do you think love is immature?'

'Not in itself.'

He rubs his greying head. The hair on his chest, she remembers from last summer, is greying too, above and about his nipples. He has a young man's belly. Like a tree in autumn he is withering from the top down. Not since the upheavals of puberty has she been so aware of men, the presence of the male, as now. Is it because she has a lover now? Maybe all women feel like this. And men? I still know next to nothing about love, she thinks: and I'll suffer for it.

'You always said to take love lightly,' she says.

He sighs, breathing smoke out. 'I can't be sure I can even go on hiding my feelings at home.'

'But that's not a reason to leave! That doesn't make sense!'

'Why doesn't it?'

'If you can't hide it, tell her. She probably knows.'

'No, I'd know if she did.'

'She always has before.' He stares at her. 'I never told her. Of course not. She never told me straight out that she knew. She just – hinted. "I think you're like me," she said last time. "I let lying dogs sleep," and we laughed. You didn't take it seriously, so . . . And that's what she's doing now.'

'Why didn't you ever . . . ?' He shrugs.

'Tell you? You *know* why. I didn't tell Mum what you told me either, did I? You both trusted me. And I would never have dared, anyway. Why do you think I wanted to live in at College? Because I was out of my depth at home.'

She sees herself wading for the first time beside the huge white legs of her mother and father into cold green slabs of water that tilted high and hurled her off her feet. Screaming, she clutched a hand, a knee, clambered on a slippery thigh. They carried her back to the sandbank. Lapped in pale water, she sat there alone wailing while they waded back in without her, deeper and deeper, until they disappeared.

'Secrecy. Lies. Hints,' her father is saying. 'Why wouldn't she say, if she knew? I didn't want to hurt her, that's all.'

'Oh, *what* can I say? Can't you just wait a while? You can't spring a thing like this on her. At least, give her time.'

'Time! That's just it. I'm afraid Sandra won't wait.'

'Won't wait?'

'Won't wait, I mean, if I go off to America for months with your mother.'

'Why not?'

'It'd be asking too much of her credulity, she says.'

'But if she loves you?'

'It's faith that she lacks. Not love. Faith and hope.'

'It sounds like she's blackmailing you.' He is silent. This is what he sometimes suspects. Resentfully, in spite of himself, he pictures Sandra curled and smug on her bed reading at this moment, the lamplight around her in flounces of smoke like a mosquito net; while he fights his daughter for her sake. 'Blackmailing you,' Anne says. 'She'll wait, if you go alone.'

'You still don't understand.'

'*Tell* me.'

'I can't not take your mother, can I,' he mutters, 'if I'm living at home?'

'You can't mean that you want to take *Sandra* to *America*!'

'Annie, enough now. Please. This is dreadful.'

'You do! You do! How *could* you? You can't *mean* it.'

'Annie, for God's sake.'

'You're my father and I love you. You know that. Maybe more than Mummy. But if you leave her, I'll be on her side. I won't even see you again.' She wonders as she says this if it is true; and if he would care. 'I mean that.'

'*Well!*' He pushes his untouched plate away in turn. The boy opposite pauses to stare curiously from the cold tangles of spaghetti to their faces, and back. 'What shall we talk about now?'

'Nothing. I'll go.' But, as he half-expects, she makes no move to. He fills the glasses, drinks his down, and lights a cigarette.

'Big match tomorrow,' he tosses defiantly across the table.

'Yeah!' The boy grins back at him.

'How do you like your chances?'

'Gunna win!' The boy looks for approval at his mother, who gives him an imploring smile. She has finished her ravioli. 'Great ravioli, Mum,' the boy announces, clearly to please her; and she looks pleased.

'I *fear* for my mother!' Anne shouts. 'I fear for her! How will she bear it?'

'Darling!' Shock makes him spill his wine. With his napkin he stanches the dark puddle, wondering if she can be drunk. After all, she has eaten only the bread. He gapes at her in such evident mute dismay that again he strikes her as boyish, an elderly bad boy, and a spasm of laughter crosses her face. Yes, she is, he decides. Grinning with relief, he throws his arm around her shoulders to pull her to him for a moment and she smells suddenly the drenching sweetness in the armpits of men who smoke. But she draws back from him.

'Gunna win, no worries.'

'I don't know, though,' her father teases. 'You're up against the best team, just about.'

'We aren't, they are! And my dad's playing!'

'Your dad, is he? Go on!'

'He's the captain!'

'Is he now? What's his name?'

Again the boy refers to his mother, then leans forward and whispers it.

'He's your dad? Well, good God!' The woman nods, ruefully,

CAFFE VENETO

it seems to Anne; the dark eyes glimmer and close. 'You going to be as good as your dad?'

'Better!'

'Going to see him play?'

'Too right!'

'Might see you there.'

'Finish, finish.' His mother nudges him: heads are turning in the red haze. He scoops up his last shreds of ravioli, while her father turns his jovial smile on the mother. 'His dad's a magnificent footballer. One of the greats. And you,' he tells the boy, 'must be very proud!' The boy nods gravely, wiping his chin.

The woman springs up. 'Yes, goodnight.' Her voice shakes and she opens her pale palms in a beseeching gesture. 'We going now.' She stoops to the boy's ear. 'Come on. We going.'

'Oh? Can't I have a *gelato*?'

'Yes, in a cornet. Please, the bill.' She tugs the waiter's sleeve. But the boy wants to hear more. She wavers, but bends her head, blotting her cheeks with her black lapels, and rushes alone to the counter.

Anne leans forward. 'Your mother wants you.'

A black suede arm is beckoning.

'Yeah, I better go.'

'Well, nice meeting you.' Her father puts out his hand; the boy's tawny hand is lost in it. Confused, he stands smiling at them, glancing now and then towards his mother until at last he can detach himself and run to her.

'How about that?' Her father sits back. 'Nice kid. If he turns out half the man his dad is!'

'I think she was crying.'

He looks round, but they have gone. 'Sorry?'

'She was crying. That's why she rushed off.'

'Why would she be?'

'I think, because of you. All that about his father.'

'He's a great player. Why shouldn't his kid be proud of him?'

'He takes after her,' Anne says. 'Both honey-coloured.'

'So are we in this light.'

CAFFE VENETO

'Dark honey. Like a Byzantine Madonna and Child.'

'I thought they looked Indian.'

'Yes? Or Maori.'

'Maybe.' He considers. 'Or Indonesian.'

'The thing is, they were so happy. A dinner out at the Caffe Veneto. She should have been safe.'

'From?'

'She was hurt. Shamed.'

'Why, though?'

'Who knows? The boy's father may have *done her wrong*. Anything. It's none of our business, that's all.'

'Well, she's not his wife. I've met his wife.'

'My point.'

'Anne, all I did was pay tribute to a marvellous bloody footballer!'

'You overdid it.'

'*Did* I.'

'What right had you to make her cry?'

'How was I to know?'

'*I* knew.'

'Well, *I* didn't, I'm afraid. Sorry.' Stung, he makes a hurt face. 'I see nothing I do or say tonight is going to find favour. Poor me.' His lined eyes meet hers. 'Cast into outer darkness.'

'It's all of a piece, that's all.' She tips her head back to empty her glass, and her face glows under the lamp. 'You can choose not to know you're doing it, but still the damage is done. People suffer. Lives are ruined.'

'*You're* overdoing it.'

'You really don't care.' She gazes in disillusion as he sighs. The impetuosity which all her life she has loved in him is not, after all, boyish. In the light of this evening it is shown up as shallow and rash; even, perhaps, brutal. 'You ride roughshod. You'll always get away with it.'

'All right. I'm a clumsy galoot. That boy's mother's life is ruined. *Mea culpa*.'

'In a small way it does go to show,' she says, and holds out her glass for more, 'that you can make strange errors of judgement. Admit that. May I have some more American wine?'

'Just what I was about to say of you.' He fills her glass. His suddenly amused lips look as if they are bleeding, black from the wine. He watches her turn her glass so that the glow of wine moves on the table. 'Can this be our practical Annie?'

'Why can't it?'

'Burning incense to the Madonna of the Caffe Veneto.'

'She thought we were lovers quarrelling.'

'Did she? She can't have heard much.' He glances round. 'I'll bet she was on your side.'

'Being practical,' she says, 'if that's what's expected, tell me: have your loves ever lasted? Has love ever made you happy for long?'

He takes her hands. 'What has happiness got to do with love? "To love is to suffer," didn't Goethe say? "One is compelled to love, one does not want to." ' She shakes her head and pulls free. 'Annie.' But she turns away, one hand folded to hide her face.

He foresees himself at the moment when she will stand on tiptoe to kiss him goodnight holding her by the shoulders and pressing with his closed lips a kiss of finality on her stained lips; holding her away, then, to look in her eyes and compel not only resignation. Consent, absolution, belief. When he sees that she can't move first, he holds the bottle up under the lamp and shakes it. 'All gone,' he pouts. He sniffs it: the dregs have a smell of olives. She looks at him. 'Like a coffee?'

'No, thanks.'

'Sure?'

'No, I'd better get back.'

He glances at his watch. 'Let's go? It's after ten.'

While he pays she droops at his side staring at her shoes on the bare planks, in an attitude of reproach, as he notes wryly. Whatever gave me the idea, he thinks, that I could convince her of the imperatives of love? My shy and scrupulous daughter, of all people! No, her mother's daughter now. He holds her coat open for her to grope into. 'Drive you back to College?'

'I think I'll walk.'

'Walk you back?'

'All right.'

It is clammily cold. They walk on a wide path past shadowy trees holding their few brown leaves still in the mist. A full moon glimmers. His daughter's shoulders are folded in; her hair hangs in two rusty skeins along the line of her nose. At eighteen she is no longer a girl. Prettier now, yes, but shedding her young freshness. She will be late, as fearful of hurt as she is, to come to ripeness. She has a shrouded look, he thinks; her eyes, when for a moment she glances up, seem full of sorrow and foreboding.

'Give my love to Mum,' she says once. 'Tell her I'll ring.'

'I will.'

'You'll come to the play?'

'Of course. You'll see to the tickets?'

'You have to go to America. Don't you?'

'Yes.'

'With Mum or with Sandra.'

'Yes.'

'What's she like?'

'Beautiful.'

'You were my household gods,' she says as if to herself. 'Warm and luminous. One each side of the fire.'

'Oh, Annie.'

'Oh, I grew out of it.'

She has her hands in her pockets and is staring down at heaps of leaves as she shuffles through them, not close enough for an arm round her shoulders to seem unforced. She is exhausted, of course; so is he, barely able to speak. He breathes long trails of smoke out, thinking of Sandra reading; and of Margaret, at home with his sister's children, waiting.

They come round the crescent and the brick hump of her college stands black on the glow of the sky. Under the trees it is deeply dark. She catches a plane leaf as it floats loose: brown on one side, pale with brown veins on the other, like an imploring hand.

'Have a wish?'

'You know.' She looks at him. 'Daddy, you won't do it. Will you?'

'No.' He turns his stubbornly pleading face to her, but she is looking down again. 'No, I don't suppose I can.'

'You mustn't.'

'I won't. No.'

On the gravel at the entrance she turns abruptly and kisses him, her hands on his shoulders, and runs up the steps. Her mouth tastes of tears. I never asked about her love affair, he thinks. He starts back, his shoes crunching in the mist. But she is inside the blurred glass door, which is slowly closing. Her shape stoops, signing in. The light goes out, and the lock clicks.

MILK

I was nine when my father first took me to Greece for a summer. He came from a northern village. There were, as he had promised, animals everywhere. And my grandparents did love me. Yiayia, my grandmother, read me stories and spoiled me. My grandfather, Pappou, was deaf, so we didn't talk much. But he took me everywhere. My cousins, the other grandchildren, all lived in the city and were only visiting. Sometimes they were nice, sometimes they teased me. They picked fights. They sulked.

'Niko's our boy,' Yiayia said. 'He's flown thousands of miles just to be with us. So don't be mean.' They groaned. 'You all have mothers,' she added. 'Niko hasn't. His died when he was three.'

When they'd gone home it was better. As well as feeding the animals we did heavy work in the fields, Pappou and I. I helped load bales of lucerne and hay on the cart, and lay the pipes for watering, and hoe the tobacco. My father helped too. I wanted us to stay forever, but he said no.

My father and I took Pappou to the market town and bought him a cow with a calf. Whatever we and the calf couldn't drink, Yiayia could make into cheese or yoghurt, or sell. Not many people in the village had a cow then, though there were goats and sheep with pink bags of milk between their legs. Our cow, all hide and bones, had an udder so huge that she looked, Yiayia said, as if she was perched on a barrel. She was put in the barn next to the house with her calf and Pappou's old horse. I helped with the milking. We let the calf suck first, to start the milk flowing. When we hauled him away, the calf propped and pranced and the cow gazed round in dismay, both of them mooing. After the milking we set the calf free to finish off. Once

MILK

in his rush he knocked Pappou over in a pile of wet black dung. I shrieked with joy. Pappou sat there and cursed me.

'Niko! Niko!' Yiayia was furious. I blushed and said sorry to Pappou. He was looking sheepishly at me. Niko was his name too, of course. I was named after him. Who did she mean? Bemused, we looked at her. She laughed then.

Yiayia asked me to hang up the curd cheeses at night in their white cloths, high up on a pole near the grapevine that shaded the porch, so that cats and dogs couldn't snatch them. I wished I didn't have to. Up there near the porch lamp beetles rattled against me as I tied knots. Cobwebs clung. The whey dripped in my eyes and down my arms.

'Good boy,' Yiayia said. 'That's fine. Up there nothing will get them. Not even the wolf.'

The wolf. My cousins had told me horror stories about a wolf: a *lykanthropos*, a werewolf that they said lived in the village.

'Is there one here, Yiayia?'

'Lots. Ooooh.' She made a howl and laughed up at me, her eyes lost in yellow wrinkles. 'Not in summer, silly. There are in winter.'

'Why?'

'Why? It snows here, that's why. They get hungry.'

'Where are they now?'

'Up on the mountain. And there they'll stay till you've gone home, so you can get down now.'

I slipped down. The mountain hunched grey beyond the river, the lights of its villages twinkling and fading like fireflies.

'Have you ever seen one, Yiayia?'

'One or two. There was one last winter as big as the calf. it was full moon like now, but on snow, so I saw it clearly through the window. The men went after it with guns. You'd have shot it for us, eh, cowboy?' She said it in English, *kaouboyee*. 'It'll be back.'

'Did it kill anything?'

MILK

'It couldn't get in. The foxes were worse. It only came for the donkeys.'

'How did it get in?'

'Oh, not in a barn, no. On the other side of the river. They were tied.'

'In the snow?'

'Yes, poor things.'

'*Why?*'

'What use is a donkey in winter? There's no room, no feed. They say it's cheaper to buy a new one in spring.'

'So they feed the old ones to the wolf?'

Yiayia shook her head. That meant yes. No was when she tossed her head back, frowned and said tsk.

'They didn't have to tie them,' I whispered.

'Yes, they did, or they'd have come home.'

I gazed in horror.

'If you aren't your father all over again!' she said. 'Here in winter there's nothing all round but snow and ice. People die too.'

'I'd go and untie them!'

'God love you,' she said. 'They'd die anyway.'

'I'd feed them!'

But she'd gone in. Layers of mist were floating blue and silver over the rooftops. I shivered. The porch lamp blinked. Cobwebs full of beetles hung from it. The muddy cups of swallows' nests were empty of birds. Dogs barked. It seemed to me that the night had a chill already.

A fat donkey jiggled past. The rider, her face turned away from our house, was Kyria Tassoula.

Kyria Tassoula never spoke to my grandmother. It was some old quarrel, my father said. Women and their quarrels. Her house was just over the road. Some of the family would say hullo as I went past, but as if it embarrassed them to, so I mumbled and scuffled on. Their boy Stelio liked me.

One afternoon, too hot to sleep – we all slept after lunch – I

MILK

found an old woman in the kitchen with Yiayia eating yoghurt. She hobbled over to me, peering hard, and patted my cheek. Her breath was sour. Like all the old women, except Yiayia, she was wrinkled, toothless, all wrapped in black. They were talking, but it wasn't Greek. I ate some yoghurt and watched them. Yiayia dressed in colours and left her white hair uncovered in a bun bright as a snowball in sunlight. Only close up her red cheeks were cracked with lines. She smelled of rosewater.

She told me later that that was Stelio's grandmother, his father's mother. She sometimes came over in secret and if she wasn't well enough they kept in touch through a neighbour. She was Kyria Tassoula's mother-in-law, but she hated her too. She was glad I was friends with Stelio.

I wasn't really. Stelio, though bigger and older – nearly fourteen – had played soccer by the river some evenings with me and my cousins. Once, seeing that I was fascinated by the fireflies, he chased and caught me one. In the red ridges of his palm it glowed weakly, a little battered grub.

'What is it in English?' he grinned. He was a greasy boy, always grinning, heavy yet loose and light-footed.

'Firefly.'

'Fyah flyee. Fyah flyee.'

He walked home with us, so I had to keep the firefly. From the corner he lagged behind. Frightened of his stepmother, my cousins whispered. Kyria Tassoula, she beats him, and she beats his father too, and one day you'll have a stepmother, too, Niko. I hoped not.

There were always night noises. Cats fought on rooftops, roosters crowed at the moon, donkeys burst out in sudden sobs and groans. Tractors roared past from daybreak, then the early bus. When, that night, frantic yells and snorts woke me I thought, I hoped, it was just a donkey. I thought of the *lykanthropos*. My father ran to open the shutters. The screaming blasted in then, loud, agonised.

'What is it, Dad?'

'I don't know.'

MILK

Yiayia and Pappou were on the porch staring over at the yard of Stelio's house, where torches glowed and thrust agile shadows among men and thistles.

'It's all right,' Pappou said. 'It's only a donkey. Tassoula's donkey. *Yennaei*.'

Laying an egg. I knew that word. But Stelio's stepmother's donkey wasn't. It was shrieking with pain.

'Oh my God!' my father said. 'Can't they do something?'

'Tsk. Not now. It's finished. Listen to it.'

Lights went on in house after house. Dogs barked.

'If they bring a *haïvan-doktor*?'

'Tsk. Too late.'

I clutched my father's arm.

'Oh God. Why don't they shoot it?'

'Them?' Yiayia grinned. 'You don't think they'd waste a bullet? Slit its throat maybe. That's more like it.'

'Sssh, Sevasti,' Pappou said.

'It's my bet she poisoned it.'

'Ssh.' Pappou took her inside and turned out the lights. My father locked our shutters. In the dark I crawled into bed with him and he made room, one arm tightly round me. The screams and sobs were quieter after a while.

'She's getting better, Dad,' I said. 'Isn't she?'

'Yes,' he said. 'Go to sleep.'

'What was wrong with her?'

'It's over now. Sleep.'

The bed smelled of my father, as he smelled when we were in Greece. Of sweat and dust and hay.

In the morning, helping Yiayia to search the barn for eggs, I found out the truth. The donkey had not got better. It was gone. At first light it was carted to the hill.

'*Pethane, totes*?' It died, then? I still wasn't sure.

'*Psofise*, little one,' she said. 'Not *pethane*.'

'*Psofise*?'

'*Pethane* is for when people die.'

MILK

'What if you say *psofise* when people die?'

'No, you mustn't, it's an insult.'

'Then it's an insult for animals too.'

'Don't be silly,' she said. 'People are more than animals. People have souls.'

'Well I'm saying *pethane*.'

'Tsk.'

I had to see for myself. I sauntered past their yard and just glanced in. The tall thistles were all trampled and torn up. There in the midst of them stood the grey donkey. *Den pethane*, I said aloud, it didn't die, so there. It trotted to me, breathing hoarsely, and pushed its gazing head through the barbed wire. It came up to my middle. At last I understood. It was a baby, a newborn *gaïdouraki*. I rushed home and told her.

'I think it's hungry,' I added.

It was sure to be. It had stayed by the mother's corpse all night and sucked it. My skin prickled.

'Will the wolf eat the mother, Yiayia?'

The wolf or something else. Weren't they all God's creatures?

'Yiayia, can I please feed the *gaïdouraki*? There's plenty of milk!'

It was too small. It was best to forget it.

'With a baby bottle, please, Yiayia, I know how!'

No, it was a waste of time. It wasn't ours. Stelio's stepmother would stop me. The whole village would laugh at us both. But she gave in and wearily found me an old bottle with a teat and handed it to me to fill with warm milk.

The *gaïdouraki* stumbled to me with little sobs and wheezes. I held his head. At first his lips fumbled, then they clamped on the teat. As he gulped I stroked his fluffy back with the dark cross on it. His eyes watched, river-brown eyes lined with black. I patted his rough nose.

'What are you up to, Niko?'

Stelio was always there before you saw him.

'It's hungry, isn't it? What's its name?'

'Hasn't got one, silly.'

'What'll we call it?' I asked him. It was their donkey.

'I know!' He grinned. 'Fyah Flyee.'

'Firefly. All right.' I liked it. Stelio laughed. When the bottle was empty I climbed out. Through the wires Firefly nudged me, panting. I looked back. Stelio waved.

On the next market day Pappou and my father went on the bus but I stayed home to feed Firefly. Preparing his bottles – he was becoming insatiable – I chattered on to Yiayia, though as usual she wasn't listening. She often wasn't happy. She had been very quiet all that day. As I turned to go she put her hand on my shoulder.

'Wait. Are you going over there?'

I just looked at her.

'Well, look, do something for me, eh? Will you, Niko? Stelio's grandmother's sick in bed. Take her this yoghurt.'

'Yiayia, I *can't*. I've never been to the house. I go to the yard not the – '

'Stelio's your friend,' she said. 'His stepmother went on the bus, I saw her. I can't go, you know that. Come on, Niko, you do it for a donkey, won't you do it for a poor sick old woman? Niko, please?'

I left the bowl with its embroidered cloth over it on a fence post while I fed Firefly, and Stelio found it.

'What's this, Niko?'

'Oh. It's for your grandmother.'

'What's in it?'

'Yoghurt.'

'What?' He had a look. 'Yoghurt for my grandmother?'

'She's sick, isn't she?'

'She's sick, so what? We've got food.'

'Oh.' What would Yiayia say?

'You idiot, take it home. What next? Ha ha.' His voice when he laughed was a yodel. 'See if Firefly wants it.' Firefly poked his head between my legs and Stelio doubled up. 'See! He thinks that you're his mother. Ha ha ha! You are now, aren't you, Niko?'

MILK

I hoped Yiayia would give up then, but no. She would take the yoghurt herself, but I had to come and carry it. She ignored my whining protests. Stelio gaped when he saw who had knocked, but he led us in politely and left us there. It was hot in the dark inner room, its windows and shutters all locked. There was a bad smell. Yiayia kissed the head lying above a tangle of dim sheets. 'Sophia,' she murmured. I heard an answering croak, but I understood nothing of what they said. When Yiayia said '*Yiaourti*,' I stepped forward with it.

'*Ligo*,' the voice struggled. A little. '*Ligo*, Sevasti.'

Yiayia went to look for a spoon. I hurried after her. She stopped short. Kyria Tassoula stood there, Stelio behind her.

'You?' she said to Yiayia. 'You sneak in here when I'm out, do you?' Then she saw the bowl. 'And what's that?'

'Yoghurt,' I whispered. 'For Stelio's grandmother.'

'*What*?' Kyria Tassoula grabbed it, strode into the bedroom with it and hurled all the yoghurt on the bare floor. It splashed in lumps like vomit.

'You old fool!' she said. 'You beg food from *her*, do you? Then eat it.' She swung round to us. 'You think no one else can make yoghurt?'

'*Fonissa*,' hissed Yiayia. I didn't know that word.

'Get out. You and your brat.' She gave me the bowl. 'Mad old women.' She smiled. 'Do you find each other by the smell?' Stelio's laughter whooped.

Yiayia said nothing on the way home. She locked all the doors and shut herself in her bedroom. No one was home. I sat in silence praying that my father would come soon. In the end I made coffee, thick and sweet, I knew how, and took it in to her. She drank it. She was crying. My father and Pappou, when at last the bus came back, sent me to hang up the cheeses while she told them. When I'd finished, Yiayia was whimpering into my father's shoulder. Pappou sat grey and stiff.

'Tassoula came home in the bread van,' he was saying.

'When I was little,' Yiayia said, as if she hadn't heard, 'I thought she was a princess. Sophia's clothes! Her braided hair!

MILK

In church the priest couldn't think straight.' Her yellow lips shook. 'You should see her now. I've kissed corpses with more life in them.'

Kissed corpses. My own grandmother.

'She says Tassoula's poisoning her,' Yiayia said, 'and she won't eat or drink. *Fonissa einai*, she said.'

'Since when?' asked my father.

'Since the night the donkey died.'

'What!'

'She said it was a sign.'

'Mama, you know that's nonsense,' my father said. 'She's sick, she's dying of cancer, haven't they told her?'

Cancer was a word I knew. *Karkino*. My mother had died of that. It was something inside you that ate you, not like a worm, like a giant wart. You couldn't catch it from anyone who had it. You died slowly.

'Is hungry sick, *paidi mou*?' Yiayia's lips stretched in a yellow grin. 'Is hunger a cancer? Is it? That's what she's dying of.'

'Mama, she has cancer. The doctor told me.'

'Tassoula wants her dead, that's all I know.' She looked at Pappou, who looked down.

'Mama, if she won't eat – '

'She would have eaten the yoghurt.'

The house over the road had a horror in it now. Not during the day, just as the cemetery had none then, but lay there sunny and green beside the gravel road that led to our tobacco fields, its stone crosses crowded by thistles with mauve flowers and the singing of furred brown bees. After dark came the horror. Rattling home in the cart I could never look at the cemetery, and to shut my eyes was worse. I gazed ahead at Marko, Pappou's horse. I saw nothing but Marko's bouncing rump and the swung black hair of his mane and tail. We turned at the church, its storks' nest sprawled on the tower. Then past Stelio's house with a clatter. I looked away. At last, our own bright porch.

That night I was in the fetid room again. An indistinct shape

MILK

in the bed mewed words I didn't know. Yiayia sobbed. Kyria Tassoula leapt into the darkness. Pale yoghurt splashed. I begged for the light to stay on. My father said no, it would bring every mosquito in the village. So he let me come into bed with him and talk till I felt better.

I asked him what *fonissa* meant. I thought it might be something like *lykanthropos*. Kyria Tassoula had pointed eyeteeth and, in my dream, gold eyes.

'A *fonissa*,' he said, 'is a woman who kills someone. A murderess.' He hesitated. 'Your Yiayia was very angry when she said that, Nick. She didn't mean it, you know.' I didn't answer. 'You mustn't talk to people about it. All right?'

'Yes.' He turned over. 'Dad? Did my mother – smell like that?'
'*What?*'
'That old lady smells – dirty.'
'Oh no. God, no. Your mother was in hospital. The nurses took good care of her. Jesus Christ.'
'Why doesn't Stelio's grandmother go to hospital?'
'Well, only people who might get better go to hospital here. If they're too sick they come home. She's lived in that house for fifty years. She'd be frightened anywhere else.'
'She's frightened of Kyria Tassoula.'
'No, no. She doesn't like her, that's all.' I said nothing. 'She gave you a fright, I know. She has a bad temper. But that doesn't make her a *fonissa*.'
'Yiayia said – '
'I know. But Tassoula does her best. Most people do, Nick. That's what I think.'
'Yiayia doesn't think she has cancer, does she?'
'You can't change an old mind. It's no use trying. So go to sleep, Nick, will you? It's three o'clock.'

Yiayia gave up. The next couple of days she woke late, and in the afternoon heat when we went to bed she lay crying. My father prepared meals. The dirty washing rose out of its basket like dough. Yiayia wouldn't help with the milking, but sat inside

MILK

while Pappou clashed buckets and cursed. She groaned, the second day, when he brought the milk in, that milk was more a burden than a blessing. Pappou hurled it, bucket and all, through the kitchen window. We had none to drink. I gave Firefly water. When we came in from the fields that evening we found her in the last red light from the window, peeling potato after potato into a pan of water. Again, nothing was cooking. On the table at her elbow a hen flounced and jabbed at crumbs. Yiayia's cheeks were wet. Pappou and my father bent over her.

I found Firefly gasping with hunger, grieving.

'Yiayia!' I burst in, frantic. 'There must be some milk somewhere!'

'Are you thirsty, little one?' she droned.

'For the *gaïdouraki*, Yiayia.'

'Ach. You and your *gaïdouraki*.'

'Please, Yiayia.'

'Come on, Nick, don't bother Yiayia,' my father said in English.

'The *gaïdouraki*,' Yiayia muttered. 'Why should I feed their *gaïdouraki*?'

'It's starving,' I said in English, and burst into sobs. 'And it's bloody not fair!'

'Nick, that's enough!'

Pappou, plodding in for a bucket, looked at me.

'What's wrong with our boy, eh?' he said.

'*Aman!* That *gaïdouraki*,' Yiayia snapped. '*People* can starve there and no one will lift a finger.'

'You want some milk, is that it?' I shook my head. 'Come and help and I'll give you some.' He patted my shoulder and bent over Yiayia, but I heard. '*Ela*, don't be hard on the boy, Sevasti *mou*. He's going soon.'

I stared at my father.

'Are we going soon?'

'Of course. You know we are.'

'When?'

'The day after tomorrow.'

MILK

'*No!*'

'Yes, we have to, Nick.'

In the barn I was not much use, but Pappou gave me the milk. I asked if he needed a donkey. No, he had a horse. He slapped its rump. He had no room, no feed, no use for a donkey. He said he was sorry. He was, I saw.

It was dark in the yard by then. Stelio was chasing Firefly with whoops and cracks of a whip. I said hullo. He stopped short with a giggle.

'Fyah Flyee. Here's mummy with your milky.'

He went on, though, cornering Firefly at last and trying to mount and ride him. When at last I had a chance to give him the bottles, he gobbled them and pressed hot and shaking against me.

'He loves his mummy,' Stelio sneered. 'Did you miss me yesterday, Niko?'

I shook my head and grinned back at his oily face.

'Know something, Niko?'

'What?'

'Your grandmother's mad. Everyone knows that.'

'Do they.'

'You know what else?'

'What?'

'If my father sees you here again he'll shoot you.'

That was a lie too. They didn't waste bullets. Besides his stepmother beat them both. I wished I could watch.

'You're going home this week, I hear. Poor Fyah Flyee.' He pulled up one long soft ear and crouched to yell. 'You hear that? Your mummy's going home.'

'WIll *you* look after him, Stelio?' I wheedled, but sick, hopeless. 'Look, he likes you.' Firefly cringed.

'Me? *I'*m not a donkey's mother.'

I picked up the bottles. He was still hungry. Would I dare come back with more? Stelio's chant followed me home.

'Niko's Fyah Flyee's mother. Niko's a donkey's mother. Eh, Niko?'

MILK

He saw me turn by the porch lamp.

'Niko, *tha psofisei, xereis?*'

Niko, he'll die, you know? I knew.

'I'll eat him alive! I'm a *lykanthropos*. Ooooh!' He laughed, howling. I went straight to bed.

The next day, our last, Stelio's grandmother died. Her corpse would stay at home until the funeral, my father said. If I met any of the family I was to shake hands and say sadly, '*Zoï se sas*,' long life to you. But I kept well away. Yiayia, her face like iron, sat on the porch watching a file of old people shuffle into Stelio's house. Finally she went herself. No one spoke to her or tried to stop her, she told Pappou. Who would have dared? I wondered if she kissed the corpse. She came back remote and eerie, a listless stranger, even her cheeks pale, and her white bun loose in wisps. She sighed, pouring me milk.

'It's my fault,' she murmured. 'I meant well. Am I to blame? But no one was a better friend to Sophia than I was.'

'They wouldn't let you help her.'

'Even so.'

'Yiayia.' I clutched the bottle and in spite of myself said it. '*To gaïdouraki mou tha pethanei.*'

'Ach, little one, yes.' She hugged me. 'Yes. *Tha psofisei*, poor thing. Ach, Niko *mou*.'

'*Yiati tha pethanei*, Yiayia? *Yiati?*' Why? But my last hope, gone.

'What can we do? It has to be so. We all have to die. We die, and donkeys die, even wolves die.' Tears shone in her eyes. 'Your own mother died, on the far side of the world, and I thought I'd go mad when they told me.' She smiled, a difficult smile. 'And you're a big strong brave boy now.'

For the last time I brought water in buckets to the cow, the calf and the horse. I hung the cheeses high among the cobwebs. I fed Firefly five times, the last time at night, a hard cold night with stars. I didn't see Stelio again. Candlelight moved behind their shutters. A dog howled. The mountain crouched black, spangled, a new moon above it.

MILK

We stayed up late after the bags were packed and we'd had dinner and drunk our milk and honey. My father and grandparents talked for so long, I woke in bed with my father at dawn before I knew I'd slept. We had coffee, all of us yellow and rumpled under the lightbulb, trying to hurry, but when we carried our bags to the bus stop the porch lamp was a blotch on the wall and the morning hot and white. Firefly's head was bowed through the wires. He moaned when he saw me coming. Even after we turned the corner I could hear. When the bus came Yiayia, in tears, kissed us goodbye. Pappou hugged her.

'They'll be back, they'll be back,' he said. 'Won't you, Niko?'

'No,' I said.

It made them smile.

MELPO

When I married Magda, Jimmy is thinking, all our family danced. We roasted kids and lambs in our whitewashed oven outside. We drank ouzo and new wine by the demijohn. The whole village was there. My mother had cooked everything. Cheese pies the size of cartwheels, meatballs, *pilafia* . . . In spring she picked nettles and dandelions and stewed them with rice, for Lent. In autumn she brewed thick jams from our apples and figs and windfall apricots. Tubs of yoghurt and curd cheese sat wrapped all day in blankets by our stove. On feast days an aged hen seethed, tawny and plump, in the pot. Until the Germans came, and then the Civil War.

The day I married Magda, my mother led the line of dancers holding the handkerchief, making her leaps and turns barefoot on the earth of our yard, by the light of kerosene lamps.

When our family planted out tobacco seedlings in the dry fields a long cart-ride from the village, we started at daybreak and rested in the heat of the afternoon under the oak trees at the spring. We ate hard bread, and cheese and olives, and drank spring water. Once when I was small I picked up a tortoise where it lumbered among pale clods of earth. It hissed, spurting hot urine on my hands. I dropped it, then picked it up again. *Mi*, Dimitraki! my old aunts shrieked in their black scarves. Melpo! *E*, Melpo! But my mother lay there with earthen feet, in shade as cold and thick as the spring water, fast asleep. My mother, Melpo . . .

'Now your mother wants to meet me,' Kerry is saying, 'Why now?'

Kerry looks taut, as if angry, Jimmy thinks; but she is only disconcerted. Flecked with brown, her pale face is blushing. A green glow off the water, wavering up, lights her bronze hair.

'Darling, she didn't say.'

'Well, why do you think she does?'
'She said so.'
'Yes, but why?'
'She didn't say.'

Jimmy, balancing his rod on the warm concrete of the pier, lies back, his head in Kerry's lap, his heavy eyes closed against the falling sun, the swathed still sea.

'You know she wouldn't hear of it before.'
'She asked me your name again and said, "Dimitri, you sure you want to marry this woman? Really marry, in our church?" '
'And what did you say?'
'Kerry.'
'Oh yes.'
'And yes, Mama, really marry.'
'What have to told her about me?'
'Nothing much. Red hair,' I said. 'Australian, not Greek. Divorced, with one son called Ben. A teacher of maths at the same school where I teach Greek and – '
'Did you say anything about the baby?'
'No. Not yet.'
'Well, I'm not showing yet.'
'No.' He hesitates. 'Eleni and Voula have not told her either. I asked them.'
'They *know*?'
'Well, yes. I told *them*, they're my sisters. They said they'd guessed, anyway.'
'Oh, come on.'
'Yes. When they met you at the dance. They like to think they can always tell. They are pleased. A daddy at forty-five, they keep saying. Better late than never. They like you. How about after school on Thursday? Is that all right? Nothing formal. Just in and out.'
'All right.'
'You're blushing.'
'I'm nervous.'
'Try out your Greek on her.'

'I hope you're joking.'

'Me? I never joke.'

'You said she speaks English!'

'She does. She even makes us look words up for her. She hardly ever speaks Greek now, strangely enough. But very broken English. Nothing like mine. Mine is not bad, after only twenty years here. Would you not agree?'

'For a quiet life, why not?'

Shafts of sunlight are throbbing through the water as outspread fingers do, in fan shapes.

'She wants to meet you now,' he sighs, 'because she is dying.'

'Oh! You've told her!'

'She wanted to know. I think she knew, anyway. Don't be shocked when you see her. She is wasting away, and her mind wanders. I wish you could have known her when she was young. Her life has been – *martyrio*. *Martyrio*, you know?'

'Martyrdom?'

'Yes. Martyrdom.'

'Because of the War?'

'Oh, yes, the War. Many things. The War was the worst. I was only about eight then. My sisters were too little to help. Our baby brother was sick. We were evacuated from our village. My father was a prisoner. Can you imagine it? His mother, my Yiayia Eleni, minded the little ones. I sold cigarettes, razor blades, *koulouria* – those rolls like quoits with sesame? – on the streets all day. My mother did cleaning, sewing, washing for rich women, to feed us all. But we were starving.'

'Can you remember so far back?'

'Of course. Everything. One night I remember my mother was mending by the kerosene lamp in the warehouse we were living in, in Thessaloniki. My grandmother put her hand on her shoulder.

' "Melpo," she said. "It is time you thought of yourself."

'My mother lifted her red eyes but said nothing.

' "You are young. Your whole life is ahead of you. And what about your children?"

' "Mama," my mother answered. "Don't say this."

' "It is what I would do. He is my own son, my only son. But it is what you will have to do sooner or later. He will manage somehow, he is a man. Think of yourself as a widow, Melpo. The War will go on for years. You are still beautiful. There are good men who will help you. It is not a sin. You have no money, no home, no food. I mean what I am saying."

' "No. Your son believes in me and I have always deserved it. I always will."

'Yiayia shook her scarved head and said nothing more. Her eyelids were wet. My mother went on sewing. My baby brother cried out and I rocked and hushed him back to sleep. When I looked back, my mother was still and sagging over her work, so Yiayia took it away and laid her down to sleep and pulled the flour sack over her. She saw me watching, and hugged me.

' "*Aman, paidaki mou*," she wailed, but quietly. "You must be the man of the family now."

' "I know, Yiayia," I said. "I am already." '

He lies still. Kerry bends over and kisses his brown forehead. 'I'm nervous,' she says again. Her long soft breasts nudge his ears. He feels her shiver. The gold spokes of sun have gone out of the water, leaving it black.

'Don't be.'

'Have we known each other long enough? Can we be sure? Long enough to get married?'

'Well, let me see. How long is it?'

'Ten months. No, eleven.'

'Is it eleven months?' He smiles. 'That sounds enough.'

'What will your mother think?'

'That we should wait. But I don't want to. You don't, do you?'

'No. She might like me, you never know.'

'Yes. Don't be too hard on her, will you, if she is rude? And by the way, better not wear pants.'

'Pardon?'

'Pants. Trousers? Overalls? "Womans should wear only dresses." '

MELPO

'Oh God!'

'It is her old age.'

'I don't have a dress. Or a skirt. I don't *own* one.'

'Oh. Well, never mind. Don't look like that. No, listen.' He sits up, agitated. 'Forget I said it. She can hardly see. Glaucoma.'

'What flowers does she like?'

'Oh, anything.'

'Roses?'

'Yes. Fine.'

'Oh God! I hope we come through this!'

'Darling, of course we will.'

'Do you love me?'

'Yes, of course. *Kouragio!*'

She grins back at him, pushing her fingers through the shaggy grey curls at his temples. Shadow lies all over the bay and the far city. High above, a gull hangs and sways, silent, its red legs folded, still deeply sunlit.

Eleni and Voula, exchanging looks, have served Kerry iced water, a dish of tough green figs in syrup, a glass of Marsala, then Turkish coffee. They have exclaimed over her roses and argued amiably about vases. Flustered, Kerry waits, avoiding Jimmy's eyes. She feels gruff and uncouth, awkward. A bell rings three times in another room. '*Pane*, Dimitri,' Eleni hisses. Jimmy bounds away. Kerry grins blindly at the sisters.

When he comes back and leads her to his mother's room, hot behind brown blinds and stinking of disinfectant, she misses the old woman at first among the jumbled laces and tapestries, the grey and golden faces under glass: a skull on a lace pillow, mottled, and tufted with white down. Only her thick eyes move, red-rimmed, loose in their pleated lids.

'Dimitri?' The voice a hoarse chirrup. 'This is Keri?'

'Kerry, yes. I'm glad to meet you, Mrs Yannakopoulou.'

'Good. Thank you for the roses.' Rumpled already, they sag in dim porcelain, mirrored. '*Keri* is candle in our language. *Keri* is wox.'

'Wax, Mama.'

'Yairs. Wox for candle. Dimitri, *agori mou*, put the lamp, I carn see Keri. Now leave us alone. We tok woman to woman.'

The door closes. Yellow folds of her cheeks move. She is slowly smiling.

'*Katse*, Keri, siddown.' Kerry sits in the cane armchair by the bed. 'My daughters they tell me about you.'

'They're very nice.'

'Yairs. They like you. They say good thinks about you. She hev a good heart, this *filenada* of Dzimmy, they say. She love him too much. She good mother for her little boy. Where your husband is, Keri?'

'My ex-husband. In Queensland, as far as I know. We aren't in touch.'

'Why he leave you? He hev another womans?'

'I don't know. He's been gone years.'

'You doan know?'

'No, Mrs Yannakopoulou.'

'You were very yunk.'

'Twenty-two. My son is nine.'

'How old you say?'

'Nine. *Ennea*.'

'Ach! You speak Greek!'

'I'm learning.'

'Yairs. Is very hard lenguage. How old you are, Keri?'

'Thirty.'

'Thirty. Yairs. You too old to learn Greek.'

'Oh, I'll manage. *Echo kouragio*.'

'*Kouragio!* Ah bravo.' A giggle shakes the bedcovers. 'Good. You will need *thet*, if you love Dimitri. He is quiet man. Mysterious. Always he joke. You will need to be stronk. You are, yairs. Not *oraia*, that doesun mutter. How you say?'

'*Oraia*? Beautiful. I know I'm not.'

'Better not. You not uckly. Too *oraia* no good. They fall in love with they own faces. They mek the men jealoust.' A smile bares the wires around her loose eye-teeth. 'Lonk time now Dimitri tellink me: this woman, this Keri, Mama, I want you to meet her. Keri? I say. Her name Kyriaki? No, he say, she Australian woman, she not Greek. Not Greek, Dimitri? I doan want to meet her. But he keep saying please, Mama. Orright, I say. If you thinkink to merry her, orright. Because now I hev not lonk time to live.'

'Oh, Mrs Yannakopoulou – '

'Orright. Is not secret. Everybody know.' Her hand clamps Kerry's arm. 'And before I go on my lonk, my eternity trip, I want to see my boy heppy. That is all I want now. My boy to be heppy.'

'Yes, well – '

'You are also mother. You hev a mother heart. You want what is best for your boy. You do anythink for him?'

'Yes, but – '

'You good woman. Good-heart woman. You hev *kouragio*. So mek me one favour. For *my* boy.'

'What?'

'Tell Dimitri you woan merry him. You love him. Orright. I understand love. Love him. Look after him. Live with him, orright. *Aman*. Doan merry him.'

Kerry pulls her arm away. The lamp casts a wet light on the ravelled cheeks and throat.

'So I'm not good enough.'

'You *good*. I doen say thet. But divorce woman. Not for Dimitri, no. Not for merry.'

'But he's divorced!'

'Doesun mutter. Is different. She *putana*, thet woman. He loved her too much, but she go with our neighbour, our enemy. Is shame for all our family. We come to Australia for new life. Is not Dimitri fault.'

'Yes, I know. He told me.'

'Hwat he tell you?'

'It was twenty *years* ago.'

'His heart *break*. Some children they find them one night together in the pear orchard: Magda with our enemy. They mother tell me. Dimitri was away. When Magda came home, I tok to her, I tell her I know, all the village know. I cry for my poor son. He will kill you, I say. She cry, she scream. She say she waitink baby. I say we want no *bastardo* in our family. I pack all her *proika*. I say, go and never come back. When he come home, *I* tell Dimitri.'

The scaled eye close, wet-rimmed. Kerry sighs.

'He told me about it. My divorce wasn't my fault either. And I don't play around.'

'For Dimitri next time should be only *parthena*. Veergin.'

'Isn't that up to Dimitri?'

'Is up to *you* now. You know thet, Keri. You can say no. Say *wait*.'

'And then what?'

'I know Greek girls of good femilies – '

'No. You tried that before. He told me. He wasn't interested, was he? Why arrange a marriage these days? I love Jimmy. We want to get married fairly soon. I'm going to have a baby. Jimmy's baby.'

'Hwat? You waitink baby?'

'Yes.'

'Hwen?'

'August.'

'August. I understand now.'

'So you see – '

'You should be *shame*!'

'Ashamed of a baby? Why, what's wrong with it? We aren't living in the Dark Ages. Jimmy's very happy. He likes kids. Ben adores him. He'll be a good father.'

'I understand now why he want to merry you. *Apo filotimo!* For honour. Because you trick him.'

'No. That isn't true.'

'You know hwat womans can do if they doan want baby. You know.'

'I *do* want the baby. So does he. You have no right – '

MELPO

'I hev the right of mother. The right of mother who will die soon! My only livink son! Doan break my heart!'

Kerry, her face hot, pats the writhing yellow hands and stands up.

'I'd better go, Mrs Yannakopoulou. I'm sorry.'

'Wait! Listen to me: I hev money. Yes, I hev. They doan know nothink. Inside the bed.' She claws at the mattress. 'Gold pounds! Hwere they are? Take them. Hev the baby. Leave Dimitri alone. Hwere they are?'

'No, thanks.' Kerry pulls a wry face. 'I'm sorry about all this. And I was hoping you'd like me.'

The old woman is moaning. Her eyes and mouth clamp shut, and she starts shaking. Kerry shuts the door softly on the dense lamplight and goes on tiptoe to the kitchen. It is full of shrill chatter. Saucepans hiss, bouncing their lids, gushing sunlit steam. All over the table sprawl glowing red and green peppers ready to be stuffed. Jimmy, Eleni, Voula, and three children, all suddenly silent, stare with identical eyes like dates; stare up in alarm.

'Someone better go to her. Quickly.'

The sisters hurry off.

'Darling, what's wrong? What happened?'

'Ask your mother. Can you take me home?'

'Of course. Just let's wait till she – '

'It's all right, I'll get a tram. Will you come round later, though, please?'

'Yes, of course. Unless she – '

'Look, if it's all off, fair enough. But you're not to punish me. I *wasn't* hard on her.'

'Oh, Kerry, punish? Why would it be all off?'

The children are gazing open-mouthed.

'She'll tell you.'

'You tell me.'

Kerry shakes her head, reddening.

'You are punishing *me*! Why are you angry?'

'Oh, later!'

The bell rings three times. Jimmy bounds down the passage.

'Mama?' His voice breaks. 'Mama?'

'Leave me alone all of you. And you, go with your *putana*. Leave me alone.' She struggles to turn to the shadowed wall. '*To fos. Kleis' to fos.*'

He turns off the lamp and ushers his sisters out, though they linger, he knows, whispering behind the door.

'She had to go home.'

'Good!'

'*Min klais, Mamaka.*' He smooths her sodden hair. 'No. Don't cry. Don't cry. No. No.'

'Give me a tablet. No, this ones. Water.' He slips his arm behind her knobbled back as she gulps, flinching. 'Ach. *Pikro einai*. Bitter.'

'Tell me what happened.'

But she is silent. He picks up the photograph on her dresser. It is one of the last photographs of his father. His father is sitting in the doorway, feeding Eleni's two little daughters spoonfuls of bread-and-milk. They coaxed him in baby talk for *paparitsa*. It was his *paparitsa*, not theirs. It was all he could eat by then. A white hen is tiptoeing past them. Wheat was heaped in the long room that year, a great trickling tawny mountain; the barn was too full already of barley and sesame. The best harvest since the War, his father said. Bravo Dimitri. None of them has seen the hen yet. In the light at the door they are like three shadow puppets on a screen. He alone looks frayed, dim, melting in the air. His death is near. He regrets, Dimitri thinks, that I have had no children. No grandchild of my sowing, no grandson to bear his name. Still, he is smiling.

In the photograph the bread-and-milk bowl is white. In fact it was butter yellow and, catching the light, glowed in his father's hands like a harvest moon.

'Mama?' he says softly.

'*Nai.*'

'Tell me what happened.'

'She can tell you.'

MELPO

'*Ela. Pes mou.*'

'This Keri. She hev not the right name. She not wox. Wox? She stone. Iron.'

'Why?'

'You want *her*? Hwat for? She not yunk. Not *oraia*. Not Greek. Not rich. For *proika* she hev hwat? A boy. A big boy. She zmok.'

'No.' He grins. 'She doesn't.'

'Australian womans they all zmok. Puff poof. Puff poof.'

'Kerry doesn't.'

'Dimitraki, listen to me. I know you like I know my hand. You my son. You doan love Keri.' She hesitates, then dares: 'Not like you love Magda.'

'Leave Magda out of it.'

'Thet time I save you.'

'Magda is gone. I was too young then. Forget Magda. I love Kerry now.'

'She waitink baby.'

'Yes.'

'Why you doan tok? You should be tell me this, not Keri. Is too big shock.' She sighs. 'If is your baby.'

'It is.'

'How you know? She maybe trick you. Australian womans – '

'Mama, I know.'

'*How* you know? Divorce woman!'

'Mama, I love Kerry. I trust Kerry. I need Kerry. All right?'

'*Thet* is how?' He is silent. 'You engry?'

'No.'

'Yes. You engry with me.'

'No. You will see in August if it is or not.'

'*Aman*, Dimitri,' she moans.

'Enough, Mama, now.'

'Orright, enough. Enough. Merry her, then. I am too tired to fight. Do hwat you want. But you wronk, you know?'

He waits.

'I hope so she hev a boy. For the name, your Baba name. Is

100

good for his name to live. August, *aman*! You think I livink thet long, to see your little boy?'

'Mama, you will.' He squeezes her hand. 'My little girl, maybe. My little Melpo.'

'*Ochi*. If is girl, I doan want the name Melpo.'

'Kerry does.'

'Tell Keri if is girl, she must not call her Melpo.'

'You tell her. Next time she comes.'

'I *never* see her again.'

'Ah, Mamaka.'

'No. Sometime you askink *too* much.'

'You know,' he sighs, 'that if I have a girl, I will call her Melpo.'

'I doan want you to!'

'You do so.'

'*Aman*, Dimitri *mou*. Put me *rodostamo*.'

He tips red rosewater into his palm and sits stroking it over her cheeks and forehead and whimpering throat, the thin loose spotted skin of her forearms.

'Her heart is stone.'

'No. She is strong. Like you, she has had to be.'

'She will control your life, you want thet?'

'I *think* I can get used to it.'

'Well. I done my best. I hope so you woan be sorry, you know?'

'Thank you, Mama.'

He bends and kisses her ruffled cheek. Her eyes close.

'*Ela pio konta*,' She whispers. 'Closer. I have gold pounds inside the bed. Your Aunt Sophia's. Ach, if I had them in the War! The baby died from hunger. Take them, *paidi mou*. Doan tell the girls. Take them for your baby.'

'*Aman*, Mama. You and your gold pounds. You gave them to Magda. You drove her away. And I forgave you. Remember?'

'For your good. For honour.'

But only after years, Mama, he thinks. Bitter years.

'Sleep,' he says.

'I carn. I pain too much. Go and tell Eleni to come. Bring a clean sheet, tell her. When she goes, come back. Sit with me.'

'Can I do anything?'

'Nothink. Maybe Keri waitink you?'

'She will understand.'

'No. Go to her. When I was yunk, I was stronk. My God. Remember? And *oraia* also.'

'I know. There was not a woman like you in all Makedonia. You had a spirit like fire.'

'Hold my hend, Dimitri.'

One day when you are not tired, Mama, he thinks, I must ask you: do you remember the storm, that last summer in the village, before the War when I was five? You sat on the porch in this cane armchair suckling Eleni. The rain was a grey wall. Hens shot past us slithering in the brown mud. The clouds were slashed by lightning and by spokes of sunlight. Afterwards I led the horse out, fighting to hold his head down, but he tore at the grapevine, splashing rain in clusters on us all. White-eyed, his dark silver hide shivering, he munched vine leaves. I was angry. You laughed so much, Eleni lost your nipple, and kicked and wailed. Then I laughed too.

Remember how we stood in the river thigh-deep, slipping on bronze rocks. You taught me to catch little fish in my hands. We threaded them on the green stalks of water plants.

DARLING ODILE

On the way from Sydney to Tahiti I stood for hours every day at the ship's rail and gazed into the wake: Tahiti, the Island of Love. Whales, under their mirroring roof of waves, the tossed balloon of the green sun, must be shrilling, wallowing, coupling. I tried to see dolphins and flying fish. At night, hot in a daze of red Algerian wine, I watched the mast point creaking to this star and that, while under the lifeboats red cigarettes glowed, faded, glowed like far lighthouses. A ukelele twanged and voices sang.

I had brought a sleeping bag but Hamid, the Madagascan cabin 'boy' – Hamid was fifty if a day – said not to think of sleeping on Tahitian beaches, whatever I might be used to back home. No, he said, let me find somewhere safe for you, *chérie*.

Before lunch all the last week Hamid, cringing in the dark behind bulkheads, had beckoned me into a cabin where he had glasses and ice ready, a bottle of aniseed *pastis*, and *casse-croûtes* of crusty flute bread with camembert and frills of sweet pink ham. He knew my lunch in fourth class would be stale and greasy, inedible: he wheedled or stole his treats from the larder chef. He was the first black man I'd ever met.

While I nibbled and made conversation he sat taut and trembling. Then right there on the hot bunk he pounced and spread me out and lay on me wriggling until with one sharp squeal he subsided like a clockwork monkey. The first time I thought he was having a heart attack; that's what a sheltered life I'd led. He stained my dress. I kept all my clothes on – a silken summer dress was all – and clutched his curly grey head to stop him kissing me. He hissed. His wild eyes were red-threaded, his teeth furred green.

Through the port-hole came splashes and squalls of birds.

By then – I would turn twenty in Tahiti – I felt that my formal education was complete. The day after my final exams I sold my textbooks to buy silk dresses. It was time for my *éducation sentimentale*. In theory, I knew what to expect. I had liberated views for those days – 1960 – and read widely. In practice I was a virgin; indignant young men had even called me frigid. (Was it true? Masturbation was a word in Freud to me.) But I had read *The Second Sex* from cover to cover in the original French. I had read Colette. I dreamed of becoming one of Colette's *grandes nonchalantes*, a *chère artiste*, a Léa. I wanted my defloration to be a slow and sensual, transcendant rite of passage. Where else but Tahiti, which was not only French, but Polynesian (I had read Margaret Mead)? I would be taught *le plaisir*, *l'amour*, *l'amour libre* – *libre* because untainted, there, by commerce or by force – in the tawny arms of a tropical man.

I was lucky. Tahiti would have remained nothing but a Gauguin daydream but for my mother's new lover, a bookmaker just widowed, who adored her. It was bliss and orchids every day, and champagne, French champagne, always there like a green cannon in its misty silver ice-bucket. 'This is the lap of luxury, Rosie,' she sighed. As a graduation present she offered me a fur, but I wanted a sea voyage.

'But darling, not on your own?'

'Mum, I've hitch-hiked all over Australia on my own.'

'But why Tahiti?'

'I can practise my French. Do some skin-diving. Please.'

'I don't know. I don't understand my own daughter. All this gadding around. I was a married woman at your age. Look at all the girls in your year that are married already or at least engaged. You've go an Arts degree, so what? You've still got a lot to learn. You're a worry to me, Rosie.'

'Oh, Mum, come on. It'll broaden my mind.'

'Well, I don't know.'

A few days out of Santo a telegram came from my mother: I had passed my final exams. NOW WHAT? she had added. That night I drank too much of the crude Algerian claret and sat on the rolling deck in a fever. Now what, indeed? Adventures on these high seas? A teaching job in Sydney? But first, Tahiti!

Là, tout n'est qu'ordre et beauté,
Luxe, calme et volupté.

That's a strange word, *volupté*. So is defloration, because it isn't like a flower at all, this female hole we have. Perhaps like a brown-fringed sea-anemone with a wet red mouth. Or a velveted clam. When the ship left, mother gave me one long-stemmed rosebud that looked like withering before it could bloom. I held it to the tap in the cabin basin and pressed its red mouth open. Swollen drops glowed on it as it stretched out sipping like a crimson snake. When my pubic hair first grew I stooped and peered with a torch and mirror at the coral frills of those lips ringed with whiskers. It is like a heart, its red folds and chambers. The membranes open like the petals of my rose, but shielded, husked with fur.

At our last lunch before Papeete Hamid grabbed my hand and offered to set me up in his apartment in Paris, in the Arab quarter. Was this *love*? But Paris! There would be weird drumming African music in the grey air, and the smell of baking bread and coffee; on the sky, those grey trees I had seen in so many films, scribbling themselves in the slow river, fading in mist. Rows of lights glistening in the boulevards. He'd be at sea a lot. Regretfully, I turned him down. Why did I? I might have been better off, who knows?

He didn't seem to hold it against me, anyway.

After all the passengers had disembarked and been through customs he sneaked me back on board and into the cabin. Gaudy girls in *pareu* dresses were sitting there, sipping *pastis* or ruby-red grenadine with ice. They were prostitutes of course – what other girls would Hamid know in Papeete? – with bodies like egg-loaves just out of the oven and tasselled black hair with a tongued hibiscus flower pinned in it.

I was taken aback at first. Prostitutes, here? Then I felt proud that Hamid believed that I was so enlightened I could chat with a pack of whores and never turn a hair.

'Hamid, *chéri*,' cooed one. 'She is *sensass*, your little *Australienne*. What are you worried about? I'll take care of her myself.'

DARLING ODILE

Sensass was slang for *sensationelle*. Good. I wanted her to like me. She was fat and half-Chinese, paler, cooler than the others. Her eyes were the black enamel of a goldfish's under fine faint eyebrows. Her doll's mouth cooed broken French. Her name was Odile.

On the quay she waited smiling while I said goodbye to Hamid. I let him kiss my neck. Don't cry, Hamid, *chéri*, I murmured. I'll write to you. I promise. He pressed a wad of Pacific francs into my hand, as I had known he would, and he wouldn't let me give them back. I licked the tears from his poor red eyes while he whimpered in my arms like a puppy.

In the streets of Papeete women sat on the footpaths plaiting green baskets. At one end of the quay a replica of the Bounty was moored, looking too small to be real, as corpses and waxworks do. Her blurred spars and shrouds were winter trees twigged with yards on which her dusty sails were scrolled. At night she sat in a pool of oily light. MGM was making another Bounty movie. American extras with long hair swaggered along arm-in-arm with *vahines*, or slouched with them sipping beer in waterfront bars while Tahitian men glowered. Marlon Brando was said to be at large in this bar or that. All the footpaths said in long chalk letters: MGM GO HOME.

Odile took me to stay with her at her aunt's, in a big household full of women, children, ducks and black piglets with one ambling sow. It was one of a cluster of thatched and plaited *fares* with electric light but no glass in the windows, their hibiscus hedges draped with washing, on the outskirts of Papeete near a river and a black beach.

Those first long indolent days were filled with a hot, a golden light. We had nothing to talk about. We lay on sand that was the black ash of volcanoes, long plumes of palm shadow stroking us, and wrapped in *pareus* swam and wallowed in the still lagoon, twisting among bubbles, her gold body and mine still white undulating side by side. Fish slipped by, mailed and supple, trailing their silky fins. In the sunlit shallows they breathed dappled water.

DARLING ODILE

'Rosie, you'll get burnt.'

'Will you put more oil on me?'

Her hand stroked the scented oil, *monoï*, on me, then mine on her.

Sometimes we fell asleep, waking with a hot headache, cross and surly. One afternoon a hot wind blew and the sand fluttered with the sound a wood-fire makes, burning us. Once a burly *vahine* waded thigh-deep with a net heavy with fish. Cats sat waiting at the waterline. The sky at sundown tightened and cooled on the sea like the skin on hot milk.

In the last orange light we had showers in the bath-house with the ducks. We dressed up and brushed out our hair, songs on the radio, French and Tahitian. Odile taught me to dance the *tamure*. By the lamp at the window she put on mascara, white eyeshadow, lipstick. Arm-in-arm we strolled into Papeete, to this or that waterfront bar, Quinn's, Le Col Bleu, Bar Léa.

Once Hamid's money ran low, Odile was amazed, then scornful, that I refused all offers from men: not in the name of virtue, but of *amour*, or *volupté*. She was offended that my refusals pushed my supposed asking price up to five times hers. A white girl, a *vahine popaa*, was a novelty in the bars back in those days.

'Rosie, why not? After Hamid, he looks good.'

'After Hamid, who wouldn't?'

'Et alors?'

'Non.'

We both shrugged and pouted. I was not going to admit to virginity. Besides, I didn't like their attitude: that gross and condescending, sly black sailor plying me with wine punches, that silky Chinese millionaire, that rowdy Bounty extra. She soothed and cajoled my rejects, taking them in turn to a room she rented overlooking the quay. Most nights I walked home the long way alone.

Barefoot on the soft dust of the road I breathed the night's hot breath of jasmine and nectar under the stars. The hibiscus flowers were all curled up, all tightly folded. Strangers sauntered past talking, singing, plucking a ukulele: *bonne nuit, vahine papaa,* smiling at me. Sudden downpours of warm rain sent us all scattering with shouts and laughter to break off banana leaves for umbrellas. Afterwards the rain had washed a sweetness of strange flowers into the starry silence. Those flowers open only at night, Odile said once, pointing up, and then they wither at daybreak. No, that can't be true, I said. It's too beautiful. *Si, si!* She swore it was.

The first night that she came home at dawn I had lain awake all night, afraid. What was that pattering across the lino? Oh, a spider, Odile shrugged. Or a little mouse. She sighed, lying down beside me on the *pareu* bedcover, a Gauguin blue-and-yellow on the double bed her aunt had honoured us with. She was translucent as butter, so fat, so smooth, carved out of pale jade, my golden Odile. Her great breasts swung, blossom-tipped.

'I have borne a child,' she said. 'You can tell by my nipples, of course.'

Could I have? I wondered how.

'He is nearly two. My mother is raising him. They live on Bora Bora, where I grew up. Willy is his name.' She had a sad smile.

'Were you in love, Odile *chérie*?'

We girls in the bars called the whole world *chérie, chérie*.

'Love? No. Not with that one. No.' She looked sidelong, those glossy eyes of her narrowed. 'But now I am in love.'

'Mmm? Tell me about him.'

'He is American. In the Navy, the Seventh Fleet, I think it is. They were here on a visit last month. He lives in Hawaii.'

'Is he in love with you?'

She shrugged, and again that smile.

'Well, what's his name? Is he good-looking?'

'Yes, of course. *Sensas*. His name is Stéphane.' She took a letter from a mother-of-pearl jewel box by the bed.

'Oh, a letter! What does it say?'

'It is in English.'

Darling Odile,
Got your photo today, gorgeous. It goes everywhere I do. Wow, am

DARLING ODILE

I missing you! I can't get to sleep these nights thinking about how hot and wild you got me. We sure did have ourselves some good times! Honest to God, no woman ever made me feel the way you do in my whole life. What wouldn't I give to be sinking my you know what into that hot little Chinese pussy of yours this minute!!! I'm saving up real hard for your fare over here, honey, so don't you let me down now. Soon, soon, soon. I'm going to grab hold of you and eat you all UP! Write me, OK? French, Tahitian, Chinese, what the hell, so long as you write me, OK? The photo smells like your hair. Baby, words fail me.

Here's looking at you, kid.
Steve.

'I think he loves you,' I said.

'Ah *oui*? What does it say?'

'Oh, you poor darling!'

I translated it. Tears of happiness rimmed her eyes with light. Mangoes when ripe have just that glow of red in their golden cheeks as Odile had. The sun was striking through the banana trees: I ran my fingers along her sumptuous breast and flank as daylight brimmed about in in the room.

'Sleep well, *ma pauvre petite* Odile,' I whispered.

But she lay stirring, sighing, for a long time.

Most mornings, while Odile slept in, I wandered round the market. There fish as tall as men hung from hooks by their horny lips, their huge silver eyes soaked in blood. I bought red and yellow bananas, and scented mangoes, and grapefruits with skins like pitted green balloons. Pale green flesh glowed in them. We always ate lunch at one long table with Odile's relatives: fruit and breadfruit, avocadoes from the tree, taro, raw fish. I learnt to make the raw fish, tuna or bonito, soaked in lime juice and coconut milk. Odile's aunt would never hear of my paying board, so I gave money to Odile to pass on to her.

At night if we were hungry we bought fried food from trolleys on wheels or ate *maa Tinito*, Chinese rice and red beans, in family restaurants with four or five tables, a basin on the wall, and one stand-up *cabinet* for everybody in the yard beyond the kitchen. Money was short.

That afternoon was stormy, not beach weather, so when Odile woke we went early to Quinn's. Sleepy girls drifted in from time to time and sat around gossiping, writing letters, lazily sipping beer. The band was rehearsing for the floorshow: the drums, the steel guitars, ukuleles, a hoarse baritone. The tables had a nap of golden dust. Between storms wet sunlight probed thickly through any gap into the languorous red glow cast by the stage lamps. Their crimson gloss coated all our hot skins.

I wrote postcards to my mother and to Hamid. I saw Odile's lip curl. Then we wrote Steve a letter in English. Odile dictated, and I embellished.

'Steve darling, I miss you too.'

Steve darling,
I can't forget you. I remember everything about you, everything we did. It scares me to think we might never meet again. Tell me we will.

'I shut my eyes and keep remembering how you made love to me. I dream that you're here beside me.'

I shut my eyes and keep remembering how it feels when you're inside me. I stroke you all over in my dreams, thinking you're here beside me.

'When they're lying on me I shut my eyes and think of you. You're the only one I love.'

When they're lying on me I shut my eyes and think, oh, Steve, Steve. You're the only one I love.

'I want to be with you. I'll come when I can. You know I will. Trust me.'

I want to be with you. I'll come when I can, and we'll make a new life away from Papeete. You know I'll come. Trust me. My Australian friend Rosie is writing this for me.

'I love you, Stéphane, no, put Steve. Your Odile.'

DARLING ODILE

> *I love you, Steve.*
> *Your Odile.*

The days that followed were too hot to go trudging to the beach. After calling at the Poste Restante we walked to the river instead. Beyond the ford of pebbles there was a deep pool where we floated helpless as watermelons in the churning, froth, our *pareus* billowing. We landed in the shallows, thrown together, our bare skins grazed. Once a snake lashed on the pebbles as I lay gasping, no, a thick grey eel, then flickered away. Shadows arched in the water. We were green-lit there like Gauguin's strange white horse stooped to sip the coiled surfaces of water.

Once the whole family came with food in banana leaves. We all splashed and dived, giggling. I heard Odile's cousin, a sleek boy whose voice was breaking, ask her something about me: I heard 'Rosie'. She replied in Tahitian, grinning scornfully, and finished with a jeering laugh. Then she saw my face. Ah, *te voici*, Rosie, where were you? She took my hand and waded to the bank to plait out of leaves a crown for me and other for her, and pressed them on to our dripping hair.

Was Odile not to be trusted? I dismissed the thought.

On my twentieth birthday there was a letter for Odile from Steve at last at the Bureau de Poste, and a letter and a cheque for me from my mother, with best regards from the bookmaker. 'Wishing you many happies, pet,' she had scribbled. 'How's my free spirit? Not too free, I hope! Thank your Odile for me, won't you, for looking after my girl. Be seeing you soon. Don't do anything I wouldn't do!' Of course, I hadn't written much about Odile in my postcards home, as she'd only worry. We cashed the cheque at the Banque de l'Indochine and went to Quinn's, where I wrote Odile a translation of Steve's letter.

Darling Odile,

Just a short note to say I love you. You are just the sweetest juiciest woman I ever saw. You are. I'm sending you a little something by registered mail: wear it for me, baby. I mean, all the time. You promised.

DARLING ODILE

Write me again real soon, another letter like that. I can't wait. I can't get to sleep for thinking about you. I just want you like crazy the whole damn time.

Mad about you, kid.
Steve.

P.S. *Dear friend Rosie, thanks a million and keep up the good work huh?*

There was a photo too, of a grinning, heavy, broad-shouldered man, Polynesian dark brown, wearing a crown of leaves on a blue beach with coconut palms.

'What's he sending you, *chérie*?'

'The ring, I suppose.'

'The *ring*!'

I bought us a prawn dinner to celebrate, and later back at Quinn's we ordered French champagne. Odile was wildly dancing, laughing everywhere. Half-stifled in the crush, the smoke, I sat numb in an icy, foaming dizziness of champagne. A hot, fuzzy yellow light floated among the tables: in the aisles men of all races were crammed to watch the floorshow, Ruita on the red stage dancing the *tamure* to thudding drumbeats. I felt a nudge on my bare shoulder and, glancing, saw a man's black trouser-legs. Absurd to object. I sipped more icy foam. He rubbed gently at first, then harder and harder, until I heard a sigh above my head. My shoulder felt briefly damp when he moved away.

A group of Tahitian men from behind me, surging across, grabbed a table near by: I wondered which of them it had been. One stared back at me with burning eyes. You? I thought. Are you thinking you've defiled me, using me? I tossed my head. You haven't.

The way home was long, dark, cool. My dazed head cleared. I watched the moon set, paddling in sand and the frills of waves among the many-breasted coconut palms, tripping in the starlight over coconut husks and the out-riggers of canoes. A man with a ukulele fell into silent step behind me.

'*Bonsoir.*'

'*Bonsoir, monsieur.*'

'You like Tahiti, *vahine popaa?*'

'Oh yes, I love it.'

He was Tahitian, very tall, smiling with broken teeth.

'Your are *Américaine?*'

'*Australienne.*'

He hummed a song, walking close, strumming his ukulele. The way home wound past hibiscus hedges, the *fares* here and there beyond them still glowing gold. At a bend in the sandy path suddenly his arm came tight round my shoulders. He dragged me stumbling through swordgrass to a banana grove. His ukulele fell with a cry.

'Stop it!' I gasped, clawing him. 'No! No! Don't!'

'*Je veux de toi.*'

'*Non! Je veux pas!*'

'*Je veux de toi.*'

He shoved me down in the rough grass, lifted my silk dress and wrenched my thighs apart. I felt him bore between my soft dry lips. His palm clamped down on my nose and mouth. Struggling, kicking, frantic for breath, I scratched and bit. He grunted, riding me the harder for it: he lunged and rasped inside me. Then his hand lifted. He shuddered and lay limp on me.

When he got up three more men were waiting.

'Oh, please,' I begged him. 'Don't let them.'

He put his arms round their shoulders, muttering in Tahitian, but they scoffed and pushed him to one side. The others watched, smoking, as one by one each man unzipped and lay on me, pushed his cock inside and thrust briefly. I shut my eyes. I was bruised all over, soggy and aching inside. None of them was brutal, and one who took too long was reproached by the others. I opened my eyes: it was Odile's sleek cousin. He was hissing, wet-faced. *E hoa*, moaned the others; get a move on, friend.

When it was over the three men left me alone again with the first man. He knelt beside me, lifting my head, intent.

'*Ça va?* You're all right?'

DARLING ODILE

I nodded. Then he did it to me again, riding my white body gently, his mouth – not his hand – over my mouth. He squelched in blood and semen, moving inside me. When he finished he straightened my dress and patted my torn, gritty hair.

'Go home, *vahine popaa. Va vite. Vite.*'

He slapped me on the rump, picked up his ukulele and went.

I cried, staggering home in the starlight, not daring to go and wash in the river or the sea. The tears boiled over in my eyes against my will. My teeth clenched on a child's whimpers and wails in the face of loss, injustice. No one saw me creep to the bathhouse or to bed. I told no one. They may have found out, I suppose. Odile may have known all along. There were no more late nights at Quinn's after that, no more night walks. I stayed in the *fare*, reading by lamplight, until I slept.

So much for my defloration. As for *plaisir, volupté*: they were lies in books.

In the shadows of our black beach I wrote one more letter for Odile. I did my best for her, though my heart wasn't in it any more. I mistrusted her now.

Steve darling, darling Steve,
I want to be with you so much, it's hard to wait not knowing when we can be together again. I think of you all the time. I think of how your hands stroke and hold me, and the look in your eyes then. I'm the same all over, but you're all different colours, brown, russet, yellow, black. I want to kiss you all over everywhere. I kiss that mole near your left nipple, and the one on your thigh. Then – guess where! I kiss the freckles on your nose and cheeks. Do you like that? And of course I'll wear your little something when it comes. I said I would, didn't I? Chéri, je t'aime.

Your Odile.

PS This is Rosie signing off and wishing you two all the best, Steve baby. Sounds like you're real hot stuff! Rosie.
PPS I'm blonde.

In a day or two my ship docked.

DARLING ODILE

I'd been only vaguely aware of the date and the passage of time until suddenly there she was: not the one I came on but a sister ship, throbbing and glittering at the quay, loading copra. I packed my bag and said my goodbyes. We had one last day, on a white beach. Marlon Brando was there with cavorting *vahines*. I didn't swim. I was bleeding. I wasn't pregnant. I could see the ship's doctor for VD tests. Coated with sand we ate slices of yellow watermelon. The slanted black eyes that were its seeds shone in its pale flesh.

I watched Odile roll in the sea. Sometimes in the cold rough river, when her legs had tumbled apart, I had seen the hairy blossom between them glistening. That, and her lips, and her nipples, were the only red on her. She was the same all over. How had she been broken in? How had she borne it? Could she honestly love a man? The memory was sour in me of thrusts and shudders, and poor Hamid's soft squeals. Men are at women's mercy then, the strongest men: wise women made the most of it. My mother did. I should have asked Odile to teach me her trade. A whore, she knew love's bitter mystery. Odile *chérie*, I should have said, before it was too late: teach me what I must know. Teach me pleasure.

In the chatter on the crowd by the gangway Odile hung a mother-of-pearl heart on a chain round my neck and hugged me, sobbing and sniffling. I knew I'd never see her again. I went on board and waved to her. The ship's strung lights lay spindling in the water. A band was playing. In the distance the *Bounty* was a ghost ship. Long before we sailed Odile was gone. She was at Quinn's.

Jostled, I watched the quay drift away, and the lights of Papeete, and Tahiti's black towers of mountains hung with clouds. Thrown garlands of white flowers tossed in the wake. Stars floated. Eels were weaving in their dark caverns. Steve and Odile, I thought, the brown and the golden: soon you'll be heaving and coupling like the whales, the long sun aslant over you.

AT THE AIRPORT

Her son clatters into the airport building, impatient to go. She gloats over him, his wheaten hair, his eyes the same colour of dark honey that his father's are, his sturdy long body and legs. He is eight and she will not see him again for three months. Again he is going with his father, who used to be her husband, to spend the winter, the Greek summer, in his grandparents' village. He will write to her.

Dear Mum haw ar you good you shod come one day it is relly fun we have watafites and jamp off the hen house. Grand Dad is all ways snoring i can not go to sleep! Zzzz i wish we cod stay here. love from me and Dad and Grand Mum and Grand Dad and the rest off the famaly XXXXXXXXXX PAUL

He will send photographs of himself and his grandparents, who were fond of their foreign daughter-in-law. She will see him grinning into the sun in villages and on beaches that she will never go to again. As time passes they are becoming like the house she keeps dreaming of, which has never existed, she is sure, yet which she recognises when she goes there.

She will miss him. He will not really miss her. They no longer live together and haven't for four years. He stays at her flat on weekends and school holidays. For all this, her ex-husband blames her. Her son, more than anyone else, blames her.

Her ex-husband, flustered and tired, waits in line to check in his luggage. The girl he lives with now fills in his immigration cards for him. To give the couple time alone, her son and she go to the cafeteria. On the way they buy a doll for a new baby cousin in Greece whose godfather her son is going to be. She herself will never see this baby girl. Photographs will show him taking a wet and oily naked baby from the bearded priest, just as six years ago he was taken, splashing and furious. She buys a coffee, and a trifle for him. She asks for a taste. He gives her spoon for spoon of it, sandy, soaked in wine.

'I thought you liked trifle?' She is disappointed.

'Oh yes, I do.'

'But you've given me half?'

'Well, you like it too. Don't you?'

His smile is sad. He is sorry for her, because he is going and she is not.

They are stopping over in Bangkok. She remembers her son at two on his father's shoulders at a rainy temple in Bangkok, a flounced and gilded temple full of a statue of Buddha. A cat lapped a puddle in which grey pigeons and the gold robes of monks were reflected, fluttering. He climbed down to stroke the crouched cat.

She remembers him that year on the shoulders of an uncle emerging from the dark vault of a mulberry grove into the noon heat. He munched, stained with juice. His hands made crimson prints on his uncle's bald dome. They washed each other at a tap in the yard. His white hair trickled. Seeing her, he opened his arms and leaped into hers. He was glossy, cold-skinned. *'Moura,'* he said. Mulberries.

That year he was baptised in the font of the village church. He was given his Greek name, his grandfather's: Pavlo. And Greek nationality.

After drinks at the bar and hasty kisses and farewells they are gone. She is left with Vanessa, who lives with them now but has never gone with them, not yet. She and Vanessa go back together to sit in the bar beside a window through which they can see all the plane. It is late taking off. She is sipping riesling and Vanessa vermouth. They are not alike in any way. Even the man each of them has loved in her time is not the same man. She looks in the pane at the sleek eyes and hair of this younger woman warmly nestled, looking out. No sadness is showing.

AT THE AIRPORT

She sees herself, looking no less calm. Their glances, meeting, jump away.

The plane taxies and turns. They stand to watch it hurl itself up. Then they take polite leave of each other.

She pays her parking fee at the gate and drives on to the freeway. Planes in the foggy air blink their lights and rise and sink. There is a dim full moon. It will shrink and fill again three times before his father brings him back. He must, he has made promises. No self-pity, she thinks, having worked hard to keep her composure, the outward sign of dignity, intact. It is her crust, her shell. Her carapace. Loss and the fear of loss assail her.

'Daddy wants us to go and live in Greece now,' she remembers him saying a while ago. 'But you can come too.'

'I couldn't go and live in Greece, Paulie.'

'You used to.'

'Ages ago. I don't belong there now.'

'Why not?'

'I just don't.'

'*I* do.'

'Yes, I know.'

'I'm Greek.'

'Half-Greek.'

'No. I'm Greek.'

'Well, I'm not.'

'You can speak Greek.'

'That's not enough.' She hugged him. 'You belong here too.'

'There's better, Mum.'

'Why?'

'Well, *there's* a family.'

In the next two months she is patient. She goes to her job in a coffee shop and then to classes. She hands in work on time. She sleeps late. She walks along the winter beaches. On the grey sand she finds mussel shells, feathers, dulled glass. She sees a yacht trail close in to shore. Its heavy sails move cloud-coloured, the late sun in them. Out past the shore water shadowed by this or that drift of wind, a red ship hangs in midair.

She remembers their summer beaches. She dwells on the time when he was four, only four, and they were in Greece for the last time together. She blew up his yellow floaties on his arms, took his hand and swam with him in tow far out into the deep water where a yacht was anchored. Puffing, they clung to a buoy rope that threw bubbles of water in a chain on the surface of the sea. Scared and proud, they waved to his father and the rest of the family, those dots on the sand, aunts and uncles and cousins. The yacht tilted creaking above them. On the sea, as if in thick glass, its mast wobbled among clouds. They glided back hand in hand. Used to waters where sharks might be, she had never dared swim out so far before. Here there were none. They passed, mother and son, above mauve skeins of jellyfish suspended where the water darkened, but not one touched them. Bubbles had clustered, she saw, on the fine silver hairs on his back, on his brown legs and arms and on hers.

She often dreams of this swim now. It was a month after it, back home in the early spring, that she left home. Her son was asleep. When he woke he thought Mummy was playing hidey. He laughed, looking in wardrobes. Then his father told him. 'Your Mummy's sick in hospital,' he said. Her son told her all this later. 'Well, what I should say?' his father shouted at her. 'You walk out, you want I say that?'

She found a flat in South Melbourne, two hours' drive from their town, and a job in a hotel. 'I thought you'd be a good mother,' was what her mother said. 'You were at first.'

Her son's black kitten, black but for the circles of gold round his eyes, sits and nibbles one paw. He has been entrusted to her while her son is away. He is used to her now. He falls asleep on her lamb's fleece stretched on his back. When he wakes the bell at his throat will tell her so. At night she sits and studies. A cowled white lamp peers over her shoulder at the shadow of her hand writing. The kitten wakes – chink – and gazes. He eats crouching, his sharp little shoulders almost bald. She lets him out during the day, but is anxious. At night he must use the litter box. He prowls in it and flips the granules over the carpet obsessively. Nothing must happen to him while he is at her place. Growth, of course, must. He is becoming a stolid cat. Will her son still love him? Will her son come back?

On her balcony she listens to a slow sonata, a hollow clarinet, watching a sunset douse its cold flames in the bay. The bridge has its gold lights on. The moon, when it rises, is nearly full again. The moon she sees tonight shone a few hours ago over her son. Does he ever think of her? Remember me, she says. Miss me. I miss you.

The pot of basil they gave her for her balcony before they left is still there, but black and dry. Basil dies in winter. Her balcony faces the sea wind. The lane opposite is always full of dark rainwater. The sunset shows in it. Night fills it with lamps.

'It's breaking your mother's heart,' a neighbour reproved her when she first left. It was true, in a way. Her mother's little clockwork voice was always on the phone.

'I've talked to a lawyer,' it piped. 'Act fast, she says. The longer you delay the more weight it gives to the status quo.'

'Delay – what?'

'You have to *apply* for interim custody. You can't wait till the divorce.'

'Oh, Mum, no, I can't contest custody.'

'What do you mean? He's not going to hand you the child on a platter. He'll fight you for him.'

'He talked about that before I left. Even if I won he wouldn't let me get away with it. He'd kidnap him and go home. He would.'

'There are laws – '

'Constantly being broken. You know that.'

'Well, try, at least. What's got into you?'

'That'd turn him completely against me.'

'So *what*?'

'Mum, as things are, he lets me see Paul. And he lets *you* see Paul. He's sorry for us.'

'Why should anyone be sorry for you? You've brought it on yourself. Where did I go wrong? A real mother would go to hell and back to keep her child!'

She writes to Paul about his kitten and the football and the village. She knows it amazes him that she knows the village. He forgets that she went there before he was born and then twice with him when he was little. With an incredulous grin he looks at slides of her in the village with his family, when he comes to visit, as if she was there by some magic. She knows how he feels.

She takes out the old projector and looks at the slides again. She gets photographs from him in the mail and studies them. She gets a letter.

Dear Mum haw ar you i am very well evry day we go to the beche, evry after noon the weves have gron hiarh and hiarh and moore hiarh and hiarh. i went very deep on tuesday. how is my cat. there is a kitten here its names psipsina. i was bitten by a wosp on the neck twis i was pritending i was drackula. any way love from me and evry body XXXXXXXXXX PAUL

He used to ask her why. Why don't you love my Dad? Why did you leave us? (Why didn't you wake me? Take me?) Won't you ever come back? Why not? Will you always be my mother?

He would understand one day, she used to answer: it was a long story. She doesn't ever want to show him wounds or admit to the rage and spite that caused them. Nor, she thinks, does his father. They both cringe under their son's accusing gaze. They have stopped accusing each other, and now make what amends they can. They trust each other to behave well. It was not always so.

What matters after all is that there came, in their anger and terror and despair, a point of silence one night in which she went to her sleeping child, kissed his cheek, picked up her suitcase. Left. This is what counts. Might it have been otherwise? Yes. No. Whatever happened before it belongs to one life, which is over. What comes after is another. In dreams, what is meshes with what was and what might have been; as in dreams she goes to a remembered house which does not exist. What might have been cannot be.

Since Vanessa moved in, he has stopped asking questions.

She brought him to stay at her new flat and took him to the Zoo. Politely they gazed at the animals, especially the sandy, sleepy lions. He rode on the train and on a white pony. On the spiral slide he made her go up with him the first time and clung on to her as they spun down; then he went up alone again and again while she waited to catch him at the bottom. They had hamburgers and milk shakes. Then he had to go to the toilet. The Men's, he insisted. She promised to wait but after a while she called out that she was just going to the Women's: wait, she said. When she came out he was not there. She stood in the smelly shade until a man looked in and told her there was no little boy inside. She rushed over to the lions, then to the slide, the ponies, the train, the toilets again. A microphone blared. Reception! she thought and hurtled along crowded paths. There he was, red-faced. He turned his back.

'A lady brought him in. He said his Mummy went home!' the woman at reception accused. 'Of course I said Mummies don't do that, but he was that positive! "Why ever would she?" I said and he said, "I don't know." '

'I was only in the toilet,' she explained.

'You were not!'

'I was. I called out.'

'You did *not*!'

'Darling, I *did*! You just didn't hear.'

'No, you never! You did not call out! Oh, why didn't you?'

She tried to hug him and wipe his eyes. Sobbing, he pushed her. But he walked beside her out into the sun.

'Remember our long swim?' she asked as they watched lions.
'In Greece?'
'Yes. Remember?'
'No,' he muttered.

One afternoon the cat doesn't come back in. She wanders, calling, along streets filled with cars and darkness. The lamps twitch on. The pairs of gold eyes that she stalks and chases all belong to strange cats. His cat must be lost. The wind tugs and hurls cold sea-spray. She blunders through puddles.

At home in the lamplight she can't concentrate on work. She can't finish her letter to her son. A child is wailing in the flat next door. Mama. Ma-ama. Every half hour she goes to the door and calls the cat.

Once as her son stepped out of her car after a visit with her, he saw his kitten playing on the road. He called, but the kitten lifted his tail and danced away. 'If I catch him I'll kill him!' Her son's face was dark red. 'He knows he's not allowed out! I'll kill him!'

'Oh, Paulie,' she said.

'I will. I mean it. I'll flush him down the toilet!'

'He'll come back,' she said.

He just looked at her.

Before she goes to bed she opens the door a last time and calls out. Suddenly the cat is there, flattened against the wall in the wind, thin and black as his shadow. He struts in and prowls, purring, and folds himself on the lamb's fleece.

After the divorce, when her ex-husband took her son home to Greece, her mother would not be consoled. Paul was gone, her only grandchild. He was as good as gone before that. But now his father would never bring him back.

'Mum, he will.'

'What make you think so?'

'He just will.' Compassion, she thought. Respect for the tacit bargain: you keep him, but *here*. Even mercy, for the defeated opponent. 'His business, for one thing.'

'Why did you have to go and marry a Greek?'

'Oh, come on. You always liked him.'

'Can't you work something out?'

'No.'

'I can't get over it. How could you do it?'

'I had to.'

'It wasn't that bad.'

'It *was*. I was spending days staring at one corner in one room. The sun never came in. Everything was grey. Shadows moved, that was all. Nothing mattered, not even the child, and he was so persistent. When footsteps came near me, I banged my head on the window frame until it bled or they went away.'

'You should have seen a doctor.'

'A doctor! When my *life* – '

'A doctor, yes. Depression can be treated, you know.'

'I've come alive since I left.'

' "I, I, I." When you realize how selfish you've been all along, and how *weak*, when you finally think of the *child* – '

'It's best for him not to be fought over.'

'You *hope*. Oh, the easy way out, as per usual. You're a callous and self-centred woman. I'm ashamed you're my daughter.'

'You make better chips than Vanessa,' her son told her on a visit a few months ago.

'That's good. Who's Vanessa?'

'A lady. She lives at our place. She's got this dog. Its name is Roly. Guess why.'

'Short for Roland?'

'No. Because it's always rolling! Mum, if my dad marries Vanessa, will Roly be in my family?'

'I suppose. Vanessa. She's not Greek, is she?'

'No. She comes from Sydney.'

'Has she been to Greece, do you know?'

AT THE AIRPORT

'Yes. She loves it. She'd like to live there, she says. Could she take Roly?'

'I don't know. Maybe. Is he friendly?'

'Oh, yes. You make the best chips I've ever aten.'

'Eaten.'

'Eaten.'

They did come back from Greece that first time, and the next. Her son loved her mother just the same after the divorce, and she spoiled him. Now, two years since her death, he often mentions Granma, his voice hushed and sorrowful. He remembers her best cooking dinners when they visited, ladling gravy, hovering over a sizzled chicken. He knows he will die one day. He buries dead birds and crickets, and saves moths from his cat.

One morning in September she has a good dream. She is at the house she is always dreaming of. It has a deep veranda of sagging boards that looks on to muddy grass and bare trees. A window burns with light. As the sun sets she strolls in and opens a door of gold wood that she has never opened in any previous dream. She knows the moment before she looks that her son will be in there. He is asleep, his cat at his feet. He wakes and looks up, smiling.

She lies awake breathless with joy in her rented bed. She wishes she could tell her mother this dream. Some time, she hopes, her mother will be behind a door, in one of the bright rooms in this house.

Dear Mum haw ar you we ar coming back 15 september. its at 4 oclock in the morning. pleas meet us at the air port. i wont you to.
XXXXXXXXXX *PAUL*

She rings the number Vanessa has given her, but is told that Vanessa is up in Sydney because her mother is sick. So Vanessa won't be at the airport. On the night she wakes to the alarm with a sour headache at three, crams the cat into his basket and drives through the dark under all the faint lamps of the city. The airport building, full of light, is crowded already. Voices boom,

AT THE AIRPORT

echoing. The plane has landed. After an hour passengers start bursting through the door with luggage trolleys. Her eyes are crusted, dazed. They will keep watering. Her ex-husband and her son push through last of all. Her ex-husband looks smaller, gaunt and grey. But her son! So big, so brown! She is full of exclamations and this delights him. He thinks she is crying, though she says no. They all talk at once and wish aloud for coffee, but there is nowhere open, so they go out to the car park. She has forgotten where she left her car. In the cold wind and half-light they all wander over the painted asphalt, looking. Her son sees it first. He wraps himself in his sullen cat. The sun comes up, a gong on the rim of the sky.

'Glad you're back?' She hugs Paulie.

'Yes, if you are.'

'I am. I'm very glad.' To her ex-husband she says in Greek, 'There are times when – ' she can't speak. 'Life – ' she tries again.

'Oh, life. Life. Well yes.' He smiles wanly.

The trees toss and swill the gold light. Their eyes glitter with it.

INHERITANCE

Here I sit in your armchair shrouded in shadows of grey lace; my glass of red wine glows on the sill; the garden is starlit beyond the mirroring pane.

Again and again you were taken to the hospital and came back determined not to die. My father each time grey with terror that you soon must. Your mind, half-dead since your stroke, stumbled on among twisted words and phrases, hostilities, old affections, shards of memory. Some querulous love left for your garden and for my little girl, Claire, whom you kept calling Paula. Splutters of anger or distress when anything was out of place or time. My father in his closed room tinkered with clocks and radios, played scraps of Bach on his piano, studied the stars by telescope. He died years ago and is charred bones now.

Up at the hospital they said that this time you would die. You'd given up. Why?

You used to ask me to promise not to look at your dead body. 'That's not how I want you to remember me, Paula,' you said. You didn't look at your own mother, who died young. 'What remains is only the husk,' you said, 'the soul being ascended unto the Father.' We went with Auntie May one cold afternoon to put lilies on your mother's grave, cold white folded lilies. I crept among the staring statues in bony drapery. The cypress trees had seeds like snails on their black fronds.

'Promise you'll have me cremated,' you said.

The first time you didn't want me to know that something serious was wrong. I was in the middle of examinations at university and must not be put off my stride. But Auntie May rang me in college.

'Paula, if they won't tell you the truth I will,' she shouted. 'It's *cancer*. Your mother might die under the knife. *Yes*. You ask your father.'

Cancer was what I had always most feared for you. You smoked such a lot. You rolled your own. Godgies, I called them. (You loved my baby talk.) Pipes and lipsticks and lollipops were all godgies, and the little stalks that boys could pee through, but not my father's bicycle pump which was the hogfig. Daddy hated your godgies too. You lit the first, convulsed with deep coughs, at daybreak. I delayed opening my bedroom door and letting in the smoky breath of the rest of the house. In winter on the way to school – streetlamps still gold, a grey light spreading – I watched in disgust as white smoke poured out of me.

In the holidays when we went to the city for lunch and a show I wouldn't sit in a smoking compartment and flounced on my own to a non-smoker. Perched on a green seat by a shuddering double window I watched bridges and factories trundle beyond my dusty shadow. On the city platform you were waiting, breathing smoke through an angry smile.

At ten, on some dull visit, leafing by lamplight through old magazines while you grown-ups played cards, I read that cigarettes caused lung cancer. I tore the page out. 'Oh, what rubbish,' you said. Tearful and urgent, waiting on the corner that frosty night for a brown bus home: 'Mummy,' I whimpered. 'Please, please stop. You'll get cancer and die. Daddy, you tell her.'

'It's your mother's own business, Paula. Just keep quiet.'

You never got lung cancer. Eight years ago after your stroke the doctors made you stop smoking. My father and I weren't mean. We kept quiet.

When I rang from college, my father denied that it was cancer you had.

'You know what your Auntie May's like, lovey. Always got the wind up about something,' he soothed. 'Mum's got to go in for a minor op., that's all. A fissure of the anus. Now you do your best. We're proud of our girl.'

But it was cancer of the bowel. You survived the colostomy

and learned to fasten plastic bags to the new hole cut in your belly. You've had to do it for nearly twenty years. You were both cool after that with Auntie May, for having interfered. But my results weren't bad.

By then I was deep in first love and that was all that mattered. He was married. I never told you. He behaved like a gentleman and paid for the abortion. In all that summer of muggy heat and secrecy I only wrote you a letter or two. I'm sorry.

When that was over I hitchhiked down to see you in your bedroom that Dad had moved out of by then. In the hot noon darkness crowded with old furniture you lay asleep, tangled in bedclothes, your lamp still on. Your mouth gulped, grimaced, when I stepped inside.

'Hullo, Mum.'

'Paula! Is that you?'

Tears, glowing, trickled down your furrowed throat.

'Are you all right, Mum?'

'Paula!' Your voice blurring in the pillow. 'Why didn't you ever come?'

Later, after your shower, you called me into the bathroom to show me by its furred yellow light. I had never seen you naked. You hesitated, frail and shaking, your knees slack; then took the towel away. Your eyes rolled up in appeal. From hip to hip your belly grinned at me with crooked lips. On one side, your new anus, a puckered bud, a hole. Your nipples lolled, pink eyeballs staring down. Under the belly's sag nestled the shaggy grey chin of your groin.

'Is it still sore?'

'Not too bad.'

'It doesn't look too bad.'

You smiled at last, and I kissed you. Your wet suede cheek.

At Claire's age, at seven or so, I remember reproaching you for looking so flabby, wrinkled and sick. Why don't you look pretty like other mothers? I persisted. You were close on fifty, no longer pretty, but loved. The grocer sold you more butter, the butcher more meat, than you ever had coupons; old ladies poking in their dry flower beds straightened stiff backs and held you up with gossip; neighbours were in and out all day for coffee. The tram conductors on our way to the second-hand bookstore told you their life stories. One whole summer in the hot twilight before bedtime you read me and my playmates *Alice in Wonderland* from my faded green copy that smelled, still smells, of autumn leaves.

Daddy read me music in bed. Scales, crotchets and quavers. FACE and Every Good Boy Deserves Food. We hummed the first bars of sonatas he was going to teach me. But I had no ear, and disappointed him.

Waking in terror of cages and shadows and furtive rustlings I would call out to you. It was always he who came, he the lighter sleeper. 'Mu-um, my leg's got cramps.' His knee joints crackling at every step down the dark passage. He would switch on my dazing light and sit rubbing my calves, wryly yawning.

'Not better yet?' he would sigh.

'No. Daddy, can I come into your bed?'

'No, lovey. Back to sleep now.'

'But I'll dream about the hospital!'

'No, you won't.'

'Will you leave the light on?'

'All right. The passage light. Night night, Snooks.'

He would kiss my cheek and stalk crackling back to the dark room you two slept in. Snoring in counterpoint.

I was always dreaming about the hospital. This great terror of hospitals, all my life. At five I spent six weeks in one with scarlet fever. You dressed me in my best brown jumper and skirt and Daddy took me there in a taxi. A nurse bathed me in phenol. The children's ward was long, cold, dim. Its balcony had a high wire fence that I clambered up one day for a dare. I was caught, punished with isolation; the nurse had short red hair and an angry contempt that stunned me. You rang the matron daily. No visitors were allowed for fear of infection. The fenced ward was our prison. Often I overshot the bedpan and rubbed the sheet for hours after, to dry it; the white cage of my bed jiggling, tinkling. I could see one skylight with stars behind it turn blue, grey, gold each morning. Nurses sponged us and replaited our plaits tightly. When Daddy came for me at last, I refused to speak. My brown jumper and skirt were brought out folded. I had given up hope of ever seeing them or home again. It was a sunny day. A stiff wind blowing.

As he aged and in retirement became remote – brittle, silent – his nights were more disturbed and the crackling of his joints woke me several times a night as he crept outside, but by then I never called.

My knee joints crackle too. I take after him. Daddy's girl. We were skinny, to your plump. Daddy's little skinnamalink. He dinked me on the bar of his bicycle to vacant lots where in other summers circuses had appeared overnight, soiled elephants shambled; to clamber through the golden skeletons of the new houses. He lifted me high into our gumtree to pick off its crouched caterpillars. He built bonfires like haystacks and lit Catherine wheels warily. He held my cheeks in rough palms to guide my gaze at galaxies and constellations. Our trees waved giant hushed shadows over skyfuls of stars.

You weigh five stone now.

On that last day, when you trotted in right on time with his morning tea, he lay flung half-off the bed in an attitude of terror, his grey eyes wide; heart pills all over the sunny floorboards. I was two hours getting here. An aged, sorrowful child, you sat numbly for hours by the window; scurried to pack away his clothes; on the telephone mumbled over and over broken self-reproaches, despair. You had squabbled over breakfast. He had trudged back to bed in a sulk. Feeling sick, he said.

'Mum, you couldn't have known.'

'Should have. Should. Oh yes. Oh.'

Once his clothes were packed off to the Brotherhood, the piano and telescope sold, you asked me to find you a flat near ours in the city. I looked around on my days off: it had to be a ground-floor flat because of your heart. There was nothing suitable. After a couple of months you said you'd changed your mind, you weren't helpless, thanks all the same. You'd stay put.

I wish I was one of those women who give up their lives to care for the old and sick.

You always hoped I'd want to be a nurse when I grew up. When I got out of hospital you had made me a nurse costume. When I was twelve you talked me into spending Saturday afternoons helping at the hospital with friends from school. The patients were old, paralysed, incontinent, blind, abandoned. We folded linen and peeled potatoes. We hacked off the green shells of pumpkins, polished and grooved, with orange seeds and rags of flesh hanging in their wombs. One afternoon the nurses asked me to feed a young blind man his custard. It was a privilege: nicknamed Freddie, he was their favourite. In my awkwardness I let hot custard trickle down Freddie's neck and puddle in his pillow as he lay smiling up. Tears spilled from his white eyes. Frantic, I mopped his raspy throat and chin, I was too ashamed to ever go back. He kept asking after me, my friends reported. 'Oh, Paula,' you said. Shaking your grey head. 'You are heartless.'

We were down here just last Sunday. Whimpering, you bared your sore, swollen ankles. 'Oh don't want. Turn into a vegetable.' Your veined eyes round as you faltered, saying that. You spent most of the day in bed and refused to eat. On Tuesday the Meals on Wheels man found you lying on the kitchen floor and called the ambulance. The matron rang me at work.

'Can you come down? Doctor says her heart's grossly enlarged. She's very weak.'

'She'll be all right, though, won't she?'

'Well, we can't say. Come down if possible. She's asked for you.'

You'd asked for me.

I took time off and drove down with Claire to the little bush hospital. A day of midwinter spring, with the lamps lit all afternoon along the shore. Kookaburras and magpies in the shabby gumtrees in the grounds. From your window, late sun glazing the hollow sea. Woodsmoke from chimneys in the hills towered.

When you had your stroke a few days before Claire was born, we had been estranged for months: my child would have no father. I lumbered in to visit you in the city hospital, kissed your cheek and flopped gasping in a chair with my offering of daffodils. You could hardly move. Slowly your stiff mouth drooled words.

'What, Mum?'

'You. Go. Now.'

'What did you say?'

'Want. You. Go. Now.'

I flung the gaudy flowers down and went.

Last Sunday Claire found some of your old photographs. She brought one in to show us, the one of you and Auntie May smiling on a staircase. Two little sepia girls with frilly dresses and bows in their hair.

'Have you still got that dress, Mummy? Please can I have it?'

'No, that was Granma's dress.'

'But you've got it on!'

'No, that's not me. That's Granma. When she was your age.'

'Oh. Have you still got it, Granma?'

You smiled, shaking your head. That was all. Later I found the photo in the rubbish bin. I took it out, stained and creased, when you weren't looking.

A while ago I played all the tapes that Dad had made, mostly of broadcasts of organ recitals. His beloved fugues wheezed, thumped and groaned. In the middle of a slow passage I heard him sigh. I played it again. There it was. His deep sigh, embedded in the music.

I told you about it. Would you like to hear it? I'd play it for you. You shook your shaggy head. Were your eyes blank, or hostile? You would have loved to hear his voice, wouldn't you? You would have.

You turned your head away.

This time I brought red tulips propped in a carafe on the locker like five sunlit glasses of red wine. They are opening unseen beside you now, showing their yellow throats. Inside each are six rods of black velvet like the legs of an upturned insect; and a three-pronged tongue, its colour lost in the glow.

Your mottled hand crawled to huddle in mine, a dry claw for all these years plump again now with the same fluid that was welling in your ankles. In your lungs.

'Sorry dear. Accident. Shower.'

'You fell in the shower?'

'No, no.' Shaking your angry matted head. 'Accident. Bowel. Mess in bathtub.'

'Oh, Mum, that's nothing! I'll clean it up!'

'Disgusted.'

'Of course not. You couldn't help it. Don't be silly!'

You rolled your filmed eyes up to gaze at me.

'Thank you. For coming.'

'I'll be back tonight. Now you get some sleep.'

I kissed your hollow cheek. Your cropped grey hair sodden, fetid, all on end. You nodded and twisted to watch me go back to Claire, anxiously on tiptoe in the doorway. We waved to your mute face watching. Watching us go.

I dropped Claire at the Smiths' to play and came back alone to sit here drinking as night fell. The wine was dark as blood by lamplight. Remembering.

I drove back alone in visiting hours. I was too late. Your body, wracked as if in childbirth, was heaving up off the bed with every gasp; your mouth a mute howl; your eyes bulging, blood-stained. I called you. Nothing. No hope now, the doctor said. Did you know I was there? When I was holding your swollen hand, could you feel my hand? You'd asked for me. Did you want me to go now? I'd always promised not to look. I crept away.

What should I have done?

I picked Claire up. Fast asleep by their fire, she hardly stirred when I carried her to the car and then to bed. 'Read me *Alice*,' she mumbled, but fell asleep again.

I sat up gulping wine. Your wracked grimace accused me. So weak, how had you found such strength, such anguish, to fight for each breath, each heartbeat, one by one? I sat slobbering with shame and dread until the telephone rang and the doctor murmured that my mother had passed away, and suggested an undertaker. So it was over, you had cast your loose old skin: it lay there stiffening in warm sheets. Nurses will sponge you now and stop up all your openings – the warped anus, too, in your seamed belly. You used to apologise to new nurses for it. At home you flinched as wind purred out, escaping the taut bag; with strained composure visitors would ignore the sudden smell.

Stars roof your luminous garden. The trees are still. Empty snail shells, small brown skulls, litter the flower beds and the frosty grass. A blue glow covers the fuchsia with its dangling bells, the japonica's red paper petals, the studded daphne. Pale lilies are coiled around their dusty rods. Soon your dry wisteria vine will hang out its frilled mauve pods in bunches.

In one of the grey snapshots by the bedlamp in your room you and Dad walk elated hand in hand past the pillars and steps of the GPO, just married at forty at the start of the War. In the other you grin squinting into the sun on the verandah, your only baby, bald and glum, cuddled in tentative white-downed arms. My lifetime ago.

The shower taps are smudged with brown. You told me. The soap as well. Splatters here and there blotch the grey enamel of the tub. With rubber gloves on I scrub away the hard brown spots, pour boiling water over and wrap gloves, soap and steel wool in newspaper before I ram them in the bin.

Stooped here in splashing yellow water, sludge oozing from

your hole and between the puffed finger that tried to hold it back, did you decide to die?

Rust is tarnishing the steam-furred mirror. I am shiny under the dusty globe, my lips black from the wine. The dim skin of my eyes is bruised, wilted. My bones are yellow ridges. Hollows lie dark along my jaw and throat.

Claire's tread thumps down the passage. In the mirror her sleepy face that was mine once. Her warm hair all on end.

'Granma just died, darling one,' I say.

'Won't we ever see her again?'

'No. She wouldn't like us to.'

'Does she look horrible?'

I shake my head. She leans frowning in the doorway:

'This is our house now, isn't it?'

'Yes.'

'Are we coming to live down here?'

'Maybe in summer.'

'Where's Granma's soul now?'

'I don't know.'

'Not here!' she shrieks.

'No. Not here.'

'With Granpa's?'

'Nobody knows.'

'Can I come into your bed? And leave the light on?'

'All right. The passage light.'

She comes and presses her hot face against me.

'Mummy,' she whimpers.

MARIA'S GIRL

I had not heard from my sister Maria for thirty years when a short letter in Greek arrived from Melbourne announcing her death of a brain tumour. Dear Uncle Manoli, it said. Her daughter, Niki, hoped her letter would find us. As the only child, she felt that she should let the family know. The name of the village had been on her mother's papers. She and a friend would be in Greece in January on their way to London and could come and visit us, if that was all right.

'Not a man friend, Manoli?' my wife said.

'It says *filo*. Yes.' I peered down at the letter. So Maria had had a child. 'Write to her, Vasso, will you. Tell her to come.'

Vasso sniffed. She wrote that same night.

After the letter the dreams began. I have seen others die Maria's death, slowly, in silence. Cancer eats the brain alive like wasp maggots in a spider. Her body, like mine, must have sagged, aged, all its hair gone grey. Grey corrugations mat my skull. My face is like a withering potato with white slit eyes. Night after night I shamble, my head thumping, to gape in a mirror aglare with yellow light at a grey face and blood-streaked eyes. Yet Maria in the dreams is twenty-six years old as I last saw her. Souls may not grow old when bodies do. I have a vision of yellow, speckled hands folded in death.

She was three years older, but once we were grown strangers often took us for twins. We lived here alone for a time, as close as twins. Our mother had died of pneumonia in the winter of '41. When our father was killed in the Civil War three years later I was still only sixteen. I carried my pistol everywhere. Relatives wanted to send us to the city, but we insisted we could manage. We treated each other, now I look back, with the tender respect of an engaged couple. Until the night of the fire.

Her guilt and shame forced her away. Not all at once, a gradual estrangement. As in a clear pane that crumbles before your eyes, the image beyond is lost in a mesh of white crystals.

When she left for Australia on the bride ship I went down to see her off, a gruff and grubby peasant jostled on the floodlit wharf with the city aunts and cousins. She was scarved and dressed in black, a widow already at twenty-six. Her eyes were wet. When my turn came to kiss her goodbye, she flinched. Neither of us ever wrote. Silence, for ever.

I watched the ship dwindle, flickering its golden lights.

Vasso must have noticed my dreams and wild awakenings, but we never discuss them, or much else these days but the goats and the firewood, the apple trees that need pruning, simple things. The violent years are behind us. Vasso has been a good wife and mother. She was always a cold woman, not like Maria, poor Vasso. If she has dreams of her own, she keeps them to herself. She is lonely now, I think. Each summer our sons arrive back in shiny cars from Munich and Zurich with their painted wives and little children. Each has named his eldest son and daughter after us. The children feed the hens and goats, chase fireflies on the river banks at nightfall, pick the fat, hairy mulberries, ride with me on the haycart. They cry when the time comes to leave. The little tragedies of children.

It is deep winter now. The river trickles, congealing, its banks heaped high with snow. The black trees could be wrought of ice and iron. Even at noon the whitewashed houses have lighted windows glowing under their crusted eaves, patching the snow with gold. The air is grey. In the yard our few white laying hens, almost invisible, jab at the frozen snow.

Niki is delighted with the snow.

Niki is just as I had imagined her, the image of Maria, the same age, and even dressed in black. The same golden skin and long, honey-coloured eyes and hair, banded hair glowing. How well I remember her, dressed for church, stooping low to iron the ends of her hair straight, the old flat-irons heating on the stove. She speaks good Greek in Maria's own voice. She is still wearing mourning for our sake, I think. It is our custom.

The whole village has exclaimed over the likeness, and made much of her. Only Vasso is critical at times, but Vasso is not from here. She never knew Maria. They are going on to London soon, anyway, Niki and her young man. They make no secret of sleeping in one bed, and stay there half the bitter white morning. Her Bill is forgiven a lot, not being Greek. He is well-liked, in fact, tall and blond, with his stutter and his glasses, his few words of Greek, his way of wheedling the old folk to pose for his camera with their carts and looms. In the *kafeneion* he buys beers all round and tries to dance to the juke box. They have been invited everywhere, even to the school. They are both schoolteachers. They are hoping to find jobs in London and come back to us in the summer.

Over coffee the other day I showed them my old photograph of Maria and me on old Marko the horse in the vegetable patch. There was our old apricot tree, and the sunflower beside it, as tall as a man.

'Mama looked old, Theio. Older than you.'

'Well, she was three years older. But she was only twenty then. Our father had just died.'

'No, I mean now.'

Yet I know I look old for my age, though I am strong as rock.

'Fifty-six. That's not very old.'

'No. Poor Mama.' After a while, handing it back, she said. 'Is that a sunflower? Mama always had sunflowers in the garden.'

'It comes up every summer.' I wiped the pane and pointed out the spot where it will rear its shaggy golden head. The snow fumed in a dark wind. Icicles glinted on the barbed wire fence. On all my land I see, with an inner eye, golden seeds lying in wait.

Niki is shocked by our poverty, the relentless cold dour poverty of our village. In the house we heat only one room, the front one with the old black fire-stove that lives on apple wood. Vasso grills bread and chestnuts on the top, boils the lentils and beans and an occasional hen, heats the bathwater, bakes her famous *pita* in its black depths. Vasso and I sleep in that room, and she takes the young ones a *mangali* of hot embers at bedtime, and squabbles when they open the window a crack behind the shutters.

'You'll catch your deaths!'

They look warm enough to me under Vasso's wedding *flokati*, like two humped, shaggy sheep, as she says goodnight and switches the light off. What a blessing that we have electricity now.

Niki hates the way the hens dart in if the door opens and flap up on to the kitchen table to peck at bread and leftovers. When she chases them they squawk and rush around, skidding on their splayed claws and dropping brown splodges. The lavatory is a problem too, a concrete hole at the back, sheltered by plastic superphosphate bags hooked on blackberry brambles. There are always splodges of brown around its sloping mouth. In summer she will hate it even more, when the blackberries bring the wasps and glittering flies buzz in the hole. During the snowstorm the other day I said to go and do it in the barn. We all do. The goats don't mind, and the soiled straw will go on the fields anyway. No, she would squat outside in the storm with a sheet of plastic over her.

The animals make up for a lot, I think. She loves them all. Our wild yellow cat pads behind her, yowling. She feeds the goats and strokes their hot white pelts and long ears while they stand smiling and spry, fixing her with their slit gold eyes. I'm fond of the goats myself. Maria loved them. How she mourned when they were taken in the Civil War.

I showed Niki the soot still on the barn walls and asked her if her mother had ever told her about the fire.

'No. You tell me, Theio.'

'Well, it was a long time ago.' I patted the hairy mudbricks. 'This was our house then, with rooms on top. The Partisans burnt it in the Civil War. But no one was hurt.'

The goats bowed and nudged me, the swollen pink bags

swinging between their legs. Niki's long-lidded eyes betrayed disgust as I squatted to pump the teats with these knotty old hands of mine. My hands are like tree-roots, at home only in the soil. She's no good at milking. You have to squeeze hard. Vasso has taught her to make cheese.

Baths are a problem in winter, too, even once a week. At first she wanted one every day, with the pipes frozen and gallons being heated on the stove. one afternoon soon after they arrived I tramped in from the barn, kicked off my boots, and, hearing a voice call in the warm room, naturally I flung the door open. The thought never occurred to me. It wasn't a Saturday. I'm getting hard of hearing now, besides.

She was stooping naked in the shallow copper pan that we all use for baths, her hair in a coil at her nape, running a shower of water from a saucepan over her long back. Her black clothes off, she glowed all over with the gold of ripened wheat.

'Maria!' I groaned.

But of course it was Niki who was crouching, turning away, shame and outrage in her eyes. My blood froze. I muttered an apology and slammed the door shut.

That night I dreamed of Maria as she stood naked in the smouldering barn. Out of her bright hair burst the great knuckly clusters of a brain tumour. She was weeping black tears silently.

New horrors were just beginning then, as the Germans withdrew. Our father and other village authorities – our father had been mayor when we were little – were taken at gunpoint, tied up, marched up the mountain and threatened with death if they refused to join the Resistance. Some, who fell in their tracks, were shot where they lay. My father was shot escaping. Others who came back safe told me. My father, who had fought beside that Partisan leader on the Albanian front, would not fight against Greeks. Next, our animals were taken. Burnings had begun at night in villages in the foothills.

That day, I remember, Partisans from the mountain had made speeches in broad daylight in the square and withdrawn as night fell, but no further than the vineyard slopes across the river. The village hummed with fear behind closed doors. Thank God, a shepherd crept home after dark and gave the warning. Five houses were to be burnt. Ours was one.

I rushed Maria, empty-handed, stumbling and splashing, to our Uncle Stathi's house. He was alone, having sent our aunt and cousins weeks before to Thessaloniki. A lame, grey man stroking a rifle. We barred the doors and shutters and huddled there like roosting hens by lamplight. Hours went by before we saw through the slats a red flame on the sky.

Our uncle growled and cursed, swallowing great swigs of his *tsipouro* and thrusting the bottle at me. That was what I needed to make a man of me, he said. Harsh and fiery, the *tsipouro* made my blood beat hard. Maria, swaying, exclaimed and wailed. I sat with my arm round her, and could not have uttered a word if my life had been at stake. I have never spilt human blood.

When he sank back in a stupor we covered him up warm and crept with the lamp to our cousins' room. We rolled ourselves in blankets on the divans there, but we could not have slept. Maria was still making a sad whimpering.

'Maria? It's all right.'
'What can we do now, Manoli?'
'It's only a house. I'll build another one.'
'I'm too afraid.'

I could only just see her face by the dimmed lamp.

'Manoli?' she whispered. 'Can I get in with you?'

I nodded. She lifted the blanket and slid in against me, her hands on my shoulders. Transfixed with shock, I burned and ached, clenched against her. She kissed me with her tongue tasting of tears, and put my hands on her soft breasts and the long, furry lips between her thighs. When I went into her she grasped me with folded legs. Never since have I felt such joy and pain and terror with any woman.

Afterwards we lay still. Her long eyes were closed. Her hair had come undone and scarved my throat with hot, itching, amber swathes.

'Let me go. Oh, my God! It's a great sin. Manoli, no.'
'You don't love me?'
'Ssh. Yes. But you mustn't ever tell. Swear.'
'I swear. Are you sorry?'
She kissed me and moved away, smoothing my blanket down.
'Are you? Maria?'
'I don't know.'

It was my first time. I wanted to tell her, but her back was turned.

At some time the lamp sizzled and went out, I remember half-waking. We woke together much later, and, without disturbing Theio Stathi's snores we crept into the first blue light of day, trailing our white breaths, jumping as cocks crew. Our house was charred, smouldering. Beams protruded, black-blistered and gnawed. Shutters and window-panes lay smashed in the mud. I thought of unseen eyes following our backs through the hot doorway. A stench of kerosene. Our feet crunched on a black flood of wheat.

The old trunk with her wedding things in it had fallen through the burnt floor of the bedroom and lay burst open on a heap of ashes. With a cry she knelt and dragged out her ruined linens and sheets and hand-dyed woven blankets, the patient embroideries and laces of all her winters. She held up a singed cloth to show me. Black tears began to trickle down her face.

I hugged her then, both of us crouching as the darkness around us crackled and fumed. Wisps of flame still glowed here and there on black tufts of sacking. I found one of the crocks of water we always kept under there, wetted the cloth and wiped her face with it.

'Let me see you,' I muttered.

She shook her head, but did not resist as I took off her black clothes one by one until she stood there golden all over and I could touch her nipples and the curls of brown hair in her armpits and her groin that I had never seen before. Sudden voices and footsteps outside brought us to our senses. Frantically she pulled her clothes back on.

MARIA'S GIRL

'Help me! Quick! Are my eyes red?'

She gave a sobbing laugh, and went out. Theio Stathi, haggard and vague, and all the family and neighbours had gathered in the yard, volubly indignant about the burning. They escorted us back with a chorus of commiserations. The sun came up and went down before they had all had their say. In the end it was decided that Maria must be sent out of harm's way to his sister-in-law the *modistra* in Athens, where she could learn dressmaking and earn her living keeping house. I sat there, struck dumb with anguish and bitterness, and not once did she look my way.

We were never alone again. They arranged a marriage for her down there, a ship's cook of forty who loved her madly, they said. I never met the man. It was at short notice, at the height of the Civil War. I rented her share of the fields from her and sent her the money. I visited her once, on business. There were others there. Numbly I watched this polite stranger fumbling with coffee cups. They had no children. When her husband's ship was lost at sea in '49 I bought her share so she could take a dowry to Australia. And for years I though about her every night.

The new house I built has walls of stone one metre thick. My shoulders will bear the scars of those stones to the grave. It is the bitterest thought to me that our sons will rush home and sell the house and land when we die.

Yesterday, as night drew in, we were sitting round the open stove in a firelight yellow as maize oil, eating the last wrinkled winter apples that Niki had roasted with honey. Bill sprawled, scribbling aerograms. Vasso was kneading a last *pita* for them. They are going in a day or two.

'It's been lovely, Theio. I'm glad I wrote.'

'Lucky you found the address. Where was it?'

'Oh, on her birth certificate,' she yawned. 'And she told me about her brother Manoli when she called my baby brother after you. She said you'd never leave here.'

I could only gape at that golden face.

'You didn't know? He only lived a few weeks. Something wrong with his heart. Mama was shattered. She called the *papas* to come and baptize him with the neighbours as godparents. Emmanuel, that's right, isn't it? After you.' She grimaced. 'My father was furious. His father's name was Yannis. He kept saying, "What right had you? What bloody right?" '

I poked sparks in the glowing apple wood.

'Were they happy together?'

'Sometimes.' She shrugged.

Last night, when I saw Maria, shreds of dead flesh hung from her, black shreds, and her black clothes. Her mouth gaped in silent shrieks. 'Manoli! Manoli!' Nothing I can say can comfort her. Throwing off the covers I stumbled shuddering outside into a black silence. The sky was hung with icicles and a white sickle moon. On the snow the shadows of trees lay in nets. A far wolf howled. Safe and warm, a goat whimpered in her sleep. My shaft of urine, glittering, pitted the white crust. Soon the thaw will set in. Heavy work brings heavy sleep. She has promised to come back to us in summer, Maria's girl has.

She will see the sunflower.

HOME TIME

By late afternoon the sky is a deep funnel of wind, damp and white. She remarks as she passes through the lamplight around his desk on her way to the bathroom: 'Doesn't it look like snow!'

'Do you think?' He squints out the window.

'That hollowness of the light.'

'It's early for snow.'

'*Casablanca*'s going to be on TV tonight at eight,' she says before he can look down again. 'Why don't we go to that bar and see it and then have dinner somewhere after?'

'Mmm.'

The room is grey; only the light around him is warm and moving with shadows. The steam pipes are silent. Whenever will they start clanking and hissing and defrost the apartment? '*Isn't* it cold, though!' she says brightly.

'Mmm.'

'Maybe I should go for a walk downtown, take some photos of the lights coming on,' she says.

'It's a lot colder outside.'

'Walking would warm me up.'

'OK.'

'Oh, maybe not,' she says. 'I might write letters home instead.' Home is Australia. It's summer there. 'Until it's time for *Casablanca*.'

He sighs and waits for silence.

She has an electric radiator on in her room – the sitting room really, but she works in here. She has twin lamps of frilly glass at twin tall windows inside which wasps sizzle and cling and trap themselves in shreds of cobweb. The table she writes at faces the windows. Three times a day she pushes books to one side and turns papers face down, since this is also the table they eat at. The kitchen is next to it, bare and icy, smelling of gas.

She pulls her radiator over by the couch and lies curled up in the red glow with her head on a velvet cushion.

Later she half-wakes: he has walked past into the kitchen. When he switches her lamps on and hands her a mug of coffee she is stiffly sitting up to make room. 'Did you get much written?' She yawns, stretching an arm warm with sleep along his shoulder.

'Fair bit.' He grins. 'Did you?'

She is glad she stayed in. 'No. What's the time?'

'Hell, yes.' He looks. 'Ten past eight.'

'Oh, we've missed it!'

'No, we haven't. Only the start.'

They gulp their coffee and help each other drag coats and boots on. 'You must have seen it, haven't you?' he says.

'Oh, yes. Hasn't everyone?'

'Then what's the – ?'

She shuts his mouth with a kiss. 'I want to see it with *you*. In America.'

He smiles at that. They fling open the door and stop short. Snow is falling, must have been falling for hours, heavy and slow, whirling round the white streetlamps. 'Oh, *snow!*' She dashes back inside for her camera and takes photo after photo from the stoop, of fir branches shouldering slabs of snow, drooping in gardens, and elms still with gold leaves and a fine white skin all over, and lawns and cars and rooftops thickly fleeced. Passing cars have drawn zips on the white road.

'Now we're really late,' he says. Hand in hand they tramp and slither the few blocks to the bar they like, bright as a fire with the lamps on. Outside it two young men are throwing snowballs. She gasps as one leaps on the other and they flounder giggling at her feet.

'Pussy cat!' one jeers. 'That's *all* you is!'

Her man is holding the blurred glass door open. Heads along the bar turn away from *Casablanca* to stare at them. He leads her to a stool, orders a red wine and an Irish coffee and stands at her back. Ingrid Bergman's face fills the screen.

The door opens on a white flurry and the young men stamping in, shaking the snow off. The heads turn and stare. 'Celebrate the first *snow!*' one young man announces. 'Have a *drink*, everybuddy!' A cheer goes up. The barman brings her another red wine and him another Irish coffee. The young men have flopped crosslegged on the carpet and are gazing at the screen.

'Oh, they're *so* young,' a voice murmurs in her ear; the greyhaired woman beside her is smiling. She smiles in answer and gives herself over to *Casablanca*. He is at her back with his arms round her. When it ends he goes to the men's room.

The old woman is dabbing her eyes. 'Oh dear!' She makes a face. 'Do you come here a lot? I do. We live just down the road.'

Do you come here a lot? I do. We live just down the road. You can see this bar from our stoop and I tell you it's a real temptation, glowing away down here. With that lantern at the door with snowflakes spinning round it and the way the elm leaves flap against it like yellow butterflies – it's like some place in a fairy tale. And here inside it's as bright and warm as inside a Halloween pumpkin. Those lamps everywhere, and the bottles burning in the mirror. And whenever the door opens, a breath of snow blows in and the lights all shift under and over the shadows. Even if *Casablanca* wasn't on the TV I'd have come tonight.

What'll you have, honey, another one of those? What is that, red wine? Jimmy, another one of those red wines and I'll have a Jack Daniels. Yes, rocks. And wipe that silly grin off your face, have you no soul, what kind of man laughs at *Casablanca*? Thanks, Jimmy. Keep it.

Look through that archway, the couples at their little tables, all so solemn and proper with their vintage wine and their candles – look, their heads are hollow, like the candles burnt their eyes out. They might all have stories just as sad as *Casablanca*, but who cares? It's *Casablanca* breaks our hearts, over and over. You cried at the end, I saw you. So did that nice man of yours. Oh, a bar's the place to watch it, a bar's the perfect place. I cry every single time, I can't help myself, it's so noble and sad and innocent and – hell, you know. I couldn't watch it at home, anyway. Bill, he's my husband, gets mad when I cry. He walks out. 'Why, am I supposed to stay and watch you slobber over this shit?' he said last time it was on. 'Most people got all they need to slobber about in real life.'

'You're what *I* got,' I said right back.

That's him there, over at the pool table. That your man he's talking to? I thought so. They're lighting up cigarettes and getting acquainted. Isn't that a coincidence? He looks a nice easy-going kind of a guy. But then so does Bill. I love Bill, I love him a lot. I've known that man thirteen years, I could tell you things . . . I'm not blind to anything about Bill, I love him anyway. He loves *me*, though it doesn't feel like being loved much of the time. He needs me. He has to punish me for that. There he is, an older man than he acts. His hair has a grey sheen and his skin hangs loose all over, see the crazed skin on his neck. He's affable and a bit loud with the drink, everybody's pal. Well, when we get home there won't be a word out of him. Under the skin and the smile he's a bitter, fearful man and nobody gets close to him.

He's a second comer, for one thing. He can't forget that. He's my second husband. Yours is a second comer too, is he, honey? Don't mind me sticking my nose in. It's just I can tell. You two are a mite too considerate, too careful with one another, know what I mean? It shows, that's all, if you can read the signs. So what if you are Australians. Oh no. Look, I don't mean you haven't got a nice relationship. But it's only the first time you give your whole self. After that, like it or not, you hold back. You've gotten wise – and you can't pretend *other*wise!

We've been married ten years this Thursday – Thanksgiving Day. You got to laugh. Cheers. Isn't that something, though. My first marriage never got to double figures. I had twenty years alone in between.

Do you remember the first time you saw *Casablanca*? Mine was in 1943, when it first came out, on my honeymoon with Andy. That's reason enough to cry. Bill knows. It's something he can't stand to be reminded of. He pretends it's only Rick and Ilsa making me *slobber*. Men – you tell a man the truth about your life, you end up paying for *ever*. Remember that.

1943! Andy was nineteen, I was seventeen, his ship was sailing for Europe in a week. Our parents said no, you're too young, but we said we'd only run away, so they gave in. We had one weekend for a honeymoon in New York City. The hotel was an awful old ruin – it still is – full of cockroaches and noisy plumbing. We were so embarrassed, you could hear every drop, every trickle. Our room was on the top floor. Through the fire escape we could see the river, and the moon in the mist like a brass knob behind a curtain, and the lights of Manhattan. So it's not a bed of roses, Andy said: it's a bed of lights instead. We saw *Casablanca* and we cried. We were such babies. He was going to be a hero and I was going to wait . . . We danced round the room like Rick and Ilsa did. We sure didn't sleep much. We didn't even know how to *do* it, you know. We were scared. Oh, we soon got the hang of it. And then his ship sailed.

He came back, oh, he came back. He'd won medals in Italy, he was a hero. But he wouldn't ever talk about it. Whatever happened over there, it finished Andy. He started drinking, then he lost his job, and soon he couldn't hold down any job, he just drank and gambled and played the black market. He'd come home once, twice a week, then sleep for days . . .

One night he started hitting me. Everything was my fault, he said. Then he cried. He promised he never would again. I was fool enough to believe it. If they've hit you once and gotten away with it, honey, you're in trouble. It can only get worse.

So, one night I woke up on the kitchen floor. The table lamp was still on, the beer that he spilt looked like butter melting under it. I remember I saw the pattern of brown triangles on the linoleum every time my eyes came open, they looked wet and red, but I couldn't see sharp enough to be sure. The window was black – so it was still night time – and had silver edges like knives where he smashed it. The curtain was half torn down, sopping up the beer on the table and moving in the wind, a white curtain like a wedding veil. *Help me*! I called out. My head felt crushed. The wind must have blown my hair on my face, hair was stuck to it. A long way away something was – snuffling. My nose was flat on my cheek, red bubbles blew out. Andy *wasn't there*. I held my head still and pulled myself up by the table leg: broken glasses, slabs of the window pane, the wet curtain, but no note. No nothing. The room was going all watery and dim as if the floor was hot as fire and yet it was so icy when I lay down, I pulled the curtain down over me to keep warm.

It wasn't till morning that I saw he'd taken all his stuff. God knows there wasn't much, poor Andy. Then I got started all over again: *Don't leave me! Don't leave me alone now! I love you*! Even now I dream – I wake up and for a moment I'm on that floor again knowing I've lost Andy, he's gone for *ever*. Oh, I've never gotten over it.

I'm sorry. Don't be embarrassed. I'll be all right in a moment. Thank you, yes, another Jack Daniels would be nice. Yes, thank you.

Funny thing was, when I got up off the floor next day and my nose was smashed and my eyes looked like two squashed plums and I was shaking so hard I thought my teeth would crack – I ran out into the street in case I could see him and maybe catch him up and all the time I was whimpering, *After all you've done to me, you just get up and go?* I looked in the kitchen window. It was empty, all shadowy gold behind the edges of glass.

Another funny thing – I had a vision in the night, a ballerina came in. (I wanted to be a dancer, I was good, but first the War started, then I got married . . .) Anyway, this ballerina in white was waving her arms and bowing. It must have been the curtain that I saw. She bent down to lift me then she lay beside me, sobbing, I remember that.

Look at us there in the mirror, like two ghosts among the whisky bottles. OK, Jimmy, laugh. He thinks I'm admiring myself. I'm not that far gone, though I'm getting there. Cheers. Is that really me, that scrawny thing with the spiky grey hair? You'd never think I was a ballet dancer. Bill hates ballet. He says that because the pain and exertion and ugliness aren't allowed to show, it's one big lie. Tinsel and sweat, he says. Dancers smell like horses, someone famous says, so Bill has to read it to me out of the newspaper. Horses aren't any less beautiful for the way they smell, I say. Horses are dancers too and dancers love them. Anyway, I say, I like the way they smell. You would, he says, you're not what you'd call fussy, are you. Now wasn't that asking for it? *No, well, I married you!* I let it pass, though, and he gives me points for not saying it: just a flicker of the eyelids, but enough.

Most of our quarrels end like that. They're harmless. Nothing Bill says or does can get to the quick of me like it did with Andy whether he meant it or not. Bill can make me ache with misery when he wants, but somewhere deep down inside me now there's this little tough muscle braces itself so the barbs can't go too far in. Bill knows. He's the same. Maybe by now it would have been like that with Andy, who knows? I don't even know if he's alive or dead. My parents came and made me get a divorce. They told him I said he couldn't see me or the kids ever again.

Let me tell you the *worst* thing – let's have another drink? – the worst thing – oh, God, I've never told a living soul this. Jimmy, more of these and have one on me, OK? The worst thing is, when he had me on the floor that night – just pushed me down – and started smashing things and yelling that he wanted *out*, I rolled over and hung on to his trouser leg for dear life and begged him not to leave me. I just wouldn't let go. I – slobbered, and howled and – and I kissed his muddy shoe. So he slammed his other shoe in my face. That's when my nose got broken. I mean, that's why.

I thank God the kids weren't home, they didn't see that. They saw him hit me other times, but not that. They were only little. Rick was about five, Ilsa was just a baby. Something like that, though – if they saw it happen, it'd leave a scar on them. 'I won't let Daddy hurt you,' Ricky used to say to me. They were at my parents' place in New Jersey because I had to get a job so

I couldn't look after them. We called them Rick and Ilsa – well, *you* know why! Ilsa's married, she's in Alaska now, she's a nurse. Rick's dead. He got killed in Vietnam. Got a medal doing it, too. If his Daddy every heard about it, I suppose he must have felt proud. Or maybe not.

Don't get me wrong, I believe in sacrifice, and love and honour and loyalty, even if it turns out they were wasted – else why would I love *Casablanca*? Rick and Ilsa, they had something or someone they'd give up everything for. I only wish I still did. Real people have their moments of glory. Time goes on for them though, they can't live up to it. But the glory lives on in memory. Bill won't see that. Face facts, he says. You and your glory and your wallowing in the past. It's shit, that's all it is, shit preserved in syrup. That's better than shit preserved in vinegar, the way yours is, I say. Oh, that's good, he says. Make with the witty repartee, babe, you know I dig that. (Bill can never let go of anything. All his past is still there inside of him, pickled.) Why better, honey? Shit's still shit, he says then. Who knows the truth? I say. You refuse to, *he* says, and round and round we go.

What you never really get over, I suppose, is finding out love's not enough. Loving someone's no *use*. And you only find out the hard way. No one can tell you. You believe in love when you're young, you believe it's forever, it's the only thing that matters, it'll save you both, if you just hang in there and give more and more. I wonder if Ilsa would have gone with Rick – given up everything and gone with him – would it have ended up with her on the floor with her nose smashed? You never know.

Here they come. Look, they're wondering what we're saying. Look at those suspicious eyes and butter-wouldn't-melt smiles of theirs! Your man's been watching you all this time. Here's looking at you, kid! Easy to see you're new. It's great while it lasts, make the most. The couples have had their wine and candlelight and now they're leaving. Don't you just love a black and white night like this after snow, when it echoes? And you slide and fall down on top of each other all the way and rub each other's feet dry and warm once you're inside. OK, fellers, home time? I've lost my coat. Thanks, honey. I feel so lit up it's a wonder you can't see me shining through it! I'm sure I don't know why I've been telling you the story of my life. You cried at the end of *Casablanca*. I suppose that's why.

'Can I read that?'

'Read what?'

Her hands have instinctively spread across the pages of blue scrawl. He raises his eyebrows: 'What you've been writing half the night.'

She passes them over her shoulder. The couch creaks and the pages rustle until at last he tosses them back on the table and goes to make coffee. She stares at them, sweat prickling her. The heating is on full.

'Thank you,' she says when he brings her mug.

'Is this finished?'

'Oh, for now, anyway. I was just coming to bed – I'm sorry. Haven't you been asleep?'

'I used to respect writers rather a lot,' he murmurs. 'Now I'm not sure.'

'You're writing your thesis on one.'

'Mmm. There's writing and writing. To my mind this' – he points – 'is more like scavenging.' He waits while she swallows hot coffee. 'Perhaps if you wore a badge, a brand on your forehead that meant: *Beware of the scavenger*? Then people would know they were fair game.'

'You think *that's* being *fair*?'

'She trusted you, it seems, with the story of her life.'

'I hope I can do it justice.'

'Justice.' He sighs.

She has nothing to say. He finishes his coffee sip by sip, takes his mug and rinses it, then comes back to stand behind her chair. Her mug is clenched in both hands; the light of the two lamps blurs in her coffee.

'I am not to figure in anything you write,' comes the smooth voice again. 'Never. I hope you understand that.'

Hardly breathing, she cranes her neck forward to have a sip of coffee, but he grabs the mug from her and slams it down on the table, where it breaks. Coffee spurts up and splashes brown and blue drops over her pages. This time she knows better than to move until his footsteps creak away across the boards. His chair scrapes. She hears a match strike in the room beyond, and a sigh as he breathes smoke in.

SNAKE

We are not told anywhere, are we, that winters in the Garden of Eden were not cold? The olive and the lemon ripen in winter and it could not be Paradise without them. Lemon and olive, sour and bitter, my mother would say: they suit you, Manya. Mama misjudges me.

I think as winter comes, why huddle here in three warm rooms? Why not go to Athens, say, and see Aunt Sophia? My dear old Aunt Sophia. Walk up to the Acropolis again. Order coffee and sit and watch the hollow city brim with a violet glow, and the lights and stars shine out. Sit on the cold stones of the theatre, high above its golden statuary, where I saw Euripides performed, Aeschylus. Or even go to Crete. It's sunny there. But I feel anxious away from here now.

Three years ago I went away. Mama and I went to the village in Macedonia when her sister Vasso died. As always when the ferry casts off in the crescent harbour of Mytilene I felt lost, speechless with dread. The Thessaloniki ferry passes between Turkey and Molyvo in the strait. I see Molyvo in the distance, its blue citadel. I never rest – those weeks in the frozen village, my God! – until we pass it again. So I might stay and see my olives through the press instead.

Aunt Vasso's own sons hadn't come down from Germany. Uncle Manoli, a dour man at any time, hardly spoke. After the funeral we were snowbound for silent weeks. I remember the full cheese-cloths hung high on the black branches of the grapevine over his front door, their icicles of whey pointed down like teats. A wolf off the mountains howled at night. We cooked what we found: macaroni, rice, icy potatoes and onions, eggs, my aunt's tomato paste and preserved pig from a crock deep in snow on the window sill. There was milk. We made cheese day by day and stored it in its crock in brine, weighed down with flat river stones. At night – from three o'clock, I remember, it was night – Mama and I huddled by the sooty *somba* roaring with apple wood until we succumbed in the stuffy dim yellow room to stupor and sleep. My uncle kept a horse and goats in the barn. An Arctic winter of darkness they lived through, shivering and crusted with excrement. He came home to milk the goats – we boiled the milk – and then sat in the *kafeneion*, glowing with ouzo, silent. The river froze. I had been there before, but in summer. Thank God I need never go again.

I keep busy all day in the garden, and at night I read. I paint a little and my work sells in town. It is not dull, just peaceful, in Paradise. And our green Lesbos is not like other islands. Lesbos was rich in art and poetry when Athens was a village and Thessaloniki still under the sea. They are as natural to Lesbos as her olive trees are, and we who love them are not thought eccentric here.

Still, I am eccentric. I am over forty and have never married. Mama has stopped her wailing over me and her tireless matchmaking. No man would have me now. Even Mitso the Idiot, who tried to rape me at a wedding once, would scowl and snarl at the thought now. As a girl I had no money, only beauty. That has gone. My dowry was my olive trees and the garden. Lemon trees grow here, pear and quince and apricot, peach and almond. We have red hens and a vegetable patch. This little house too would have become mine on my marriage, though my mother was left nothing else, as that is the custom here. Then my daughter's in her turn. I think Mama would be upset if I did marry. Not because of the house – she would stay here of course – but because we make a good couple, she and I, whatever she says. We get on.

The first few times we saw Louka and my cousin Dimitra in company Mama worried, sighed, watched to see how I was taking it. I have never told her the whole story. She guesses that, perhaps. Perhaps she even forgets now that I was engaged to Louka. She forgets my daughter. She fusses over them when they visit. She spoils their boys with sweets. It gives me no pleasure to see Louka. No pain either.

I was twenty when Louka came back from his army service to work in his father's restaurant in Molyvo. I was staying with my cousins there – Dimitra was still a schoolgirl – in their stone house at the base of the Genoese fortress, the citadel on the hilltop. In the whitewashed sun of the chapel next door striped cats lay sleeping. We could see from three windows the stone arm of the port curled round its fishing boats.

Louka had always flirted. Now he came to the house so often, and singled me out so persistently and so respectfully, that we knew he was serious. His mother called on my aunt to discuss the match. My cousins were thrilled. My aunt asked me what I thought. Yes, I said. The priest in his gold brocade came. We exchanged rings and were engaged.

It's hard to believe now what a passion I had for Louka.

He was beautiful, though, I remember, his hair so heavy and black when he let it grow, and his athlete's body dark brown and golden. After the rush in the restaurant he would sit with the tourists joking in scraps of their languages and put on music to teach them to dance the *sirto*, the *tsamiko*. The *zeïmbekiko* he danced by himself, his head sunk between his shoulders like a sated tomcat. He glanced at the women. Enthralled with Louka, they all clapped in time. There was ouzo, but most drank wine, yellow *retsina* from the barrel with its faint rankness of urine, of salt: as if the men treading it, unwilling to stop, let urine and sweat slip down their thighs into the must . . .

On still nights I could hear the *bouzoukia*. I lay awake. When the music stopped, the restaurant was closed, Louka could come and whisper at my shutters. Shutters in Molyvo are solid, not slatted. I was a good girl, and shy. I wouldn't open them. *'Den m'agapas?'* he would growl, his voice thick.

'You know I love you.'

'Then let me see you.'

'I mustn't. I can't.'

SNAKE

'Come on, Manya, open the shutters, I just want to see you, just for a moment. Manya!'

'No. Go home, please. Louka, *please*. They'll *hear*.'

Some of those nights – or mornings, by then – he must have had Valerie with him.

She was not a typical tourist. Not one of the Europeans who descend in hordes to loll on the pebble beach oiling their bones or hire donkeys and ride giggling across the headland to bathe naked at the sandy beach and the hot spring. She was staying with some Australians who lived all the year round in Molyvo. But she looked like them. She smoked and drank and slept with men. She was tall and brown with lank yellow hair and a cat's pale eyes. Her nose and shoulders were thin, red under the freckles. What would a man like Louka want with her? So when friends warned me, I scoffed. Laughing, I accused Louka, but in fun. He tried to laugh.

'Don't look so guilty,' I teased.

Shifting and shuffling, he lit another cigarette and pleaded not guilty. I said I would call witnesses. I laughed as I scored this point but Louka leapt up.

'All right then,' he said. 'So it's true. So what?'

'You're in love with *her*?'

'Valerie? Don't be stupid.'

'Then – *why*?'

'Look.' *He* would not look. He breathed smoke in and coughed. 'I'm in love with you. You know I am. These others, they're whores.' These? How many? 'They won't leave you alone. I'm only flesh and blood, Manya, for God's sake!'

'But, if you loved me, you couldn't – '

'Don't be such a baby!' He thrust his face close. To kiss me, I thought, and drew back. But no, it was twisted with feelings I could not read, of hatred, of desperation.

'*Afti me gamaei.*' She – makes love to me (so to speak). He bared his teeth to say it. Then he walked out.

SNAKE

I found Valerie sipping her morning coffee alone by the balustrade of a *kafeneion*, her eyes half-closed against the dazzle of the strait. She had no idea who I was. I sat at her table. 'Manya,' I said, pointing to myself.

'*Ego* Valerie,' she smiled.

'Louka,' I said, showing my gold ring and not smiling. She frowned. Her nose had peeled and her brows and lashes were white like cat's whiskers. She had a pocket dictionary. She looked in it and asked in broken Greek if I was Louka's wife. Not yet, I said, we were engaged, and found the word for her. She looked wise.

'Hmmm. *To paliopaido*,' she grinned. The bad boy. She shivered and picked up her towel. '*Thalassa*, Manya?' she said. '*Ela, pame*?' She really thought I'd go to the beach with her. She shrugged, grinned and flapped away down the steps. I was too amazed at the cheek of her to smack her face. I had expected to.

Louka, grown fat and bald, deceives Dimitra with tourists in summer – more deftly now, I hope – and with other men's wives in winter. Everyone knows. She will never leave him, though, nor he her. There are children, two boys: the elder a solemn bookworm, the younger a darling, a sparkling boy, and the children I do envy Dimitra. Nothing else. Sour grapes, Mama would say. No. Dimitra, each time she catches Louka out, attacks the woman. I, with my small experience, had more sense. She sobs and shrieks. She spat at one in the restaurant, pulled another one's hair. Louka takes her home and humbly swears that she's his one true love. He's lucky he married Dimitra.

At the theatre once I saw *Agamemnon*. He had led grown men to the slaughter for another man's whore and for gold. So he was returning a hero to Clytemnestra, with his slave girl in tow. I have often dreamt since of her net and axe in the stone bath and Agamemnon quietly like a great fish pumping his blood through the water. She had a right to do it. He deserved death. Never for infidelity; she was unfaithful too. Death for their daughter's death. He led her into the trap at Aulis. I would strike the blow too, in Clytemnestra's place.

But not in Medea's. One summer night at a stone theatre cut into a hill among pines, the sky clear, the sea like milk, Medea writhed and growled for us and stabbed her little boys. For this she was raised in a god's gilt chariot and sat, the moon rising behind her, and gloated. Dimitra was there. It's whispered in the family that she holds this threat over Louka's head, should he dare to leave her . . .

When my Sophoula died Louka, I suspect, was relieved. He had never seen her. 'Who says I'm its father, anyway?' I'm told that he said. I prayed for Louka's death. I screamed to God for justice, of all things. I was mad for some time. I'm sane now and no longer pray or believe. I keep the fasts. I go to church with Mama. I eat the bread sopped in wine from the priest's chalice. God doesn't lift a finger.

Lesbos is close to Turkey. I have seen from the ferry people walking in the streets of Baba in Turkey as we passed between Baba and Molyvo in the strait. Our barracks and theirs are crowded with troops. The beaches are mined. We live in dread of another war. They do too. They love children, as we do. I believe that there is one thing that might save the world from destruction: our love of children. This is stronger than hate, or nothing is. This hope, or no hope.

Louka, when I next saw him after our quarrel, was at his most easy and charming, full of anecdotes about life in the army that convulsed my aunt and cousins. I was on edge, I remember. I had come to my decision. After the preserves and the coffee I stood and announced that Louka and I had arranged to meet friends at the restaurant. He looked stunned. Outside he asked me where we were going. 'Don't ask me yet,' I said. It was a sultry afternoon, the whole town sleeping. I led him to the gullies past the olive grove where couples went. We lay on the dry grass.

'Now look, Manya, darling – '

SNAKE

'Take me,' I said quickly. 'Make me yours.'

'Do you mean it?'

'Yes. I want you. Take me now.'

He put his arms round me.

'Manya, not here. Not now.'

'Why not?' I cried despairingly. 'What's wrong with you?'

I didn't mean it the way he took it.

He pulled his shirt off, only his shirt. In the heat his body was rank and shone like varnished wood. The hair had stuck in curls round his dark nipples. He grasped me. Our teeth clashed and I shut my eyes. Tugging under my skirt, he lay on me and forced in hard and split my legs open. The pain, my God! I clung as he thudded on me. When he rolled away there was a sucking noise. He found a drop of blood and flicked it off.

'Louka?' I was close to tears.

'I hurt you. I'm sorry.'

'It's all right. I love you.' *S'agapo. S'agapo.*

Sighing, he lit a cigarette. Then abruptly he was on his feet. 'Cover yourself,' he hissed, and four boys, local children I think, burst on us there. They exploded into joyful whinnies and ran jostling and prodding to the beach.

'*Gamo to,*' Louka swore.

That was the first and the last time in my life, let the gossips say what they like. It was two whole days after it before I saw Louka. I spent them in bed pretending to be ill, but really ill, in a torment of shame and bewilderment. There was no one I could tell it to.

When he came at dawn and whispered at my window I – well, wasn't I his now? – I flung open the shutters. Appalled, Louka gazed up, swaying on the blue cobbles, Valerie clutched to him with one arm. She struggled free when she saw me, hissed furious words at him and clattered down the steps. I slammed the shutters. For a while Louka pleaded – those hoarse endearments of his – as if nothing had happened. Finally he stumbled away.

SNAKE

I didn't see Louka again for years. I left Molyvo abruptly to come here. I went for long walks alone and brooded. A broken engagement was shame enough to account for my misery, and Mama didn't pry. By autumn I knew I had to tell her. She wanted to hide me away with relatives – 'For your sake, Manya' – but I couldn't have born to leave here.

I saw Valerie again that winter (winter, but the morning heat was heavy, very still and dusty, more like summer) at an umbrella-shaded table on the waterfront, reading. Drops of sweat glazed her red nose, her forehead and the sunbleached hairs of her upper lip. She looked up.

'Hey! Hey, Manya!'

I swung away, but she ran up behind me.

'Manya! *Tha piies kafe, kale?*'

Why not? I would have coffee. Her Greek sounded better. I nodded my ironic approval and she grinned, leading me back. The coffee ordered, we were silent, facing a sea that heaved and glittered at us. We made laborious small talk, what little we could. When the coffees and iced water came, she flicked through the little dictionary she still had and asked when the wedding was to be. 'Wedding?' I was as red as she was. Did she think me such a fool?

'Louka *s'agapo*,' she said. Louka I love you? She saw my face and tried again, pointing at me. 'Louka *s'agapo* Manya.' She meant that Louka loved me.

'*Agapaei*,' I corrected. 'Yes? How nice.'

The coffee was strong and sweet and I drank the whole glass of water. In the thick sunlight her brown legs glistened with white hairs. Many Greek women are as brown as Valerie – I am white all over like cream cheese – but our body hair is dark. Some try to be rid of it; I never have. Those white-furred legs of hers Louka had opened. Did he still? I wondered, but only dully. I was weary.

'Manya *agapaei* Louka?' she was persisting. I showed her my hand with its gold ring gone. 'Ah,' and she gazed with real regret. The Athens ferry had docked further along the quay and

163

crowds with bags and boxes were hurrying there. She tipped small change on the table, picked up her bags – on one, I remember, swimming flippers flapped like an upturned seal – and jumped up.

'Manya, I must go, forgive me.' We say that when we go: she meant nothing more by it. '*Addio*.' Kissing me on both cheeks, wishing me luck. I felt too dazed and ill to speak. She looked back once in the surge of people to wave. I thought she gaped: perhaps she had just seen my swollen belly.

I had my baby in Athens and would not give her up. Aunt Sophia, our old Communist warhorse, was godmother and gave her own name when my mother refused. When I was well enough I brought Sophoula back here. For the evening *volta*, when families parade, I wheeled her along the quay in front of everyone. I suckled her for a whole year. She walked at the age of one and swam at two. Before she had all her baby teeth she died of leukaemia. I never saw a child to match Sophoula. Dying, she said, 'Mama, where are you?' I was there holding her. I have worn black since that day.

It was God's judgement on my sin, people nodded. So may their sins be judged.

In this room my child and I slept: here I laid her out and waited with her for her burial. I often sit, as I sat then, at the south window and watch the sun, the moon, then the sun again. Having lived here all my life, I need its smell of paint, its floor of striped rugs, its dark points where at night the lamp will lay a gold hand on a cracked water-jug, three red stripes, a window sill.

Here in this room I painted Sophoula naked in her coffin, among pears and apples and grapes, a bunch of blue grapes in her hand. I drew in every detail of her: the ringed nipples, each crease and nail of her fingers and toes, the lips folded between her legs, her curled ears, her eyebrows with the mole under the left one. Had I been roasting the body on a spit my mother's horror could hardly have been greater, although, afraid of her mad daughter, she let me have my way.

'The pears are rotting,' was all she said. So they were, even before Sophoula was. 'Let the poor child have flowers.'

'It's not flowers that matter,' I seem to recall saying. 'It's the fruit that matters – '

'Is this what you will do to me as well?'

'– and death is the seed inside it!'

'What will become of us, Manya?' And she refused to sit up with me. I left her to receive the few mourners who came. My mother loves her visitors. I let no one in to see the child: my mother placated them. I sat alone with the candles and kept watch as Sophoula stiffened and then was limp again and her face changed. At first I talked to her. Then I brushed and plaited her hair. In daylight I painted her as she had become. Then I dressed and covered her for the last time.

I have nearly all the paintings that I did when I was mad: all interiors with figures, as these were. Mostly they were self-portraits, mostly nude. The rooms in them are full of the whiteness that snow reflects, or moonlight; and so are the bodies. I have never shown or sold these. I can only look at them myself from time to time. I know they are here against the wall, as the dead are in the earth. I know without looking.

I still paint myself nude. I have one on the easel now. It shows the blue branchings of my veins, the shadow of bones within, the slackness of my throat and breasts and swinging thighs – all my white meat run to fat, its tufts and wrinkles and moles. It shows everything. Still, it lacks what *those* had. My best work is in landscapes these days: watercolours done in precise detail. The parapets, yellow and violet-grey, of the fortress. Hills and their trees. The leaning figures in black of old women who mind goats. Children with shaved heads of brown and black velvet. Birds and insects and snakes. Old men lapped in shadow at the tables of *kafeneia*, sea light wandering on them as they drowse, these long afternoons.

SNAKE

Dimitra came to see me before she married Louka. I was fond of her when she was little, although I had not seen her since. I would never have tolerated such questions otherwise.

'I know you were engaged to Louka once. My mother – '

'What would your mother know?'

'I don't know.' She had trouble finding words. 'She doesn't know I'm here. She won't talk about you.'

'Good.'

'I've always thought of you as my big sister, Manya.'

'Have you? Why? We never see each other.'

'I always have. I wanted to be like you. Were you – in love with Louka?' Her jaw was trembling. 'Did he – why did you go away?'

'Pride. Ask *my* mother.'

'It's just that I – am I making a mistake? Should I really marry him?' At this point she hid her face in my shoulder. She was warm to hold. I stroked her plait of hair.

'Well, but you love him, don't you? You want to.'

'But will we be happy?'

'Sometimes. Why not?' She gazed with wet eyes. 'I hope you will,' I said. This was my pride speaking. 'Look,' I said then, and turned one of the nude self-portraits that I never show around to show her. 'What do you think?'

'It's beautiful.' She blushed and looked away. 'But you should have asked me first.'

'It's not you, Dimitroula.' She looked amazed. In fact it was exactly like her but for the eyes. Hers were, and are, like brown glass; mine, like green. 'Look at the eyes,' I said.

'Yes. But, Manya, even so – ' She was white now.

'I did it years ago. How strange life is! If I painted the eyes brown I could give this to you. As an engagement present.'

'No.' She shuddered. 'Oh, don't. No.'

At a friend's wedding once, when Louka and Dimitra were showing off their first baby, Louka clinked his glass on mine, leaned over and wondered in a hoarse whisper how I had stayed so beautiful. He said I was his one true love. He was, as usual, drunk. 'Darling,' he mumbled. 'Do you still love me a little?'

'To *our* child,' I said, and clinked his glass with mine, smiling even more sweetly. 'She should have been ten this year.'

He went back to his seat next to Dimitra.

Our garden is a few kilometres out along the flat coast on a lagoon full of seaweed and sandbanks. I hardly ever leave it now except to shop in Mytilene once a week. I love the crammed old shops that smell of roasting coffee, anchovies and cumin and olive oil. Skeins of late grapes glow there, withering, fermenting. At a waterfront table I sip my coffee, knee-deep in shopping bags. At twilight the harbour water is still. Darkness frills the images of boats at anchor and of sharp-winged gulls. Boys lolling on the edge fish among lights and stars.

I visit my old art teacher shivering in her frayed villa, its tiles all tufts and nests, its windows cracked by a giant magnolia that is her pride. Excrement from empty swallows' nests trails down her walls inside and out. She is sitting for me. Children jeer at her gate and scramble to safety. 'Mad old Maria,' they shrill. Her eyes water. She turns off the table lamp to hide the tears. Maria is my name, of course: Manya, Maria. Is this how I will end, I wonder? A palsied crone mocked by children – I who love children?

My mother fears arthritis and angina. She fears death. Last year the village secretary wrote that they had found Uncle Manoli, her sister's widower, dead in the snow one morning. Mama was full of such grief, so many tears! 'Well, you have a hard heart, Manya,' she said. 'You won't even shed tears for me.' But what was old Manoli to Mama? No. It was just – Death.

Our life is calm. My companion, apart from Mama, is a cat patterned in black and white like a penguin. He lies breathing on a velvet sofa with his pink paws in the air. He is a shining seal; an owl when his black eyes shrink to gold plate with one black split from top to bottom and his blink is stern; a fanged snake when he yawns. He is everything in one, but his name is

SNAKE

Fidaki, Little Snake. As a girl I once tried, from a sense of duty, to kill a snake I found writhing on my path. I threw rocks and silently the snake dodged, jerking and scraping, its gold eyes wild. All my rocks missed. Ashamed, I stood back and let it slide into a field of maize, its tongue touching ahead of it bronze clods of clay.

Maybe snakes hunt in our own garden, but if so I've never seen one. Fidaki himself hunts, but he is belled, the birds tease him. Mama said that Little Snake was no name for a cat. I said that the Garden could do without Adam and Eve, but must have its snake.

'Well, so it has. You are its snake,' she smiled. 'Yes, you are, Manya! Its fallen angel.' Smiling, but I could see she meant it.

POMEGRANATES

'Your hair's got darker,' Kyria Sophia says, 'since you came here first. Otherwise you're the same. Your Greek is still all right. I can't take it in, how it's all those years since you left our son.'

Strolling around the village on a road that has been asphalted past balconied mansions where doughy cottages used to be, she is slow: she who strode laughing and skipped over its ruts and heaps of dung. She is almost deaf. The skin of her face is baked on, her hair dead white. A grey spider like a crab is groping over threads of it; she stands still to let the younger woman flick the spider off, and absently with ridged hands strokes her woven hair smooth again.

Passing a garden, she begs a bunch of marigolds from a young householder whose moustache just covers a tolerant smile. She grabs at running children to ask each one: whose little boy, whose little girl? Outside the bakery they meet a nephew of hers, a man bald as a brass knob who always makes much of her Australian grandson whenever his father brings him here. Merrily she screws two fistfuls off the loaf he has brought. Munching hot sour bread, talking about their boy, they all walk home in the sun.

In barn after barn left open to air, garlands of tobacco are hanging like fur coats. She and the old man no longer grow any. Their barn still has sacks of grain, bales of hay and lucerne; he keeps the old horse in there, and the cow with her calf. Kyria Sophia has her vegetable garden fenced with beans and morning glories. Her tomatoes hang in skeins among yellowing leaves. She has round peppers and long ones, deep red, and black eggplants curved like horns. Hens scratch and flounce, and two scraggy turkey cockerels. The flowers on her basil are like lilac, white and mauve.

The trees are the same, in the same warm mist as when Bell

first saw them, their leaves yellowed, even the cobwebs float among them yellowed. Mist-glossy and black, there are thorny acacias: dented gold pods, green fronds of leaves. Over the doorway the grapes are ripe to wrinkling and hum all day with insects, grapes so sweet that they parch the throat. Along the fence there are trees with round red fruits too bright to be apples and besides they have tails: pomegranates, full of red glass seeds.

It is seven years since Bell was here last; fourteen, since she first came in pomegranate time.

Kyria Sophia picks one now and breaks it open. She and this Australian who was her daughter-in-law sit on stools under the grapevine, nibbling the seeds.

'The boy kept saying when they came this summer that you had made up your mind to come. I didn't believe it. After all these years. And here you are.'

'I wanted to come before this.'

'I'll pick the pomegranates before you go. You can take some back to Australia for him.'

This is the time of year when the earth reddens, and the sun; and the moon, like an egg in a nest of clouds.

'Every summer they come I tell the boy, this or that is his mother's,' Kyria Sophia says coyly. 'Whenever we use your things.' Forgotten things are everywhere. They have just drunk Nescafe from the silver-rimmed Australian cups, with milk from the old blue-and-white striped jug. Today's yoghurt, in the red French casserole, is warm in an Onkaparinga blanket by the wood stove. Kyria Sophia has the earthenware baking-dish – a wedding present – on her lap: under a white crust is tomato paste, dried like blood after days in the sun. She is spooning off the crust of mould.

'All your things have been waiting here for you.' She sighs when silence answers her.

'What if I go and see if there are any eggs?' Bell jumps up.

'Go and see.'

She escapes to the barn, where the hens lay their eggs in the old mangers. Just inside, the black-lashed eyes of the calf bulge; it stumbles upright, its knees and belly wet with dung. The cow swings her head up from the manger with a snort that stirs the hay warmly. There are four smeared eggs stuck with straw beside the dummy egg.

She remembers the eggs she wrote 'B' on.

'She wrote "B" on the eggs!' Her sister-in-law Chloe's voice. 'Why should she hog them? What about my children?'

'Ssst.' That was the old woman. 'Here she is!'

'So what?'

'Here I am.' She saw Chloe grimace. 'What's wrong?'

'Nothing.'

'Something about eggs?'

'No, no, she didn't say anything.'

'I did.' Chloe pointed. 'That's not fair.'

'Because they're hard-boiled?'

'I'm sure it's just a misunderstanding, girls.'

'How come you need your initials on them?'

'Oh. The "B"? I always – it's for "Boiled". *Brasto*.'

'Oh.'

'So we can tell.'

'There! A simple misunderstanding!'

'I still don't see why you had to hard boil four, when there aren't any fresh eggs.'

'I thought there would be. I boiled these for the salad.'

'We don't put eggs in the *salad*.'

'No? *Sorry*.'

'They'll do for a *meze* with olives. And Magdalini will have fresh eggs,' smiled Kyria Sophia. 'Let's all go and see her now.'

'Let's go and see Aunt Magdalini?' she is about to call out now, coming back with the eggs. But there is the *papas* fluttering along the road, his coppery hair and beard as if on fire under his black stovepipe hat. 'Look! It's the same *papas*! The seaman, the red one who married us.'

Kyria Sophia's mouth sets hard. 'That's him.'

'He's coming over.'

'He would.'

Both women kiss the red curls of his extended wrist. They all recite the required greetings; then he sinks into the cane armchair with a creak to wait for the cakes and coffee.

Luckily Bell has brought a ribboned box of cakes from the city. She washes her hands and the eggs, pours glasses of water and puts a cake each on three silver-rimmed plates. This *papas*, she remembers, was a wild seaman until his wife made him study theology and give her six boys, burly farmers all. 'I ploughed the waves,' he boomed. 'My boys plough the dry land.' Barbarossa.

'He looks like a pirate!'

But the old woman sniffs, stirring the coffee.

'I ploughed the waves. My boys plough the dry land.' That time, too, he was having coffee with them both. 'Are you still liking Greece, *madame*? Yes? A very different life.'

Bell quoted a proverb: 'Where there's land, there's home.'

'Good, good. Here's the place to raise children.'

'I hope to, father. One day.'

'Soon, if God wills.'

'We'll see.'

'Mmmm. How many years is it?' Scratching his bright beard, he leaned forward. 'You do have contact with your husband?'

'Contact? He lives here!'

'No: contact. She doesn't understand!' He rolled his eyes at her mother-in-law, who shot them both a shifty look.

'Contact? Mama, he can't mean – '

'Of course he does!' hissed the old woman.

'Oh.' She felt her red face gape stiffly in a grin. 'Yes, I do.'

'It's the will of God then, eh?' he said gratefully. Both women glared as he took his leave.

'And what's more, your mother put him up to it!' She was still angry when her husband came home. 'What she really wanted him to ask was if I'm on the Pill!'

'Don't start this again,' muttered her husband.

'It's *her*. She never stops.'

'Ssst. Perhaps it was a misunderstanding.'

'Sure.'

'OK, so she wants grandchildren. What's so terrible about that?'

'Like when she took our dirty clothes – '

'She wanted to help you wash – '

'– to see if some disease was stopping me conceiving!'

'You hurt her that night. Shouting, crying, shutting yourself in.'

'Asking if I'd like to see a doctor! "This stain here on your pants – are you sure nothing's wrong?" '

'Oh God.'

'Oh yes, God, oh yes. "The will of God".'

His curly beard is sprinkled with icing-sugar; he rubs his hands and a veil of it falls. 'Is it the will of God,' he intones now, 'that the churches in your country should have women priests?'

'No!' says the old woman. 'Jesus was born a man. He wasn't born a woman!'

'Mama. He had to be born one or the other.'

'Exactly! And he chose to be born a man. He said woman was born to be man's hostage!'

'What? Hostage!'

'He said so in the Bible. And now the Protestants have women priests! Blasphemers! God will send his fire to Earth!'

'Because of that?'

'The world will end soon in storms of fire. That's the nuclear holocaust. No wonder, when mankind has forsaken his way and let communism and divorce and women's liberation run wild. They worship the Antichrist! May God send the fire to burn them!'

'Well now, Kyria Sophia, time I was on my way.' The *papas* sighs. 'Duty calls. Have you got the names?'

'I'll bring them, father.'

POMEGRANATES

Tomorrow is Psychosavvato, Souls' Saturday, when he will hold a morning service for the souls of everyone's dead. Their names will be read out, and each family's *kollyva* shared among the mourners. Kyria Sophia will be the first one there.

After the afternoon sleep they go to see Aunt Magdalini, who insists on picking all her best roses and presenting them with a hug of welcome. She scuttles in the blue cave of her kitchen dishing out cherry *glyko* on glass saucers, mixing coffee, pouring iced water.

'*Aman*, Magdalini.' Kyria Sophia slaps her saucer down. 'This cherry *glyko* of yours. Nobody can eat it. Throw it away.'

'I boiled it too long,' cackles Magdalini.

'Is it *glyko* or glue?'

'Don't eat it, dear, if you don't like it,' Magdalini tells the visitor.

'Oh, but it's lovely!' she answers. It's more like toffee than jam. She scoops up the last threads and bites them off her spoon, grinning at Magdalini, who is more than ever a gnome of a little old woman. Kyria Sophia hunches her shoulders and her black brows. Magdalini, as ever, is impervious.

'I haven't boiled my *kollyva*,' she says. 'Have you?'

'Oh yes,' says Kyria Sophia.

'I haven't even cleaned the wheat.'

'Bring it here, then.'

Magdalini brings in a pan of rustling wheat. The three women sweep it with their hands, picking out stones and husks and seeds. The mist hovering in the doorway turns cool blue.

Kyria Sophia has a bowl of *kollyva* with a lighted candle stuck in it, as if for a birthday; and a little brass incense holder which she stuffs with red hot coals from the *somba* before setting in it a bead of red incense like a pomegranate seed. She takes them from room to room. The smoke trails after her muttering shadow.

Back in the kitchen, sighing, she strains the evening milk and puts it on to boil.

POMEGRANATES

The old man comes in cold from the *kafeneion*, hungry for chestnuts before dinner. He smokes with his eyes closed, waiting. Kyria Sophia has to remind Bell where to find the chestnuts. She remembers without being told how to slit them with a knife and shuffle them round on the iron top of the *somba* until they scorch. Singeing her fingers, she peels them then, enough for everyone; waxen, wrinkled and sweet, they sting in the mouth.

Kyria Sophia cuts bread and cheese and heats up the vegetable stew left over from lunch. The old pots flutter their lids and whistle, now and then uttering a faint crow as of roosters in the distance. The milk, as always, boils over, surrounding the pot with a frill that crackles and burns brown. They eat eggplants and peppers and beans and mop up all the red oil with their bread. The cheese is a salty white honeycomb, the grapes ripening into raisins. To celebrate her coming, they pour what's left of last year's ouzo from the demijohn, and drink it watered.

While Bell washes up, Kyria Sophia decides to inspect the eggbound hen. 'I hope she's managed to lay it. If not – ' She holds up the knife. 'I'm not letting her die on me.' Soon squawks and one screech come from the henhouse. A bundle thumps on the kitchen windowsill by the pot of basil: red cords poke from speckled shoulder feathers. Kyria Sophia throws open the window – oil-yellow smoke drifts out among needles of rain – and with a pot of boiling water at her elbow she plucks and cleans the hen.

'Rain at last. Well, we'll eat her tomorrow.' She crams the carcase into the refrigerator. (They have one now, and a television set too.) 'In red sauce? Or egg-and-lemon, maybe.' Her bloody fingers hold up a bright pomegranate: no – the egg that she pulled out. 'Pity,' she says.

She sits by the *somba* reading the prayer book aloud in her cracked treble, glancing over her glasses now and then. The visitor goes and leans over the sill to breathe in the cold air made lemony by the wet basil. In the mud below, the cat's eyes flash green; it sends up a yowl for more of the tattered hen. Both the old people are snoring.

So many village evenings spent yawning beside the *somba*, to the sounds of cats and snores and night birds. She has put off going to bed, because this is the same old bedroom, and the bed. Those are the two cane armchairs that made up a cot for the baby the first time he was here. These are even the honeymoon sheets that they rumpled and soaked with sweat all the first summer, night and afternoon. Now she opens the window and the hinged shutters: she leans on the sill. The rain has stopped. Drops fall from the grapes into dark puddles.

On the chest by the bed are old photographs of them all together, here and in the city and on beaches. She is holding one of her boy tossing wheat to hens long since killed and eaten, when his grandmother creeps in.

'Some hot milk?'

'No thanks, Mama.'

'All the good times.' She points at the photograph. 'Don't they matter any more?'

'Everything matters.'

'Can a woman just walk out on her man these days, and her little boy? Don't you remember how it was?'

'I remember, or why would I be here?'

'I can't take it in.' She turns away. 'Hang anything you want in this wardrobe. See, we have a wardrobe now. I'll just take my coat for church, then I won't have to wake you tomorrow.' Her voice is still reproachful. Once she would have added: Or will you come with me? She holds up a slim camelhair coat, silk-lined. 'Isn't it beautiful?'

'Yes. Let me see it on.'

She slips it on and lets her white plait loose.

'Yes, Mama, you look very elegant.'

'I'm old.' Peering in the dull wardrobe mirror: 'Look at me. Is my hair much whiter now? Whiter than when you first saw me? It must be.' There are tears on her cheeks.

'No.' Bell puts her arms round her. 'It's the same.'

A MAN IN THE LAUNDRETTE

She never wants to disturb him but she has to sometimes, as this room in which he studies and writes and reads is the only way in and out of his apartment. Now that he has got up to make coffee in the kitchen, though, she can put on her boots and coat and rummage in the wardrobe for the glossy black garbage bag where they keep their dirty clothes, and not be disturbing him. 'I'll be an hour or two,' she says quickly when he comes back in. She holds up the bag to show why.

'Are you sure?' His eyebrows lift. 'It must be my turn by now.' They were scrupulous about such matters when she first moved in.

'I'm sure. I must get out more. Meet the people.' She shrugs at his stare. 'I want to see what I can of life in the States, after all.'

'Not to be with me.'

She smiles. 'Of course to be with you. You know that.'

'I thought you had a story you wanted to finish.'

'I had. It's finished. You know you don't have time to go, and I like going.'

He stands there unsmiling, holding the two mugs. 'I made you a coffee,' he says.

'Thanks.' She perches on the bed and drinks little scalding sips while, turned in his chair, he stares out at the sky.

His window is above the street and on brighter afternoons than this it catches the whole heavy sun as it goes down. He always works in front of the window but facing the wall, a dark profile.

He says, 'Look how dark it's getting.'

'It's just clouds,' she says. 'It's only a little after three.'

'Still. Why today? Saturday.'

'Why not? That's your last shirt.'

'It's mostly my clothes, I suppose.' It always is. She washes hers in the bathroom basin and hangs them on the pipes. He has never said that this bothers him; but then she has never asked. He shrugs. 'You don't know your way round too well. That's all.'

'I do! Enough for the laundrette.'

'Well, OK. You've got Fred's number?'

She nods. Fred, who lives on the floor above, has the only telephone in the building and is sick of having to fetch his neighbours to take calls. She rang Fred's number once. She gets up without finishing her coffee.

'OK. Take care.' He settles at the table with his back turned to her and to the door and to his bed in which she sleeps at night even now, lying with the arm that shades her eyes chilled and stiff, sallowed by the lamp, while he works late. Sighing, he switches this lamp on now and holds his coffee up to it in both hands, watching the steam fray.

Quietly she shuts the door.

The apartment houses have lamps on already under their green awnings. They are old three-storey brick mansions, red ivy shawling them. Old elms all the way along his street are golden-leaved and full of quick squirrels: the air is bright with leaves falling. The few clumps that were left this morning of the first snow of the season have all dripped away now. As she comes down the stoop a cold wind throws leaves over her, drops of rain as sharp as snow prickle her face. The wind shuffles her and her clumsy bag around the corner, under the viaduct, down block after weedy block of the patched bare roadway. The laundrette seems further away than it should be. Has she lost her way? No, there it is at last on the next corner: DK's Bar and Laundrette. With a shudder, slamming the glass door behind her, she seals herself in the warm steam and rumble, and looks round.

There are more people here than ever before. Saturday would be a busy day, she should have known that. Everywhere solemn grey-haired black couples are sitting in silence side by side, their hands folded. Four small black girls with pigtails and ribbons erect on their furrowed scalps give her gap-toothed smiles. A scowling fat white woman is the only other white. All the washers are going. Worse, the coins in her pocket turn out not to be quarters but Australian coins, useless. All she has in US currency is a couple of dollar notes. There is a hatch for change with a buzzer in one wall, opening, she remembers, into a back room of the bar; but no one answers it when she presses the buzzer. Too shy to ask anyone there for the change, she hurries out to ask in DK's Bar instead. In the dark room into which she falters, wind-whipped, her own head meets her afloat among lamps in mirrors. Eyes in smoky booths turn and stare. She waits, fingering her dollar notes, but no one goes behind the bar. She creeps out again. The wind shoves her into the laundrette.

This time she keeps on pressing and pressing the buzzer until a voice bawls, 'Aw *shit*,' and the hatch thuds open on the usual surly old Irishman in his grey hat.

'Hul*lo*!' Her voice sounds too bright. 'I thought you weren't *here*!' She hands him her two dollars.

'Always here.' He flicks his cigarette. 'Big fight's on cable.' A roar from the TV set and he jerks away, slapping down her eight quarters, slamming the hatch.

She is in luck. A washer has just been emptied and no one else is claiming it. Redfaced, she tips her clothes in. Once she has got the washer churning she sits on a chair nearby with her garbage bag, fumbling in it for her writing pad and pen. She always writes in the laundrette.

She never wants to disturb him, she scrawls on a new page, *but she has to sometimes, as this room in which he studies and writes and reads is the only way in and out of his apartment.*

A side door opens for a moment on to the layered smoke of the bar. A young black man, hefty in a padded jacket, lurches out almost on top of her and stands swaying. His stained white jeans come closer each time to her bent head. She edges away.

A MAN IN THE LAUNDRETTE

Now that he has got up to make coffee in the kitchen, though, she can put on her boots and coat and rummage in the wardrobe for the glossy black garbage bag where they keep their dirty clothes, and not be disturbing him.

'Pretty handwriting,' purrs a voice in her ear. When she stares up, he smiles. Under his moustache he has front teeth missing, and one eyetooth is a furred brown stump. 'What's *that* say?' A pale fingernail taps her pad.

'Uh, nothing.'

'*Show* me.' He flaps the pad over. Its cover is a photograph of the white-hooded Opera House. 'Sydney, Australia,' he spells out. 'You from Australia?'

'Yes.'

'Stayin' long?'

'Just visiting.'

'I *said* are you stayin' *long*?'

'No.'

'Don' like the U-nited States.'

She shrugs. 'It's time I went home.'

'Home to Australia. Well now. My teacher were from Australia, my music teacher. She were a nice Australian lady. She got me into the Yale School of Music.' He waits.

'That's good.' She gives him a brief smile, hunching over her writing pad.

'I'll only be an hour or two,' she says quickly when he comes back in. She holds up the bag to show why.

'Are you sure?' His eyebrows lift. 'It must be my turn by now.'

'What you writin'?'

'A story.'

'Story, huh? I write songs. I'm a musician. I was four years at the Yale School of Music. That's *good*, is it?' He thrusts his face close to hers and she smells rotting teeth and fumes of something – bourbon, perhaps, or rum. So that's what it is: he is drunk. He has a bunched brown paper bag with a bottle in it, which he unscrews with difficulty and wags at her. 'Have some.' She shakes her head. Shrugging, he throws his head back to swallow, chokes and splutters on the floor. He wipes his lips on the back of his hand, glaring round. Everyone is carefully not looking. One small black girl snorts and they all fall into giggles. He bows to them.

'I work in a piana bar, you listenin', hey *you*, I ain' talkin' to myself.' She looks up. 'That's *better*. My mother and father own it so you wanna hear me sing I get you in for free. Hey, you wanna hear me sing or don't you?' She nods. 'All *right*.' What he sings in a slow, hoarse tremolo sounds like a spiritual, though the few words she picks up make no sense. The black girls writhe. The couples sitting in front of the dryers exchange an unwilling smile and shake of the head.

'You like that, huh?' She nods. 'She *like* that. Now I sing you all another little number I wrote, I write all my own numbers and I call this little number Calypso Blues.' Then he sings more, as far as she can tell, of the same song.

They were scrupulous about such matters when she first moved in.

'I'm sure. I must get out more. Meet the people.' She shrugs at his stare. 'I want to see what I can of life in the States, after all.'

'Like that one? My mother and father – *hey* – they real rich peoples, ain' just the piana bar, they got three houses. Trucks. Boats too. I don' go along with that shit. Ownin' things, makin' money, that's all shit. What you say your name was? Hey, *you*. You hear me talkin' to you?'

'Uh, Anne,' she lies, her head bowed.

'Pretty.' He leans over to finger her hair. 'Long yeller hair. Real . . . pretty.'

'Don't.'

' "I want to see what I can of life in the States after" – after *what*?'

'*All*.' She crams the pad into her garbage bag.

'You sha' or somethin'?'

'What?'

A MAN IN THE LAUNDRETTE

'You sha'? You deaf or somethin'? You *shacked*?'

'Oh! Shacked? Shacked – yes, I am. Yes.' She keeps glancing at the door. The first few times it was her turn to do the laundry he came along anyway after a while, smiling self-consciously, whispering, 'I missed you.' But not today, she knows. She stares at somebody's clothes flapping and soaring in the dryer. She could take hers home wet, though they would be heavy: but then this man might follow her home.

'So where you live?'

'Never mind,' she mutters.

'What's that?'

'I don't *know*. Oh, down the road.'

'Well, you can tell me.'

'No, I'd – I don't *know* its name.'

'I just wanna talk to you – *Anne*. I just wanna be friends. You don' wanna be friends, that what you sayin'? You think I got somethin' nasty in my mind, well I think *you* do.' He snorts. 'My lady she a white lady like you an' let me tell *you* you ain' nothin' alongside of her. *You* ain' *nothin'*.'

She stares down. He prods her arm. 'Don't,' she says.

'Don' what?'

'Just don't.'

'Hear me, bitch?'

'Don't talk to me like that.'

'Oh, don' talk to you like that? I wanna talk to you, I talk to you how I like, don't you order *me* roun' tell me how I can talk to you.' He jabs his fist at her shoulder then holds it against her ear. 'Go on, look out the door. Expectin' somebody?'

'My friend's coming.'

'Huh. She expectin' her *friend*.' The couples look back gravely. 'My brothers they all gangsters,' he shouts, 'an' one word from me gets anybody I *want* killed. We gonna kill them *all*.' He is sweaty and shaking now. 'We gonna kill them and dig them up and kill them all *over* again. Trouble with you, Miss Australia, you don't like the black peoples, that's trouble with you. Well we gonna kill you *all*.' He drinks and gasps, licking his lips.

A MAN IN THE LAUNDRETTE

The door opens. She jumps up. With a whoop the wind pushes in two Puerto Rican couples with garbage bags. Leaves and papers come rattling over the floor to her feet. One of the Puerto Ricans buzzes and knocks at the hatch for change, but no one opens it; in the end they pool what quarters they find in their pockets, start their washers and sit in a quiet row on a table. Her machine has stopped now. There is a dryer free. She throws the tangled clothes in, twists two quarters in the slot and sits hunched on another chair to wait.

He has lost her. He spits into the corner, staggering, wiping his sweat with a sleeve, then begs a cigarette from the sullen white woman, who turns scornfully away without a word. 'Bitch,' he growls: a jet of spit just misses her boot. One of the Puerto Ricans offers him an open pack. Mumbling, he picks one, gets it lit, splutters it out and squats shakily to pick it up out of his splash of spit. He sucks smoke in, sighs it out. Staring round, he finds her again and stumbles over. 'Where you get to?' He coughs smoke in her face. His bottle is empty: not a drop comes out when he tips it up over his mouth. 'God*dam*,' he wails, and lets it drop on the floor, where it smashes. 'Goddam mothers, you all givin' me *shit!*'

'No one doin' that,' mutters a wrinkled black man.

He has swaggered up close, his fly almost touching her forehead. '*Don't*,' she says despairingly.

'Don't, don't. Why not? I like you, Miss Australia.' He gives a wide grin. 'Gotta go next door for a minute. Wanna come? No? OK. Don' nobody bother her now. Don't nobody interfere. She *my* lady.'

He stumbles to the side door and opens it in a darkness slashed with red mirrors. Once the door shuts the black couples slump and sigh. One old woman hustles the little black girls out on to the street. An old man leans forward and says, 'He your friend, miss?'

'No! I've never see him before.'

The old man and his wife roll their eyes, their faces netting with anxious wrinkles. 'You better watch out,' he says.

'What if he follows me home?'

They nod. 'He a load of trouble, that boy. Oh, his poor mother.'

'Maybe he'll stay in there and won't come back?' she says.

'Best thing is call a cab, go on home. They got a pay phone here.'

'Oh, *where*?'

'In the bar.'

'*Where*!'

The side door slams open, then shut, and they all sit back guiltily. She huddles, not looking round. Her clothes float down in the dryer, so she opens it and stoops into the hot dark barrel to pick them out, tangled still and clinging to each other. Suddenly he is bending over her, his hands braced on the wall above the dryer, his belly thrust hard against her back. She twists angrily out from under him, clutching hot shirts.

'Now stop that! That's enough!'

'Not for me it ain', not yet.'

'Leave me alone!'

'I wanna talk. Wanna talk to you.'

'No! Go away!' She crams the clothes into her garbage bag.

'Hey, you not well, man,' mumbles the old black. 'Better go on home now. Go on home.'

'Who you, man, you gonna tell *me* what to do?' He throws a wide punch and falls to the floor. With a shriek of rage and terror the old woman runs to the side door and pounds on it. It slaps open, just missing her, and two white men tumble in.

'OK,' one grunts. 'What's trouble here?'

'Where you *been*? You supposed to keep *order*!' she wails, and the old man hushes her. The young man is on his knees, shaking his frizzy head with both his hands.

With gestures of horrified embarrassment to everyone she sees watching her, she swings the glass door open on to the dim street. A man has followed her: one of the two Puerto Ricans. 'Is OK. I see you safe home,' he says, and slings her bag over his shoulder.

A MAN IN THE LAUNDRETTE

'Oh, thank you! But your wife's still in there.'

'My brother is there.' He takes her arm, almost dragging her away.

'He was so drunk,' she says. 'What made him act like that. I mean, why me?'

His fine black hair flaps in the wind. 'You didn't handle him right,' he says.

'What's *right*?'

'You dunno. Everybody see that. Just whatever you did, you got the guy mad, you know?'

They are far enough away to risk looking back. He is out on the road, his body arched, yelling at three white men: the old Irishman in the hat has joined the other two and they are barring his way at the door of the laundrette. There is something of forbearance, even of compunction, in their stance. 'They'll leave him alone, won't they?' she asks.

He nods. 'Looks like they know him.'

He has seen her all the way to the corner before she can persuade him, thanking him fervently, that she can look after herself from here on. He stands guard in the wind, his white face uneasily smiling whenever she turns to grin and wave him on. The wind thrashes her along their street. In the west the clouds are fraying, letting a glint of light through, but the street-lamps are coming on already with a milky fluttering, bluish-white, among the gold tossings of the elms.

A squirrel on their fence fixes one black resentful eye on her: it whirls and stands erect, its hands folded and its muzzle twitching, until abruptly it darts away, stops once to look back, and the silver spray of its tail follows it up an elm.

The lamp is on in his window – none of the windows in these streets has curtains – and he is still in front of it, a shadow. She fumbles with her key. Rushing in, she disturbs him.

'Am I late? Sorry! There was this terrible man in the laundrette.' Panting, she leans against the dim wall to tell him the story. Half-way through she sees that his face is stiff and grey.

'You're thinking I brought it on myself.'

'Didn't you?'

'By going out, you mean? By not wanting to be rude?'

He stares. 'No, you wouldn't.'

'What did I do that was wrong?'

'A man can always tell if a woman fancies him.'

'Infallibly?' He shrugs. 'I led him on, is that what you mean?'

'Didn't you?'

'Why would I?'

'You can't seem to help it.'

'Why do you think that?'

'I've seen you in action.'

'*When?*'

'Whenever you talk to a man, it's there.'

'This is sick,' she says. He shakes his head. 'Well, *what's* there?' But he turns back without a word to the lamplit papers on his table.

Shivering, she folds his shirts on the wooden settle in the passage, hangs up his trousers, pairs his socks. Her few things she drops into her suitcase, open on the floor of the wardrobe; she has never properly unpacked. Now she never will. There is no light in this passage, at one end of which is his hood of yellow lamplight and at the other the twin yellow bubbles of hers, wastefully left on while she was out. The tall windows behind her lamps are nailed shut. A crack in one glitters like a blade. Wasps dying of the cold have nested in the shaggy corners. In the panes, as in those of his window, only a greyness like still water is left of the day.

But set at eye level in the wall of the passage where she is standing with her garbage bag is a strip of window overgrown with ivy, one small casement of which she creeps up at night from his bed to prise open, and he later to close: and here a slant of sun strikes. Leaves all the colours of fire flicker and tap the glass.

'Look. You'd think it was stained glass, wouldn't you? Look,' she is suddenly saying aloud. 'I'll never forget this window.'

A MAN IN THE LAUNDRETTE

He could be a statue or the shadow of one, a hard edge to the lamplight. He gives no sign of having heard.

Wasps are slithering, whining over her window panes. One comes bumbling in hesitant orbits round her head. It has yellow legs and rasps across her papers jerking its long ringed belly. She slaps it with a newspaper and sweeps it on to the floor, afraid to touch it in case a dead wasp can still sting, if you touch the sting. Then she sits down at the table under the lamps with her writing pad and pen and scrawls on, though her hand, she sees, is shaking.

'Not to be with me.'
She smiles. 'Of course to be with you. You know that.'
'I thought you had a story you wanted to finish.'
'I had. It's finished.'

OUR LADY OF THE BEEHIVES

1

Barbara, in the dark beside Andoni, felt swollen all over, raw and gritty from the day's sun and salt and sand. Like a hard-boiled egg her body held the heat in. She had dreamt again that some great whining insect, a bee or a wasp, had stung her. In this dream she was asleep on the beach in the noon sun. Waking as the sting pierced her, she was alarmed to see darkness. The harsh slow sound she heard was not waves, but Andoni's breathing.

Vassilaki cried out in his sleep. She got up and knelt with her cheek against his. 'Mama?' he murmured.

'*Nani*,' she said. 'Go to sleep.' But he was fast asleep.

She sighed. It was too hot to lie awake. Instead she crept into the shadows of the sitting room, switched on the hard light and tore two pages out of her diary to write a letter to her sister.

Dear Jill (she would address it Poste Restante),

I hope you arrived safely and love Athens. We're all fine here. It was great to see you and Marcus. We've just moved into a better house, the Captain's, no less, two floors furnished. The bedrooms are upstairs, with homespun sheets and lots of chairs, a table, but the rooms are large and full of heat – bare planks for floors. Downstairs we cook and eat and keep cool. We have a marble-slabbed bench with a sink and a tap – running water! – and a portable gas stove top with two large burners and a little one for the coffee briki. *(If we run out of gas a neighbour's child will run to the* kafeneion *for us and along will come the* kafedjis *with a new bottle on his motor scooter.) The Captain and family have moved next door. His wife has left us plates, cups, glasses, cutlery, pots, pans, baskets . . . There's a large round dining table, painted shiny green, and ten rush-bottomed chairs. There are spiky bundles of herbs – mostly* rigani *– hung like birch brooms on the wall, and plaits*

OUR LADY OF THE BEEHIVES

of onions and garlic, and shrivelled hot red peppers on a string: we are to help ourselves. Her yellow tabby sits on guard day and night.

And as if all that were not enough, this house has a lid!

Well, it has an indoor staircase, as well as the usual cement outside one: an indoor ladder, really, fixed into the floor and leading to a trapdoor set in the planks above. The kapaki, *they call it: the lid. The older houses all have one. It props open on its hinges, or there's a ring in the wall to hook it into, or you can keep it shut – the sensible thing, Andoni's mother says, when there's a child to worry about. The lid looks too heavy for Vassilaki, but it's not, only awkward to lift. Besides, any one of us, being unused to houses with lids, might step into space where floor should be. (She looks on the dark side.) So we don't let Vassilaki go near it. (The Captain's wife agrees.)*

It's like Treasure Island!

For the rest: no bath, but as the Captain said, with the sea so near who needs one in summer? And in an annexe behind the kitchen there's a cubicle with a sit-down toilet, a sewered one, a bucket of water to flush it, and a plastic waste-paper basket for the used paper which we mustn't ever flush, only burn.

As for the washing, we heat water in a sooty pan of the Kapetanissa's, kindling a fire under it in the yard with twigs and brambles, wads of newspaper and (yes) used toilet paper. We wash the clothes in plastic basins and rinse them in the wheelbarrow with a hose . . . In short, it's bliss!

I wish you could come and see, but of course you have to get back to London. Tell Marcus the whole town asks after him ('that brother of yours, is it, that Marko') and please write soon.

Much love,
Barbara.

It was not what she had meant to write, but it would have to do. In the yellow glare she flicked over the pages she had written when Vassilaki was a baby. A couple of pages, that was all, in two years. She was always tired.

He lies in my arms (she read).

OUR LADY OF THE BEEHIVES

To sleep he has to suck one fist and clamp the other in my hair, or in his own.

When he cries and I pick him up he sobs, pushing his face into my armpit, like our old cat.

I unwrap his heavy napkin. He has a small pink bag, seamed and ruched, and above it a pink stalk that extends itself and squirts, like some sea creature.

With a grunt he squeezes out mustard, soft lobster mustard.

He presses on the white bags that give him milk, and opens and shuts his vague eyes.

It might be a girl this time, she thought. We can call her Eirini and that will gratify Andoni's mother. Andoni would have to be told soon, when the time was right. It was a wonder he hadn't guessed. He had something on his mind.

When she sank back on the bed in the dark, Andoni took her in his arms and drove fiercely inside her. Neither of them spoke. He was slippery all over. He hissed like a dolphin surfacing, and then subsided. They drifted back into sleep.

Tomorrow, thought Kyria Eirini, waking as the house sighed and crackled in the dark, tomorrow I'll go to the church. To the Panagia of the Beehives. For Varvara's sake.

The Panagia *sta Melissia*, as it is known, was hardly a church at all, compared to the proper one in the town square, Agios Nikolaos, the patron saint of sailors. The Panagia's was little more than a *parekklesi*, a chapel built to honour a promise by the grandfather of the man who kept the bees now. If the Panagia would save his sons in the storm that had wrecked the fishing boats – he stood watching from the hill among the torn acacia trees – he would build her a chapel, he vowed. He built it in the shape of a bee box, but with a small square tower, and mixed blue in the whitewash to make it the same colour as the hives. The oil lamp before the ikon of the Panagia would never go out, the old mothers of the town made sure of that.

Inside there was a rustling, never pure silence, even when no one was there; and when the lamps were lit for a *litourgeia* an amber light filled it. The candles on sale at the entrance were made out of pale beeswax, and smelled of honey as they burned. As itinerant artist, having covered the walls and ceilings with images of haloed saints, had painted the shawled Panagia herself with a gilded Child in skirts, in a garden full of lilies and large brown bees.

Kyria Eirini, turning over on her bed in the hot house, told herself to go and light a candle to the Panagia in the morning. Two candles: one for her dead Vassili, whose sins were forgiven; and one to ask her to do something. And this morning I won't wake Andoni to go and buy fish, I'll let him off. I'll make *imam bayildi* for lunch instead, she thought; and fell asleep again.

The Captain's daughter, Voula, lying awake in her room next door, saw the gold lozenge of their sitting room light fall on the balcony, and later disappear. It was Andoni, she thought. 'I love you, Voula, my darling,' she whispered in English, though she had only ever heard Andoni speak Greek. She saw herself on the balcony again, brushing out her hair in swathes, hair smelling of rainwater; and Andoni looking on. How could such a man have married a thin ginger-yellow oblivious foreign broomstick of a woman like Barbara?

It was almost as if he were not married at all.

She stood up. Her mother was snoring in the next room. She crept out of the cracking house, past other moon-white houses and along a dusty path fenced with sharp thistles to a beach out of sight of the town. The lights of the grigri boats were as small as the stars. She dropped her clothes on the dry sand and padded across the black suede of the wet sand with its cold pools of stars, knotting her hair in a crown as she went, to keep it dry. Then she ran straight into the thick water. The shock of it made her shudder. It was so cold it was as if she had been cut in half: she could neither feel nor see herself below the waist. She bobbed down and quickly up. Her breasts glowed, dropping glints of water. Her feet stung now where thistles had scratched them. Blood pounded in her head.

If she floated, her face lying on the water would be a mirror of the moon. But then she would wet her hair. She would be found out. A moon afloat in black ice.

The heroine of a book she had read swam alone at night. She was a sea-girl too, a fisherman's daughter, the foundling child of a mermaid; and a man watched her, watched Smaragdi in the water. But that was not why, Voula insisted to herself: I love swimming at night and I always have and I always will.

But she knew that this time she was hoping that Andoni, unable to sleep, would sense where she was and follow her.

'Who's there?' she would say, splashing to make a surface of froth to cover her.

'Andoni,' he would say. 'Did I frighten you?'

What would she say? 'No. It's all right.'

'What?' he would falter. He would not be sure.

'A little, But don't go. It's all right.' She moved her cold hands over her breasts. His hands would be dry, warm.

A whimper came from the shore. She stiffened, horrified. On the grey sand a shadow was moving towards her clothes. With a gasp she sank to her nose to hide. She could see a white body, long-legged, white-scarved: no, it was a goat. 'Meh,' it said.

With a snort of alarmed laughter Voula splashed out. '*Fige*,' she hissed, and it stared at her. '*Fige!*' She slapped its burry rump and it trotted off, its frayed rope hopping behind it. Glancing anxiously at shadows, she dragged her clothes on to her wet skin and hurried along the path. Thistles slashed her. The goat, looking back, leaped and was gone. Moonlight lay heavy and white on shuttered walls. Nothing moved. Her shadow was sharp, and at every streetlamp a dim one joined it, grew and dwindled away. It reminded her of the game she played with Vassilaki's shadow when they went to the beach; Andoni's little boy. Her step was light as the shadows falling. No one seeing her out at this time of night would doubt why.

The door creaked, but her mother snored on. She laid herself cool and dry on her bed, and yawned. Bubbles of blood stung on her ankles. The moon was blue stripes on a wall.

A loud door creaked, waking Barbara, but no other sound followed. The house creaked a lot as the night cooled. She lay and thought that the air in the room was like coal in a fire, black and steadily smouldering. It would be good to walk through the grey dust of the streets now. The boats would be converging out at sea, gathering in the net. *Savridia*, she thought; *kefalopoula, marides, barbounia, fagri, sardelles*. She knew more fish in Greek than in English. It would be good to wade into cold black water flickering with fish. But there would be a scandal if anyone saw her. Besides, she was tired.

With a sigh she turned her soaked body over. A donkey sobbed, a goat gave a sudden meh-eh-eh. Soon the roosters would wake. Soon Andoni's mother would knock on the door and call Andoni to go and buy fish, unless she slept in. Soon Vassilaki would wake, waking them all.

She closed her eyes and slept.

2

Voula met Andoni coming out of the water with his speargun and flippers, pushing his mask up to his rough hair. 'Hullo, did you catch any?' she said.

'No. None there.'

'Bad luck.'

'You're looking very beautiful today.'

'I look very beautiful every day.'

'Is that so?'

She only smiled and swung away, ruffling the surface. That he was watching her made her aware of all her colours and shapes intensified in the morning sea. In a few minutes he waded back in and floated and swam lazily some metres away. But neither of them spoke again.

This morning as usual Barbara had clothes and napkins to wash, soaking in a basin on the back *taratsa*. She wrung them out and with a grunt hurled the dirty water into the vegetable garden. Hens skittered. She poured powder and hot clean water on the clothes and pumped and kneaded them. There were ripe grapes already in the vine above her head, and flies crowded in them. The morning sun shone through grapes and leaves; she looked on the ground for green reflections, as if they were made of glass; but the shadows were black. They were sharp in the still light. Strange, thought Barbara, brushing sweat off her eyebrows, how shadows look sharper on a still day, as if a wind would blur air as it blurs water. Bubbles catching the sun in her basins of clothes were like white opals.

Kyria Eirini swept the leaves and hens' droppings off the dry earth of the yard with a straw broom with no handle, then rinsed and wrung out the clothes with Barbara and helped her hang them out. Then she went in to tidy up. When she opened the shutters and panes to air her rooms, the sun fell in thickly and whatever was inside glowed, furred with gold. No matter how often she dusted, more dust drifted in and settled. At least it's fresh dust, thought Kyria Eirini. Insects buzzed in and out.

She was glad when Barbara and Vassilaki went to the beach at last, to the same spot as always, so she knew where to find them. She would rather stay and be alone in the Kapetanissa's kitchen. She boiled rice in milk and honey to make *rizogalo*, stirred it and poured it on to plates to cool before she tapped cinnamon over its tightening lumpy skin. Andoni and Vassilaki loved her *rizogalo*. She sliced doughy eggplants and salted them, sliced onions and garlic and tomatoes. She breathed in the smell as the olive oil smoked in her hot pans. 'God be praised,' she muttered. 'Everything we need, he gives us.' She slid slices of eggplant in and the oil frothed over them.

Barbara came to life only in the sea. Her speckled body glowed, magnified, and made its green gestures metres above her shadow on the sea floor. Pebbles were suddenly large then small as the water moved. She dived to grasp one. A bird must feel like this, she thought as she dived and twisted, gasped, the bubbles pounding in her ears: a bird flying in rain. When she came up a white net of light enfolded her lazily.

When she came out of the water she lay on a towel with another towel over her back to keep off the sun. Dazed, she watched the sea. Whenever she blinked she saw a flare of red; then the green sea, then the red flare again, as regular as a lighthouse lamp.

Kyria Eirini bent over her eggplants arranged like small black boats in the pan, ladling the filling of onions and tomatoes more carefully than usual into each one: the pan would be on show in the baker's oven. Barbara would be annoyed with her for struggling down the hot road to the bakery with it, when they could have had something easy for lunch. The thought of Barbara's annoyance was almost as pleasant as the thought of how Andoni would carry the pan home, sucking his fingers coppery with oil when he arrived because he had picked at it on the way.

So she struggled, hot in her black clothes, down the road to the baker's, exchanging greetings as she went. She pointed out to the baker exactly where she wanted her pan, and he told her that he knew his oven as he knew his own hand. She bought a hot white loaf and went on to the Melissia to light a candle to the Panagia, which was after all the real reason she was there.

The church was stuffy and dim, with a rosemary smell of old burnt incense. The glazed faces of the saints stared. Kyria Eirini crossed herself and slipped her drachmas into the box for the two candles. One she stuck in the tray of sand, for the dead; one in the iron bucket, for the living. The Panagia held her dwarfish Christ to one blue shoulder, her hollow eyes stern.

'It's not for myself,' she thought to the ikon. 'It's for my daughter-in-law. The Australian one. Fool though she is. *Aman*. Has she no pride? Enlighten her, help her, I pray. And the girl too, save her from temptation. Andoni is turning out just like his father was, whose sins are forgiven.'

As she was leaving, a bee settled on her sleeve. She shook it off. It hovered. 'Xout!' she said. They blundered together out into the sunlight.

At home she wrapped the bread in a cloth. Her dress was stuck to her. She swilled cold water from a bucket over the speckled kitchen floor to wash it. Its stones came to life, all their colours, like shingle on a sea floor. The cat that came with the house, and spent the mornings dozing under the table, sprang up on a chair and spat at her. 'Xout!' spat Kyria Eirina. The cat fled to the window sill and hunched there with a brazen scowl.

When Andoni walked in, Kyria Eirini was scrubbing spots out of the washing before Barbara got home. She started and looked guilty. 'You're home early,' she said.

'I said I'd buy the bread.'

'I bought it.'

'Why! When I told you I'd go!'

'I wanted to light a candle. It was on my way. I took a pan of *imam bayildi* as well. You can get that if you like.'

'*Aman*, Mama! You could just as easily cook it here.'

'Yes, but you like it better baked.'

'Not when it's so much more work.'

'But since it's better?'

'Tiring yourself out for nothing. It's madness.'

Andoni's reaction was all she could have hoped.

'Kyria Eirini?' come Voula's voice at the gate. Still in her bathing suit, she was hugging a pile of stripped *kilimia*. 'We thought – my mother and I thought – do you need more blankets at night?'

'Ach.' Flustered, Kryria Eirini waved her soapy hands. 'Thank you. That's very kind.'

'I'll leave them upstairs, will I?'

'Yes, there's a good girl. Thank you.'

Voula, padding into the dark kitchen, ran into Andoni before she saw him, he was so dark himself.

'Careful.' He climbed up ahead to hold the *kapaki* open.

Voula laughed. 'I grew up in this house.'

'All the same.'

'My father fell through once. He was drunk at the time.'

'Didn't you ever fall through?'

'I wasn't allowed to go near it.'

'So you never did?' He followed her and shut the trapdoor.

'No, I was a good girl.'

'Was. And now you're not.'

'Is that what you think, is it?'

'I'm hoping to find out. How old are you?'

She blushed. 'Old enough.' No, this was going too far: she looked round for something safe to remark on, and saw waxy lilies in a vase of her mother's. 'Pretty,' she said.

'Take one.' He lifted one out, its curled stalk dripping.

'Oh, no.' She stepped back. 'Are they from Kyria Magda?'

'Why not? Some old woman with whiskers gave them to your mother. Her goat got out and ate half your mother's beans last night, haven't you heard? You will. You're getting a bucket of milk too. Your mother hates them, she says, so here they are.' He nodded the lily at her. 'Take it, come on.'

'They make her sneeze,' she explained.

'Too big to wear.' He held it up to her hair. 'Pity.'

'How can I take it? It would look – I can't.'

With a stare he dropped the lily out the window. Shocked, Voula ran into the sitting room with the *kilimia*. He climbed back down to wait, letting the *kapaki* slam shut. But Voula left the house, trembling, by the outside stairs.

Andoni trudged off to the bakery.

3

It was a relief when lunch was over. Barbara and Andoni assured Kyria Eirini that the *imam bayildi* was delicious. But the baker had burnt one edge of it, and besides she thought there was just a little too much salt. They didn't think so. Vassilaki refused to eat any and filled up on all the *rizogalo*.

The washing was dry by then, hooked on the barbed wire fence among the speckled pods, green and red, of the Kapetanissa's climbing beans. Drops of water, falling from their bathers, rolled and were coated with dust. A shirt and a napkin had fallen on to the red earth. They would have to be washed all over again. Barbara sighed. Nothing seemed to dry without its earth or rust or bird stain.

The Kapetanissa had green onions and garlic growing as well as beans, and eggplants with leaves like torn felt, and cucumbers, potatoes, tomatoes, wilting melon vines. Her hens and the rooster had squeezed through the wire and were scratching and jabbing among the watered roots. Brown papery birds, murmuring to themselves, their eyes half-closed. Weary of summer.

Vassilaki had seen them too. He ran in by the gate to chase them out, but they pranced loudly into hiding. 'Xout!' he shouted.

'Vassilaki?' She had folded the clothes and was up to the napkins now. 'Where are you?' He came padding out. She pulled the wire over the gatepost. He was holding a long funnel-shaped pale flower.

'*Kitta*, mama,' he said. 'Look.' His mother had different words for everything.

'Mm. It's a lily. Where was it?' she said. Then: 'Put it down quick. Quick! There's a bee in it.'

So there was, when he looked. A bee with brown fur was crouched, its legs twitching, in the buttery glow at the bottom of his lily.

'Why?'

'It wants that yellow dust, see? On those little horns? It wants to make honey. *Meli*. Put it down now.'

'Why?'

'It might bite.'

'Why?' He held it out at arm's length.

'It might think you want to hurt it.'

'Nao,' he told it.

'Just put it down.'

'*Echo melissa*,' he called over the fence to the Kapetanissa and Voula, who had come out to see why the hens were squawking, and were packing the earth back round the roots with their sandalled feet.

'Careful, she bite you!' Voula called back, but softly in case she woke the neighbours.

'*Ela*, Voula!'

'Put it *down*, Vassilaki!'

He dropped his lily. The bee flew out, made a faltering circle and then was lost among the oleanders.

'*Paei*,' he sighed.

'Yes. It's gone.'

'*Paei spiti?*'

'Yes, it's gone home.'

'*Pounto spiti?*'

'In a bee box. On the hill near the church.' He looked puzzled. '*Konta stin ekklesia.*'

'Why?'

'*Paei na kanei meli*,' smiled Voula, shading her eyes. She followed her mother inside.

'Mama?'

'Yes. It's gone to make honey.'

'*Einai kakia.*'

'Who's bad? Voula?'

'Bee.'

'No, it's not, it's good – *kali*. But you have to leave it alone. You can pick up the lily now it's gone.'

'Nao.' They left it lying there.

He went ahead of her up the outside stairs – the wall was too hot to touch – and through the empty sitting room behind the balcony. He had gone when she came up with the washing. '*Pou eisai?*' she whispered. 'Keep away from the *kapaki*.' When there was no answer she looked in the bedroom: only Andoni, asleep. She found Vassilaki in the next room, on his back on the bed beside the black heap that was his grandmother. His eyelids fluttered as she kissed his cheek; he brushed the kiss away with a loose hand. His hair was damp. '*Nani*,' she whispered. He was already asleep. The room burned with a buttery glow like that inside the lily.

The floor creaked as she crept in, her soles rasped the planks, but Andoni stayed asleep, as if stunned, his mouth open. He had thrown the sheet off. He glistened, brown all over and shadowed with black hairs, barred as well with shadows that fell from the window over him. She lay down beside him in her dress: they would all be getting up soon. The rough cotton was stuck to her. Her breasts ached. Andoni muttered something indistinct. She sighed, hearing a mosquito whine. Our four bodies in the house, she thought, four bubbles of blood, and a fifth still forming, afloat on our white beds. A hollow light seeped through the shutters. Time and the sun stood still.

4

When they awoke, the women always brought coffee and glasses of water up to the balcony. Andoni read the newspapers there. The shadows grew longer almost as they watched, until the street was filled with them. Sometimes a sea breeze rose: the *batis*. Ach, *o batis*, people would say to each other with relief. Sometimes – especially when there was no sea breeze – the family went back to the beach for a late swim, in water warmer and brighter, tawny-shadowed and full of reflections different from its morning ones. Then the sun shrank, spilling its last light along the hoods of the waves.

This afternoon there was no sea breeze.

'Will you drink a little coffee?' And Barbara woke with a start. Kyria Eirini's grey head was at the door. 'Sorry, Varvara. Were you asleep? Vassilaki's awake.'

'Oh, not just yet, Mama, thank you.'

'Well, whenever you like.' She closed the door. Barbara lay blinking in the hot stillness. There was a crushed hollow beside her; she had not heard Andoni go. Her wrists and ankles itched and had red lumps all over them. She found a mosquito on the dim wall, slapped it, and was trying to wipe off the red smear with spit when the door opened again.

'Varvara, sorry. Vassilaki wants to go to the beach. Ach, not a mosquito? I sprayed too.'

'One. Look at me.'

'It's your sweet blood, you see. Vassilaki is insisting. Can you see any more?' They both peered up. 'No, it was just that one, Varvara *mou*.'

Vassilaki was insisting. '*Thalassa, thalassa, thalassa,*' he chanted.

'We were there all morning,' Barbara moaned.

'*Thalassa pame*, Mama!'

'Mama *nani*,' reproached his grandmother, stopping him in the doorway.

'Let his father take him,' Barbara said.

'He go to buy newspaper,' came Voula's voice in English. 'I take him, if you like.'

'Voula, would you? Come in.'

Voula came to the doorway, a coffee cup in her hand, with the other hand gathering her hair at her nape then letting it flow free. Vassilaki pushed past her: 'Mama!' Kyria Eirini made an apologetic face at Barbara and plucked at his shirt. '*Mi*, Yiayia!' And he shook her hand off.

'Come with me today?' Voula squatted beside him.

'*Pou?*'

'*Sti thalassa?*'

'Mama?'

'Mama *nani*.'

He faltered, scowling, but finally took her hand. They went downstairs to the shadowed garden to get a towel from the wire fence and find his bucket and spade. Then they came hand in hand out into the yellow evening. When he started to drag his feet, Voula dodged to make her shadow cover his, and he laughed, remembering how she always played the shadow game; and she remembered the moonlit streetlamps. 'What! You have no shadow!' she said.

'I have so!' He made his shadow escape and caper ahead.

'You have not!' Hers pounced on it again. 'You see? Where it is?'

'There!'

Families sitting on balconies looked on smiling.

Going past Kyria Magda's Voula saw from the corner of her eye that the ivory-necked lilies had gone from the pots on the *taratsa*. The white goat, tied to a post, fixed its slit brass eyes on Voula and said, 'Meh-eh.'

'Meh-eh. Meh-eh,' said Vassilaki. '*Alogaki?*' If it was a horse, then he could ride it.

'*Katsika einai*,' explained Voula, not knowing the English word. '*Echei gala.*'

'*Pou?*'

She pointed to the pink bag bouncing between the stiff hind legs; Vassilaki stooped to look, and giggled. Kyria Magda, screeching hullo, staggered across the yard with a bucket of water. 'All right then, drink, you little whore': and the goat, in its thirst, plunged its chin and ears deep, and sneezed, rearing. 'Run away, will you?' said Kyria Magda, her hands on her hips. 'I'll teach you. Yes, I'll teach her,' she told the watchers; a sour smile crossed her face.

'*Kakia yiayia,*' said Vassilaki when they were well past.

All the way to the beach Voula let him keep ahead of her with his shadow, making little rushes forward whenever he flagged, so that they arrived sweaty and out of breath. She dipped herself in the water, no more, not wanting to take her eyes off him for a moment; though he always paddled in the shallows and if he did stray further out there was a sandbank. Waistdeep, he was filling his bucket with water and spilling it on his head. It splashed all round him and sent ripples flickering up. From his hair, darker and flatter now, bright drops went on falling.

'Oooh! *Kitta*, Voula!'

She sprang to her feet. '*Ti?*'

'*Kitta! Pasarakia!*'

'*Pou?*'

'*Na!*' He pointed. There were the little fish, when she looked, first like silver needles, then like black ones. He sank his bucket in bubbles to the bottom to catch them. She lay down again, resting on her elbows. In the distance the boats were tied to the pier. A small one was pulled up on the sand nearby with an octopus spread to dry over its lamps, swarming with wasps. No one else had come down to the beach. I am beautiful, Voula decided; but he's not here to see. Over the sandbank the water was a honeycomb, a golden net. Vassilaki was intent. Now with his bucket, now with his spread hands, he bent to catch fish. *'Psarakia?'* he pleaded. *'Psarakia?'*

They stayed until the sun turned the long shoals red.

Andoni, hunched over a newspaper, saw them coming home along the street, its dark patches not only shadow now but wet dust where the shopkeepers had hosed it. At the other end of the balcony his mother and the Kapetanissa sat making lace with crochet hooks, each of them ignoring her own quick fingers to covertly watch the other's.

'When it's wet it smells like coffee,' remarked Kyria Eirini. 'The earth, I mean.'

'Here comes Vassilaki,' said Andoni.

'Ach, good!' She swung round. 'Yes, here they are!' Sounding too relieved, she knew: the Kapetanissa bridled. Did they think the child might not have been safe with her Voula, did they? She raised her heavy brows.

'Are they late, perhaps?'

'No! Not at all!' They were laughing, licking icecreams. 'Look, she bought icecreams.' Kyria Eirini made her voice soothing. 'She gets on so well with him, doesn't she?'

The Kapetanissa was not satisfied. Andoni picked a sprig of basil from the nearest pot, rubbed it and sniffed at the green mash his fingers made. His mother waved to Voula and Vassilaki, who waved back.

'I noticed yesterday what a beautiful swimmer she is,' Kyria Eirini went on, making it clear that of course he had been in good hands. 'May we not cast the Evil Eye on her,' she added, as custom demanded after praise, and pretended to spit. The Kapetanissa smiled at her, appeased.

'Yes, she's a genuine mermaid. Everyone says so.'

'Who's a mermaid?' Barbara called lazily from inside, having caught the one word *gorgona*.

'Voula. They're home,' answered Andoni's mother.

'Oh, good.' Barbara went on reading. She knew she was a better swimmer than Voula any day.

Vassilaki's chest had pink trickles on it where ice-cream had dripped through the soggy tip of the cone faster than he could suck it. Voula flapped the towel – it had lumps of wet sand on it – and hung it on the fence. 'Have a wash?' she said, and pulled the slack hose through from the garden. Vassilaki loved the first wash, the sun-warmed water in the hose. He pulled his shorts open and squeezed his eyes shut waiting for the silver water to come coiling over him. When it did he gave a yell. Voula stooped down to swill the sand and the icecream off him. But the water was running cold now and he squirmed away, giggling as if it tickled.

'Come here.' She was giggling too.

'*Nao!*'

'There is sand on you!'

'*Nao!*'

Neither of them had heard any buzzing or seen a wasp or a bee hanging, its wings rippling the air. But now Voula felt a searing stab in her thigh. She screamed with pain and shock.

'*Ti?*' shrieked Vassilaki.

Voula was slapping her thigh, staring round wildly. Whatever it was fell twitching in a puddle. She bent over it: impossible to tell now if it was a wasp or a bee. She crushed it with her hard heel.

'*Melissa!*' Vassilaki shrieked again. He peered at the crushed shell. Was it his bee? Would it dart up and sting him next? A hen jabbed and took it, spraying mud on him as she skipped away. '*Paei!*' yelled Vassilaki. '*Voula mou!*'

But this was not his Voula, cupping her stung thigh, her face red and twisted. Vassilaki stared. This was not his Voula. He stumbled into the kitchen. No one. '*Mama mou!* Mama!' He bolted up the wooden steps and raised the trapdoor.

'Vassilaki!' screamed his mother's voice. He swung around in bewilderment – where was she? – and the trapdoor fell shut with a thud above him, jamming his fingers. He screamed loudly, lost his balance and tumbled down the steps on to the floor.

5

At first everyone had thought that the screams they heard were part of the game with the garden hose. Now they all came running. Barbara scrambled through the trapdoor and down the steps to pick Vassilaki up. She sat on the cold floor of the kitchen holding him against her. For long moments he held his mouth open in a silent roar, turning dark red. Then at last sobs and tears burst out. 'Oh, oh, oh,' moaned Barbara in the Greek way that always soothed him best, rocking with each 'oh'.

'*Ponaei!*' he wailed.

'Oh, oh, *poulaki mou*,' she murmured helplessly.

Andoni crouched over him and ran his hands over the wet quivering little body, the yellow mat of hair. There was a lump there and blood seeping; grey splinters showed in the plump flesh of his arms and legs; but no bones were broken. Red tangles were printed on Barbara's dress where he had laid his head.

'What happened?' said Andoni.

'The *kapaki*. He fell downstairs.'

'I know that.'

'*Ponaei!*' Vassilaki touched his head and shrieked when he saw blood on his hands.

'Oh, don't cry, no, no. It'll be better soon.' She kissed his hair.

'*Melissa*, Mama,' he snuffled.

They looked, but there was no sigh of a bee sting.

'*Ma pou, poulaki mou?*'

'*Ti* Voula.' He pointed.

Voula, her face swollen with crying and as red as his, was standing in her bathing suit at the kitchen doorway. 'A *melissa* bite me and he frighten,' she said. 'And he hurt his self. The *kapaki* fall on him.' Her thigh bulged with a lump as big as a tennis ball: she had found the barb in it.

'Luckily he's not badly hurt,' said Kyria Eirini.

'He got a fright. I'm sorry,' Voula explained gratefully, because Kyria Eirini spoke no English. With a gasp of pain she squatted on her heels to face Barbara. 'It happen so quick!' she said tearfully; and met with shock a bitter relentless glare from Andoni.

'*Kakia* Voula!' Vassilaki hid his face.

'No, no, no,' said Barbara.

'But it was an accident,' said Kyria Eirini to everyone. 'These things happen. They can happen to anyone.'

The Kapetanissa gave her a grateful look. She had warned them about the *kapaki*, but this was not the time to say so; and besides she blamed all such accidents on the Evil Eye, but she could hardly say that either. Instead she hustled Voula home to take out the barb and dab vinegar on the sting, at the same time questioning her at length. Voula burst into more sobs: Andoni had blamed her without a word. She blamed herself, she told her mother, who stoutly told her she was being stupid. It was the Evil Eye, it was written, it was the will of God; she crossed herself.

'Yes, but they all hate me now,' said Voula.

Vassilaki, his sobs dwindling to sniffles and hiccups, was still clamped fast to Barbara on the floor. '*Ponaei*,' he whimpered now and then, when she tried to move; but it was clear that he wasn't badly hurt. When his grandmother knelt beside them with a bowl of milky antiseptic and a tuft of cotton wool, he knew what was coming: '*Ochi! Ochi! Ochi!*' he wailed, wriggling.

'Ach, *poulaki mou*.' His grandmother's eyes watered.

'I'll do it,' said Andoni.

'*Ochi!* Nao!'

'Vassilaki! Vassilaki *mou*!' His grandmother snapped on the light and ran up the steps, calling. He peered, blinking in the yellow glare, from behind his wet fists. '*Da da!*' she shouted, and punched the trapdoor. '*Da da to kapaki! Da! Da! Da!*'

Vassilaki gave a wheezy laugh. '*Da da pali*, Yiayia!' he commanded; so she beat it again, and again, until her arms ached and he decided that the *kapaki* was punished enough. And by then Andoni had swabbed the blood away.

As soon as Vassilaki was asleep Andoni inspected his head with a bright torch he had found, parting the damp tufts.

'He's all right. Really,' Barbara said.

'He could get delayed concussion,' muttered Andoni.

'I don't think so.'

'It's your job to look after him. Why did you leave it to Voula?'

'She offered. Vassilaki wanted her to take him.'

'He could have been killed.'

'It was an accident. It could have happened to anyone.'

'Did you call him to go up that way?'

'No, of course not!' Barbara jumped up.

'But you called him.'

'That was after he lifted it up.'

'I hope that's true.'

'I don't tell lies, Andoni.'

'You don't do anything much any more, do you?'

'No? Do you know why? I'm tired.'

'Tired!' He turned away.

'Tired, yes. Because I'm pregnant.'

It was some time before he turned to her; the torch in his hand threw winged shadows. He stood staring.

'You're not pleased.'

'Yes, I am. Yes. Are you sure? When will it be?'

'Mid-January, I think.'

'Does Mama know yet?'

'Most likely.'

He smiled at that.

'He's sleeping normally,' she said. 'He really will be all right.'

'I might just go for a walk, then. Just down to the *kafeneion* for a while. I'll burst if I stay here.' He bent over Vassilaki, then handed her the torch and went down into the street. From the balcony she watched him appear under each streetlamp, and disappear again.

After searching all over the sitting room, she found her diary under a pile of *kilimia*, striped red and green and black, which she didn't remember having seen before; and took out the two pages of her letter to her sister. She had more to tell her. A moth flapped at the torch, its shadow rocking the gold walls.

P.S. Jilly, I'm pregnant. I was going to tell you when you were here, but somehow it never seemed to be the right time. They will wish me kali eleftheria *when I tell them: it means* good freedom – *by which they mean* good (easy) *birth.*

> *Be happy,*
> *B.*

As they did every night, Voula and the Kapetanissa watched the boats get ready to go out in a jumble of nets and crates and lamps. Half the town was wandering along the waterfront and up and down the pier by then, dressed in their best for the *volta*. The streets were very dark now, except under the lights: people tripped over stones and tree roots. The sea held its oyster colours of yellow and grey longer, even when the caique and its little boats were chugging across to the fishing grounds, lamps strung in a row over the ringed wakes.

Later they sat with the families of the crew sharing bottles of beer and *ouzo* and plates of *mezedes* at the *kafeneion*. Moths fell against them. Often there was no other sound but the thump of the hurtling powdery moths. At every table children insisted, to the men's satisfaction, on sipping the froth from every glass of beer; soon they fell asleep in their mother's laps. Cats yowled under the chairs. Their fur twitching, they would put a calm paw on top of a cricket, then let it limp free, then cover it again. Their eyes flashed green. Beyond the yellow edges of the lamplight more crickets started creaking under the pines. Out at sea the boats gathered under a milky dome of colder light. A gull cried out; then another.

Voula, standing to pass her aunt a plate of *kalamari*, suddenly saw Andoni on the beach. But he looked away and walked on into the dark.

'Wasn't that your tenant? What's his name?' her aunt asked, munching loudly.

'No. I don't think so,' Voula said. She longed to be alone. Her stung thigh throbbed.

There were no lights on next door, when Voula and the Kapetanissa came home. They went straight to bed. The house was too hot for sleep, and held its heat and silence the whole night.

In the next room Vassilaki said in English a word like a bell, but woke only his grandmother. She could see the slatted moon from where she lay. There will be dew, she thought, by morning, and the houses will look like blocks of *feta* straight out of the brine, until the moon sets. At dawn they will be blue. I must wake Andoni to buy fish, she decided, because once the moon is full the boats know better than to go out with their little lamps. For a week we'll be without fish.

It was too hot to sleep, and besides she was no longer sleepy, having gone to bed earlier than usual when Barbara did. They had sat in the light of an amber lamp in the kitchen and eaten cold what was left of the *imam bayildi*, just the two of them mopping their plates with bread and talking quietly, almost secretively. They felt fonder of each other than they had for a long time, and they both knew this, and so were shy with each other. She thought of asking Barbara if she might be pregnant, but it was not the right time yet. When Vassilaki woke tousled and grizzling, they soothed and dandled him. They spoonfed him an egg that she soft-boiled in the coffee *briki* and on which Barbara drew a naughty face, a little Vassilaki. His pallor was gone. He sipped the egg greedily and then ate some bread with grainy honey and a peach like a yellow rose that she had saved for him. She wanted to read Barbara a prayer from the *Theia Litourgeia*, but the lamplight, heavy with moths and beetles, was making her eyes sore. They are like fish in a yellow sea, Barbara said, waving insects away. They carried Vassilaki, fast asleep, up the outside stairs to bed. She heard Andoni come up soon after.

For all she knew, good might have come of the child's fall, since Andoni blamed the girl for it; though who knew how long the good would last or what harm might come of it? In any case, it was not how she would have gone about it. The child hurt, the girl stung, the bee dead. A bee had come blundering into the sun out of the Panagia *sta Melissia*. Was it that bee? Was a bee's life of so little account to the Panagia, that she sent it to die? Thy will be done: she crossed herself. It's not for me to say. Maybe our lives are of no more account than a bee's, if the truth be known.

She must nail up the *kapaki* in the morning.

Out in the night a click of hoofs and a faint 'meh' made her sigh. There was a goat loose again. It must have come for the rest of the Kapetanissa's climbing beans; it would finish the lot off tonight, no doubt, and the Kapetanissa would talk of nothing else tomorrow. How did the Garden of Eden ever survive with goats in it? Goats eat every green shoot that pokes up. They're a ruin, goats are, though the milk makes up for it.

Is that bee alive now in the next world, she wondered; and is there honey there? Water, and milk and eggs, bread and wine? Shall we all have other forms, or none and be made of air? We boil wheat with sugar to make the *kollyva* for the dead; but it's only we, the living, who eat it. Or so it seems. For us of this world, at least, it tastes good, salty and sweet together. Like sardines fried in sweet green oil; or watermelon with a slab of briny *feta*, or any dry cheese; honey on rough bread; grapes, rich heavy muscat grapes, dipped in the sea to wash them.

Pain is like salt, in a way, she thought; it can make the sweetness stronger, unless there's too much of it. Pain and sorrow and loss.

There was too much salt in the *imam bayildi* today. Never mind. Well.

My poor Vassili, whose sins are forgiven: that was a salty old joke he loved to tell, the one about honey. Only a man could have made that joke up. A man might even believe it, who knows?

A gypsy (he put on a wheedling voice) came to an old widow, I forget why, and said, 'What is your wish, my lady? I can give you one of two things. A fine young man to marry, or a pot of honey. Just tell me which you want.'

'Now what sort of choice do you call that?' (And he cackled like an old widow.) 'I couldn't eat the honey, could I? There's not a tooth in my head, is there?' (At which he laughed angrily as if he knew all about old widows, and disliked what he knew.)

She breathed deeply of the shuttered air, cooler now with dew towards daybreak, and pulled the rough sheet up over her folded throat. In the next world may we all be young again, she fell asleep wishing. All of us young and at peace by the sea for ever.